CODE
OF THE
ASSASSIN

BILL BREWER

THRILLEX Publishing

Dedicated to you, the reader.

Thank you for choosing this book.
I hope you enjoy the story.

Praise for Bill Brewer

K. Allen

⭐⭐⭐⭐⭐ **Love this book!**

Love this book! The combination of engaging characters and detailed accounts made it hard to put down. Looking forward to the whole series of David Diegert books.

Lee Anne

⭐⭐⭐⭐⭐ **One heck of a ride!**

This book started out fast and didn't let up. An excellent book of action and suspense. Well written and engaging.

Jarod Farchione

⭐⭐⭐⭐⭐ **Made me a fan of fiction again!**

Brewer's writing reads like an action movie, while being tactical, well-paced, and realistic in all of the ways I enjoy. I highly recommend this book.

Jimmy Ray

⭐⭐⭐⭐⭐ **Assassin on the Run**

Characters are well developed, the story is exciting to follow, and it's a fun read. If you like action and adventure, you will love this one. A great story pulls the reader in, and this one had me from the first page.

CHAPTER 1

BEEP, BEEEEP! In spite of the rain, the asshole rolled down his window to shout, "Get outta the way you bloody little twat." Grimy spray from angry tires doused Mei Ling's moped. Her high wellies and long raincoat deflected the rude splash from a puddle of London rain. The large hood of her coat kept her cigarette dry, each drag illuminating her determined face as she drove through traffic on this drizzly night. At the direction of her Father, Chin Lei Wei, she was to surveil the Ambassador Hotel.

As a Board member of Crepusculous, Chin Lei participated in the control of seventy-five percent of the world's economy. In partnership with three other men, he was part of a secret group of billionaires, orchestrating the most significant economic influence on planet earth.

While bracing against the wet chill, Mei Ling thought her father's need for her to be his eyes and ears in London was a blessing and a curse. She had more freedom than she would have had in China, but her assignments carried real danger. Trained in Kung Fu and Wushu, she was capable, not only of defending herself, but also of killing if an enemy persisted. Killing was not her mission tonight. Her father had assigned her to conduct espionage, observing activities at one of London's most exclusive hotels.

Distrusting, Klaus Panzer, the most powerful member of the Crepusculous Board, Mr. Wei sent his daughter to report on the occurrences at the Ambassador. With absolute trust, he relied on her ability to observe while remaining unseen and unrecognized as a child of Crepusculous. Unlike the privileged offspring of the rest of the wealthy board members, she worked to preserve the empire, although this assignment felt like subterfuge.

The multi-paneled door of the hotel's underground garage retracted. Through the opening, a black Mercedes S550 slipped sinuously into the rain. Following the sleek sedan, a black panel van lurched onto the road, speeding off in the opposite direction. Mei Ling started her moped and followed the lithe, luxurious car.

Denise Diegert, David's mother, sat petrified in the back passenger seat of the van. The plastic zip ties were cutting off the blood flow to her hands, while the duct tape over her mouth forced her to breathe through her nose. Her seat belt held her in place, yet she could turn to see David lying unconscious on the floor of the van. What was her son doing in London? She was shocked to see him when he appeared in the penthouse of the Ambassador. He was supposed to be in Afghanistan. Frazzled at having been kidnapped, forced unto a private jet and flown all the way to London, Denise was told nothing about why this was happening and who was giving the orders. Then David showed up at the hotel, followed moments later by Klaus Panzer, a man she hoped to never see again her entire life. Panzer had raped her years ago, unknowingly leaving her pregnant and never contacting her again. He was David's father, but she never reached out to him. He forced her to have sex with him for his own personal gratification. He was never going to help her. She raised David in the home of her husband, Tom Diegert, who figured out he was not this child's father. He let the boy stay, but made his life a living hell, denying him fatherly love, acceptance and support. In the penthouse, she saw Panzer's men inject drugs into David, who now lay unconscious on a dirty sheet, stinking of motor oil. She tried not to cry, but she loved him so much. To her, he was still that curious, inquisitive little boy who loved to go on nature walks, wilderness camping trips, and long canoe paddles. David was so enthralled with the natural world; he was happy and carefree whenever he was with his mother on an outdoor adventure. Because of Panzer, he now knew the shame she had hidden from him his entire life. He was the bastard son of the world's richest man. She never wanted him to know for fear of losing him. She always thought if Panzer knew what a special boy his son David was, he would take him from her, just as he took her body for his pleasure that night. Powerful men did whatever they wanted to poor people like her. She loved David and never wanted him raised by the selfish, overbearing brute who raped her, even if he was the world's richest man. It eviscerated her heart to have to admit to David that Klaus was right when he put it together in the penthouse and forced her to confirm that he was David's father. The secret erupted from her with just a slight nod. Never did she want to admit this to David. This awful secret was supposed to be tucked away forever within her, all the way to the grave. Staring at her son, his head rolling back and forth as the van sped down a freeway he looked as good as dead. Her tears streaked the duct tape before dripping off her chin. Denise feared for both of them as they were being driven to wherever Klaus Panzer had ordered his men to take them.

The Mercedes crawled with the traffic, making it easy for Mei Ling to keep pace. The dark windows, however, made it impossible for her to see inside the vehicle.

Klaus Panzer sat comfortably in the soft leather seat. He adjusted his sleeves and smoothed his thick gray hair. From his breast pocket, he extracted a satellite phone. With this single device, he possessed the capacity to instigate a series of thermobaric bombs planted in a dozen US locations. These bombs combined heat and force to produce a super-hot, explosive impact, which ignited oxygen in the air, creating death through flaming asphyxiation. The chemistry of the bombs was extremely stable allowing them to lie in place for long periods of time, remaining undetected, yet capable of being activated by a remote signal. Each charge was strategically placed to disrupt a critical piece of infrastructure, disabling transportation, communication, banking, energy distribution, food, and water supply and ultimately governmental authority. Panzer, through his private espionage wing of Crepusculous, set up the unprecedented attack on America. The country would be severely hampered for months. It was 9/11 times twelve, all within twelve hours. From the back seat of the Mercedes, Panzer input the code which would set off the first set of explosions and initiate the entire cascade.

Mei Ling saw the blinker illuminating the right side of the black sedan. The car was moving onto the expressway ramp. She leaned her moped to the right, gunning it along the shoulder, passing all the cars including Panzer's.

Even though Panzer's original plan had someone else inputting the code, he had the sequence of numbers and letters memorized. Now that David Diegert had confounded the original plan, it was going to have to be Panzer who ignited the hellacious destruction he had planned for America. "464748DAZ," Panzer typed on the phone's keyboard. He waited for confirmation that the signal was received by his private satellite orbiting five hundred miles above the earth. The green word; ACTIVATED did not appear.

Mei Ling arrived at the base of the expressway ramp to see two police vans swerve into position. The first cut in front of Panzer's car, while the second moved in behind, trapping the Mercedes. From the vans, black-clad operators with helmets and submachine guns swarmed Panzer's vehicle.

Panzer re-entered the activation code, with no response. His driver asked, "How should I proceed?" In a moment of silence, Panzer was uncharacteristically flustered, yet he had the clarity of mind to realize that Diegert must have re-programmed the satellite phone so it would not accept the activation code. His plans were foiled, and now a London SWAT team surrounded his vehicle. Panzer initiated the phone's failsafe mechanism, sending a self-destructive charge through the circuitry, destroying all the data. A thick plume of acrid smoke rose from the disabled device. Panzer opened the car's roof, allowing the smoke to escape and the rain to enter. The SWAT team braced as the belch of smoke exited the car's roof. As he closed the roof and brushed the rain from his suit, Panzer instructed his chauffeur, "See what they want." As the chauffeur stepped out of the car, electrodes pierced his legs and torso. The jolting charge of a taser sent the man crashing back against the car, striking his head as he crumpled to the rain-soaked pavement. Through the window next to him, Panzer peered directly into the barrel point of an H&K MP5. The jacked-up operator's face was obscured by his black goggles, but his intent was clear. In spite of the threat, Panzer opened the door, stepping out into the rain. He rose to his six-foot, four-inch height. Droplets beaded up and rolled off the expensive fabric of his custom-tailored suit. The armed operators kept their guns trained upon him, but they did not subdue him. Klaus Panzer's regal bearing commanded respect even under extremely tense conditions.

A pair of detectives exited their car and approached Panzer's, looking at each other with restrained concern. The first wore a beige raincoat and a beat-up fedora. The taller of the two wore a green coat with a belt sashed tightly around his waist. His umbrella was black. They stepped past the armed operators and were immediately addressed by Panzer. "Unless you insist, I do not believe handcuffs are necessary."

"Shut up and put'em out," said the detective in the beige coat. Snapping the cuffs on Panzer's wrists, he allowed the distinguished man's arms to remain in front of him.

*****

Mei Ling watched as Panzer was led to the detective's car and placed in the back seat. Two officers loaded the unconscious chauffeur into the back of the limousine before climbing in, one behind the wheel. The first van pulled forward, then the Mercedes, followed by the detective's car with Panzer. The second van took up the rear position as the four-vehicle armada streaked up the entrance ramp, merged into the high-speed traffic, disappearing from the young lady's spying eyes. Fortunately, Mei Ling captured the event, which occupied less than three minutes, on her cell phone.

*****

Denise noticed the sign for London Polytechnic University as the van drove through the South entrance, crossed campus on Academic Drive and pulled up to a garage door on the backside of a large building.. The van sat quietly as Denise read the sign identifying the building as Culhane Hall. The garage door opened allowing the van into the building. Once inside, the doors closed.

London Polytechnic University or LPU, as most people referred to it, is a major technical university serving London since 1945. The University, built as part of the reconstruction following World War II, offered degrees in engineering, computer science, communications, medicine, and nursing as well as psychology, business, and finance. The basic sciences were represented by Departments of Biology, Chemistry, Physics, and Biotechnology specializing in nanotechnology. The University was founded by the Panzer family. The fact that the school was being built with "German" money was kept quiet in the late 40s when the planning and initial construction occurred.

For Klaus Panzer and Crepusculous, the university was the perfect place to hide in plain sight. Panzer's father designed the structures so there were unseen parts of campus from which clandestine operations could be conducted. Deep underground, in a labyrinth of secured facilities, Panzer maintained a vast network of labs, training facilities, and barracks where specialized personnel were housed and prepared for missions to support the Board of Crepusculous. It was a private paramilitary, functioning right below a bucolic campus dedicated to the open mind, the freedom of thought and the betterment of humanity. Panzer loved the contradiction and was proud of the seen and unseen capabilities of LPU.

Denise was taken from the van and released into comfortable, but secure, quarters. Her binds were removed, and she was allowed to shower and get into clean clothes before being served a fresh meal. David was slid out of the van onto a gurney, taken to medical, placed in a hospital bed and restrained. He remained unconscious while Dr. Clarissa Zeidler monitored his medical care.

*****

Panzer eyed the two detectives as the car made its way onto the expressway. He opened with, "Introductions please?"

The detective in the beige coat turned. "Shut up and don't say anything more."

The man in the green coat, who was driving, said, "I'm Agent Theodore Jackson with MI5. People call me Ted."

Reluctantly, the other spoke, "I'm Detective Robert Morrow of the London Criminal Investigation Division. You do not have to say anything. But, it may harm your defense if you do not mention, when questioned, something which you later rely on in court. Anything you say may be given as evidence."

"May I place my one phone call?" asked Panzer.

"But of course," oozed Detective Morrow's sarcastic reply.

Panzer placed a text to the head of his legal team instructing him to track his GPS and meet him at the resulting police station. Choosing to exercise his right to remain silent, Panzer said nothing more. Looking through the rain-streaked windows, he found himself fuming at the clever actions of David Diegert.

****

Diegert lay in a medical bed, twitching like a dog dreaming of chasing tennis balls, only Diegert's dream was much more threatening. He felt himself naked, lying on his back, strapped to a block of ice floating in a tumultuous sea, buffeted by torrents of cold wind from a dark, foreboding sky. The ice chunk rocked as massive waves splashed frigid water over him. Snow fell in windswept sheets, the cold sting of each flake torturing Diegert's bare skin. Twisting and turning tightened his restraints, preventing him from curling into a heat-preserving ball. He shivered with violent spasms as his body desperately attempted to generate warmth. Shaking uncontrollably, and hit by yet another wet wave, he looked up to see the clouds converging into a funnel. Was he in a snowbound tornado? The funnel cloud descended, coming right at him. Helplessness radiated from his gut as the cold power of the sky hit him with full force. From the dark center of the funnel, a face emerged. A cold gray face of a man with sharp cheekbones, icy hair, and judgmental blue eyes. The voice of Klaus Panzer chilled Diegert with an icy blast. The words were icicle daggers penetrating his heart. "Now I will show you a father's love."

The threatening phrase intensified Diegert's shivering as the cold reality of the icy grip of Klaus Panzer clamped on to his soul. The gray face rose above him, yet the cold blue eyes remained locked on his. Thunder boomed, and lightning crackled across the sky as cold wind preceded Panzer's next words. "You are my one true son. You will now see what that means to me." The words entered Diegert's ears like ice picks, with meaning as obscure as the sun in the dark gray sky. As the funnel pulled back up into the clouds, Diegert awoke when one last clap of snow thunder rolled across the expanse of his chilling nightmare.

Opening his eyes, Diegert was relieved to find he wasn't strapped to an iceberg but lay in a bed. Scanning the room, he could see he was in some kind of a medical facility. The room was light aqua green with installations on the wall for gas ports and lights that would flash in case of emergency. The bed had sturdy rails on both sides. Diegert was covered in a white sheet and one thin blue blanket. He lay there without attendants, other patients or the noises one would expect in a busy hospital. When he attempted to lift his hand, the restraints became apparent. Both wrists and ankles were encircled in soft lamb's wool with a solid brass buckle holding together the two ends of strong leather binds. There was a glowing red button next to his right hand which he pressed. He received no feedback and pressed it a few more times. His patience was practically worn out, when a person finally appeared through the curtain draping the entrance to his room. Lifting his head, Diegert saw a young woman whose unsmiling face brought no cheer to the room. She looked at him, not with concern, but responsibility. Her glasses were round, rimmed in flat black, her brown hair pulled back into an efficient ponytail. Over aqua blue scrubs she wore a thin white cardigan which she drew closed while wrapping her arms around her midsection, minimizing her breasts. From what Diegert could see, she needn't bother with such modesty.

"How can I help you?" she asked.

"Where am I?"

"I'm responsible for your medical care. I can't provide you with information." She turned and pulled back the curtain as she exited.

"Hey wait…come back here."

With her body already on the other side of the curtain, she moved the fabric from in front of her face. "Yes."

"I'm thirsty."

"My monitor indicates that your fluid level is within normal limits. Your IV is providing all the water your body needs."

Diegert followed her eyes to the tube inserted into his arm. "Well fuck that, my throat's dry."

The rudeness of Diegert's reply deepened the frown on her face. "I'll turn up the volume of your IV fluid from my computer." She snapped the fabric of the curtain closed, disappearing from view.

"Hey, come on, don't get all pissed off. I just want a drink of water. Hey! Come back."

She did not come back. Diegert watched the drips of his IV and, sure enough, the rate of flow did increase. He spent time trying to move as much as his four-point restraints would allow. His immobility brought back recollections of the past few hours when he had confronted Klaus Panzer to rescue his kidnapped mother. He had succeeded. He and his mom were exiting the penthouse, leaving Panzer locked in the bathroom. As the elevator opened, Diegert's surprise to see a trusted friend caused him to hesitate long enough to be tazed and drugged. His mom, cuffed and gagged. Now, again, he had no idea where she was and what was happening to her.

****

Inside the police station, the detectives questioned Panzer.

"Are you involved with any terrorist organizations?" asked Detective Morrow.

"What makes you think that?" replied Panzer.

"Just answer the question," grumbled Morrow.

Detective Jackson interjected, "We've received intelligence implicating you in a terrorist plot. Can you tell us why such an accusation would be directed at you?"

"I believe it has to do with certain business rivals who feel they will gain an advantage by smearing me. I'm sorry such outrageous behavior ensnared you, gentlemen."

"Will you identify these business rivals for us?" Agent Jackson held eye contact with Panzer.

Panzer blinked and turned away. "I prefer to handle my own business issues. These rivals need to learn how to conduct themselves. That is a lesson I can share with them without inconveniencing you."

"It's our job to make sure people operate within the law."

"Interesting…" said Panzer. "I think of your job as beginning when someone breaks the law."

Morrow grunted. "Our job gets interesting when someone breaks the law." He held up the disabled satellite phone. "We found this in your limousine."

Panzer gazed at the charred remains. "That device has been destroyed. A very unfortunate occurrence given the valuable contact data it possessed."

"What kind of data?" pushed Morrow.

"Business contacts, for people with whom I conduct commerce. However, it did contain proprietary data which exists nowhere else, now gone forever."

Leaning forward, Morrow said, "Yeah… that's the kind of stuff we're looking for."

"Well I hate to disappoint you," Panzer gestured toward the melted mass, "but I'm afraid you'll find nothing useful on that lump of plastic."

Panzer's lawyers arrived at the police station dressed in Kiton suits with dramatic red ties. He smiled when he saw the determination on their faces. The detectives saw their legal representatives, in low budget rack wear, casting disappointed frowns.

The Crepusculous lawyers went right to work addressing the allegations and making arrangements. No charges were filed, and a receipt was issued for the burned-out satellite phone. As he exited the building, Panzer stopped to speak with Morrow and Jackson.

"Thank you for your service. I appreciate your professionalism."

Morrow replied through gritted teeth, "Next time you're spending the night in jail."

Jackson, with a calmer tone, said, "When dealing with your business rivals, remember that enforcing the law is our job." He handed Panzer his business card.

Panzer examined the card. "I will see to it that the Police Benevolent Association receives a donation."

"Don't bother," said Morrow.

"We always appreciate the public's support," replied Jackson.

With his driver sufficiently recovered, Panzer was back in the limousine and en route to his townhouse. He called Javier Perez, connecting to the playboy's voice mail. *"This is Javier, if we have made love in the past, you are a very fond memory. If we have not, please leave your number. Chow."*

The seductive message only pissed Panzer off. He shouted, "Meet me at my townhouse as soon as you get this message. Zip up your pants and report to me immediately."

****

Javier saw the name on his screen and was not at all surprised by such a brusque demand. Being the son of Julio Perez, the man who represented one-fourth of Crepusculous, came with responsibilities. Javier judiciously avoided responsibility his whole adult life, preferring to enjoy the wealth, easily seducing women with his handsome face. That face, however, currently was battered and bruised from a violent encounter with David Diegert. Javier had possessed the satellite phone detonation device but lost it to Diegert in a vicious fight. In spite of being an accomplished martial artist and doing some damage to Diegert, Javier's blackened eye, split cheek, and fat lip revealed the outcome of his battle with the world's best assassin.

Along with his father, the other members of Crepusculous included Chin Lei Wei, the Englishmen Dean Kellerman, and Klaus Panzer, who was arguably the most influential of the four. Javier knew he would have to comply with Panzer's demand, so he dismissed a curvaceous Czech exchange student from his room at his London Townhouse and contemplated how he would manage the undoubtedly intense interaction that awaited him.

Javier, at first, paid little attention to the plan Klaus Panzer had devised to destroy the value of the US dollar. When he discovered the action included bombing a dozen US cities, he realized Panzer was going too far. Javier knew he wasn't well respected within the Crepusculous Board, but he also knew that successful economic warfare need not be fought with guns, bombs and mass destruction. He felt he must tell Klaus Panzer to use a more effective tool to devalue the dollar. He was going to have to show the world's most powerful man that he could learn something from the world's most successful playboy.

****

Mei Ling sent her video of Panzer's limousine being stopped by the police to her father through a secure link. Her note said: It took me a while to get to the police station on my moped. Panzer was not there long, as I saw him leaving just as I arrived.

Her father wrote back: Was there any resistance to his arrest? Everything in the video looks peaceful.

Mei Ling replied: There was no resistance, Panzer complied.

Chin Lei replied: Anything else to report?

Mei Ling: A van also left the hotel at the same time as Panzer. It traveled in the opposite direction. I could not follow it, but the license tag was: VS52 CZS.

Chin Lei: Very well, stay prepared for additional instructions.

Mei ling was ticked. That was it? No thank you, just an expectation to do more.

The Wei family was one of the richest in China. Her father's wealth granted him membership on the Crepusculous Board. His position with Crepusculous was unknown to Me Ling, or at least that's what Chin Lei believed. In fact, keeping her in London so she could spy on Panzer was something that Chin Lei did because he had so little trust in anyone outside the family. Expecting her not to learn about the Board when she was tasked with spying on the presumptive leader of the organization was something only a nearsighted father would believe.

Mei Ling had two brothers, Quiang her older brother and Shing, her younger. Both of them were granted great privileges, especially the older who was heir to the Wei Empire. Living in China, the two boys enjoyed fast cars and county clubs. Like the other sons of

Crepusculous, the boys lived like royals. Catered to and privileged, they were shown no reason to delay gratification. Mei Ling was given a subservient role even though she was smarter, more determined and far more capable than either of the boys. She was glad to be in London and not under the direct eye of her father and his traditional beliefs. The servants in her townhouse would have to cover for her once again as she blew off her curfew and drove her moped to the Rupert Street Bar in Soho for a night of making friends over drinks.

CHAPTER 2

When Javier arrived at Klaus Panzer's townhouse , he was surprised at the unassuming appearance of the building. It was nice, and the neighborhood was appropriate, but the dwelling struck him as just so ordinary when in fact it was the London home of the most powerful man in the world.

Javier rang the bell, and the door opened to reveal a strong-looking young man who ushered him into the foyer. The man stepped over to a screen to peruse the data, which Javier now realized was acquired as he passed through a scanner built into the casing of the front door. The man nodded and gestured for Javier to move through the residence entrance, which opened with a soft buzz.

A sturdy middle-aged, Hispanic woman greeted him with a kind smile as she said quietly, "Please follow me."

Walking through the townhouse, Javier realized that understatement remained outside. The interior was magnificent. Wide hallways, large rooms, high ceilings, and rich furnishings were evident throughout his tour. This was a home that spared no expense to make the place not only comfortable but luxurious. When they reached Panzer's office, Javier's guide stepped to the side of the door and directed him inside. The office was furnished in mahogany paneling with a hunter green carpet that softly silenced every footstep. A massive Cherry desk sat three quarters back in the center of the room. Seated in a large black leather chair was Klaus Panzer with his elbows resting on the arms of the chair and his gaze locked on Javier.

Panzer raised his voice as he began, "Your irresponsible handling of the detonation device is reprehensible and absolutely unforgivable."

Javier, still wincing from the beating he took from Diegert, looked at Panzer with a raised eyebrow over his blackened eye. "I don't need your forgiveness."

Incensed, Panzer retorted, "How dare you-"

"Your plan is foolish, outdated and unnecessarily destructive. We can achieve your aims without destroying the country and economy you seek to overtake. Economic warfare need not be fought with bombs."

"You're responsible for the biggest failure Crepusculous has ever suffered. How do you plan to rectify this?" demanded Panzer.

Javier felt the heat. He knew the power of Panzer and the damage he could do, but he had studied enough economics to realize the power of money depended on faith. A collective belief in the perceived value of an otherwise worthless commodity. Seashells, gold coins, wooden nickels, paper bills, all of them only worth the value humans agree they represent. Lose that faith, and they suddenly all become the worthless junk that they really were. Facing Panzer, he said, "We destroy the belief in the dollar by eliminating it as the world's reserve currency."

"What?"

"I said, destroying faith in the dollar as the world's reserve currency will allow us to eliminate it."

Panzer spoke slowly, his anger defusing as his curiosity rose. "How do you propose we do that?"

"We do not attack the dollar from within the US but rather from the outside. The whole world has faith in the US dollar. If we undermine that faith from outside the US, the dollar's status as reliable money is threatened throughout the world."

The deep creases in Panzer's forehead relaxed as he asked, "Yes, but how do you propose to make this happen?"

"World commodities are traded in dollars, oil, food, raw materials necessary for manufacturing the products people use every day. The price for all these things is determined worldwide by the US dollar. This forces purchasers to buy essentials with dollars or use their own currencies at the dollar exchange rate."

Panzer nodded as he waited for more.

"This type of power has nothing to do with the US Government. It is not a US policy that dictates faith, it's market driven. It could just as well be Zimbabwe dollars."

Panzer frowned.

"Ok, not Zimbabwe, but it could be Digival," Javier said with a smile. "The fact that Omnisphere has already introduced Digival as a cryptocurrency gives us an opportunity to use it on a global scale for international trade."

"You're suggesting expanding Digival?"

"Yes, let's start with oil. If oil were traded worldwide in Digival rather than dollars, all the business of buying and selling oil would convert to Digival. Companies purchasing oil would have to convert their currencies to Digival. The discussion in the media would mention Digival every day as the price of a barrel of oil was reported as having gone up or down."

Panzer folded his arms and leaned back in his chair.

Javier worked to be as convincing as possible. "Being a global corporate currency, its value is not tied to the political winds of a government. This will make its value much more stable, and the purchasing power of the currency will be universal. Oh sure, a bar of soap in Tangiers, Zurich, and Chicago would be a different price in each city, but you could make purchases wherever you are with Digival."

Excitedly Javier went on, "Right on the heels of oil we go after the trade of agricultural products. Food would be traded in Digival. Every banana, side of beef, and bushel of wheat would be priced in Digival. We can do this because we're so big. Omnisphere companies purchase so much while at the same time we are also the ones from whom these purchases are made. It was you who quietly orchestrated the ownership of both ends of the market. Owning the entire supply chain from the sprout out of the ground, to the bread on the table, to the garbage disposal in the sink and the wastewater treatment plant."

Looking at Panzer, it seemed to Javier as though a realization had come over the older man. Panzer leaned forward but held a distant gaze.

After a moment, Javier leaned in. "We have to get people to have more faith in Digival than the dollar."

A devious smile spread across Panzer's lips. On his right hand, he extended two fingers. "We must approach this from both a practical and an emotional side. We must convince financial people and everybody else. We must sell Digival as a valuable independent currency, fully supported by a known and trusted corporate entity. Then we must scare the hell out of people, so they think they are going to lose everything they have invested in the dollar. Digival will be the salvation for their emotional need to have faith in the value of a currency. The designated worthless stuff won't even be stuff anymore, it'll be numbers on a screen."

Javier's smile matched that of Panzer, and they shared a moment of mutual clarity about their goal; owning the world's currency.

"The first may be more difficult than the second," said the younger man.

Nodding, Panzer offered, "Yes, but the fact that Digival is already launched is in our favor. We've had articles in the Financial Times, Barron's and the Kiplinger Report all supporting Digival. Our CEO, Abaya Patel, met with her counterpart in Goldman-Sachs and got them to invest. Their actions will prompt the other big investment banks. Owning and operating so many of the smaller banks already gives us the capacity to get them to recognize Digival. Abaya has an upcoming meeting with the head of the Federal Reserve."

"Excellent," said Javier, "that begins to address the practical side."

"Yes, but do you really think people will have faith in what will essentially be a worldwide company store?"

"If we show them that we are serious about sharing the wealth, I think they will. Right now, people think we are selfish, untrustworthy and greedy and, in many cases, they're right. But if we show generosity and appreciation by making their financial lives better, they will believe what they experience."

Javier could see the discomfort in Panzer's face as the elder man asked, "Just what are you proposing?"

"I'm not exactly sure of the means, but we should give people Digival for free so that they can spend it in our stores and on our products so that their lives are better because of it."

Panzer's eyes narrowed.

Javier went on. "We must make using Digival a positive experience that will surprise and delight them. Digival will be a reward, easily earned for doing things everyone has to do anyway. If it has a real positive impact on people's lives, they will gladly embrace it. You can't force faith. You have to build it."

Panzer sat in silence, but the look on his face drew Javier closer.

With a sweep of his hand across the room, Javier said, "Living here as you do, with the luxury of all your power, I think you may not realize how difficult it is for most people to get enough money to live on. They experience the economic anxiety of insufficient funds each and every day. They look at us, and they get angry at our ostentatious lives. If we spun that on them and gave them Digival with which they could buy whatever they need or want, and made it clear to them that we are sharing the wealth we possess, we can shape that narrative to our advantage."

"Are you suggesting that we give away, not just a little Digival to whet their appetites, but enough to feed a whole family?" asked Panzer as he rubbed his temples with the middle finger and thumb of his right hand.

"Not only feed them, but also clothe them, educate and entertain them. If our goal is to get them to use our currency for all purchases, then we must provide for them everything they need."

"Well then where is the profit?"

Javier paused, tilted his head and focused his eyes on Panzer. "If you own all the currency, there is no profit. You must have recognized that."

Panzer's brow furrowed as he dropped his forehead into his palm.

Javier spoke softly. "The goal of owning the world's currency is to already have all the money. There is no

24

more money for you to earn and own. The real prize is the power that comes from owning all the money."
Javier paused and looked at Panzer who nodded as he held his bowed head in his hand.

"Did you lose sight of that?" Javier asked as gently as he could.

"I suppose I did," said Panzer in a moment of uncommon self-disclosure. "I find it hard to separate power and money."

"Yes, but that is exactly what you will do when the dollar is replaced with Digival. The dollar is what gives the US its economic dominance in the world. They are not going to give that up easily. We have to steal it from them by giving people an alternative that provides greater benefits."

"It's going to be expensive."

"Yes it is, but in the end, we will own it all. We have the resources to span the time it will take for this transition, but once it happens, we will own everything."

Panzer's worry dissipated, and his look of confidence returned as he said, "This is truly extraordinary, I've got some additional ideas about tanking the dollar."

"Hopefully ones that don't involve blowing up the US," replied Javier.

"No, they are financial bombs which will force the government to abandon the dollar. Like you said, once the US is no longer using their own currency, the dollar will be doomed."

Checking the time on his mobile, Panzer said, "I'm glad this meeting turned out as it did. It's late, and I've got more meetings tomorrow, but I suggest you see Dr. Zeidler in the Medical Center at LPU. She's got some stuff that will help you heal from your beating."

Javier bristled at the mention of his injuries. Panzer went on, "Just to have survived a fight with David Diegert is an accomplishment. Now don't be belligerent, I want you healed up quickly. Go see Dr. Zeidler."

*****

Before retiring for the night, Abaya Patel checked her e-mail one last time. As CEO of Omnisphere, there were always issues for her to address. To manage the volume of communications, she had an e-mail filter that tiered the messages into three levels of importance. Before heading to bed, she would check only the ones grouped into the critical category.

As an Indian woman in charge of the world's largest corporation, she knew she was a target of not only the 'Ole Boys' network of white executives but also those with extremist views who felt she was violating tradition by holding such a lofty position and not putting her family first in her life. She had to be very careful about how she conducted herself, and her security was a daily ordeal.

The e-mail she opened was from the Omnisphere Office of Technical Security. Tech Sec, as it was known, was vigilant and determined to protect the electronic assets and communication networks of Omnisphere. The constant threats were addressed around the clock, and cybersecurity was a primary budget item that was never denied.

Ken Kindler was a hands-on kind of manager. Being in charge of everything, he always had his butt in a chair and his fingers on a keyboard. Ken had written to Abaya to alert her to an intrusion into the data storage servers. He was concerned because his initial assessments revealed that the intruder was using an internal computer. The hacker, though, was talented enough to see that he was discovered and quickly hid his traces. Ken didn't feel that any harm had been done, but he wanted Abaya to know, because this type of intrusion was infrequent, and the hacker's ability to escape detection was very sophisticated.

Abaya wrote back: Thank you for keeping me informed. Please keep me apprised of your progress. I want you to identify this hacker and get him to reveal himself before we shut him down. Set a trap and catch this clever devil. Thank you.

Goodnight,

Abaya

CHAPTER 3

Diegert spent the night with little sleep and a lot of boredom, so he smiled when morning came, and along with his breakfast of eggs, toast and sausage, the young woman rolled in a cart with a large screen TV. She parked the cart at the foot of Diegert's bed. Placing the tray of food on the table attached to his bed, she rotated it in front of him before unfastening the restraint on his right arm. She placed earphones equipped with a microphone on him. Using the remote, she connected the TV to the network and brought the screen to life, revealing Klaus Panzer dressed in a gray suit, seated at a large desk in a cavernous room with dark wood paneled walls. Panzer was meticulously groomed with his thick gray hair, parted on the right and combed into a compliant sweep of obedient strands.

Diegert's appetite immediately vanished.

Panzer's ice-blue eyes roamed the space in front of him as he orchestrated full connection to the TV.
 Apparently, the image of the medical room with Diegert sitting in the bed must have appeared because a smile spread across his face as he spoke. "*Guten morgen*, my son."

"I don't speak fucking German."

"Very well, English then."

"Where the fuck am I and where's my mother?"

"Your mother is with me, and I can assure you she is enjoying her accommodations in absolute comfort. No harm will come to her."

"If she's hurt, you're dead."

With a slight chuckle and a bemused smile, Panzer replied, "I am looking forward to getting to know you, David."

Diegert, eyes narrowed, wanted to tear out the throat of the fucker who called him son but treated him like a prisoner.

"You are my son, but you're a stranger to me. Imagine, the one man in the world I've contributed to creating, and I know nothing of him. How do I build a relationship with such a unique man after twenty-five years apart?"

"You've got a fucking twisted way of building trust."

"Trust. I'm afraid we are not quite there yet. You see, in spite of the fact you are my son, you're also an assassin. A killer, a man trained to murder. That makes you very dangerous. I find that compelling, but to trust a killer, one must first forge an understanding that accommodates your violent skills and abilities."

"You want to have your cake and eat it too."

"I don't understand how this expression applies."

"You're fascinated with killing. You want to be near the action without getting bloody. You're like a football fan who has never played."

"An assassin's fan." Panzer chuckled. "I suppose I am."

"Where the hell am I?" Diegert lurched forward against his restraints.

Panzer jolted in response to Diegert's aggressive movement toward the screen. He composed himself before saying, "You are still in London. This facility is part of the London Polytechnic University. Referred to more commonly by its initials LPU. My father...your grandfather...funded the establishment of this university. This medical facility supports certain clandestine operations that are carried out from within LPU."

"Clandestine?"

"Yes, but that shouldn't surprise you since you're already familiar with the tactical necessities of some of our operations."

"No, I suppose I don't need those explained."

"David, I'm going to tell you about Omnisphere, the world's largest corporation. It's a business entity that was established by the Panzer family and which now has joined forces with other individuals who hold large corporate assets within their families. These families have formed a Board that oversees the operation of Omnisphere from a quiet, private position. The Board is known as Crepusculous. Have you heard of it?"

Diegert nodded. "It wasn't easy to find out about it, but I know about Crepusculous and Omnisphere."

"Through Omnisphere," Panzer said, "we own and operate seventy-five percent of the world's economy."

"Seventy-five percent?!" repeated Diegert incredulously.

"It's substantial, and it affords us significant power over world events. We use that power in many ways, including the support of scientific discovery. Creation Labs is a bioscience lab that produces the most cutting-edge work in the world."

"Like what?"

"Like nanocytic manipulation of amino acids altering the phenotypic expression of the genetic code, directing the structure of proteins for the molecular recreation of living tissue."

Diegert's inquisitive look gave away the lost place in which he found himself.

Panzer went on, "Using nanocyte technology, we have grown new organs, like the liver and the pancreas, inside human subjects."

"Really? That sounds amazing. I've never heard of this."

"Amazing as it is, it's only the beginning of what we can do by fusing biology with digital technology. Using software to direct gene expression allows us to alter the structure of proteins in ways that change the very nature of who we are. Creation Labs allows scientists to push the limits of discovery without being bound by convention or resource limitations."

Diegert nodded, and Panzer went on. "I believe the current state of scientific inquiry is trapped in its own ethical quagmire. Time, effort and energy are wasted on ethical considerations that stall progress in critically important areas. Fortunately, our private funding allows us to bypass these limits and push scientific discoveries into new and exciting areas like the control of cells through nanocyte transponders."

"What can you make the cells do?"

"It depends on which cells we're talking about, but we can alter protein structures, reconstituting their amino acids to change their phenotypic expression."

Diegert didn't fully understand, but he hid it as best he could.

Panzer explained, "It means we can change the way tissues appear on the body. We can also instruct proteins so that they will heal damaged tissue. We've also successfully used Digi-bio transponders to direct stem cells to form new organs. We've created new kidneys inside people."

The statement held Diegert's curiosity, because everyone knew there were not enough kidneys available for those who needed transplants. "That's cool."

"Yes, very cool."

"You can help a lot of people with that."

"Well, not really. We are not sharing this technology. It is proprietary, and we are keeping it secret."

"Why? You could not only help people, but this would be worth billions!"

"Society is not ready for the advances this will bring. But most of all, the power of having a new and unique technology gives us an advantage that is worth much more than money."

"How so?"

"Take cancer for example. We have successfully identified tumors in their earliest stages and directed immune cells to attack and specifically destroy the tumors. Then we have reconstructed the damaged tissue and restored full functional capacity. We have done this in the liver, the pancreas, and the brain."

"OK, again, that sounds way cool, but why not share this?"

"Having your own cure for cancer is a personal advantage that gives you power over all others. Power, my son, allows you to succeed in this world. Everything Crepusculous does is in the pursuit of power. Digitally manipulating proteins to cure cancer gives me power over human health like no one else on earth. I intend to maintain this advantage."

Diegert looked at the man on the screen and saw a disturbing mix of brilliance and selfishness, yet Panzer's eyes brightened with excitement as he said, "One of the greatest discoveries the lab has produced is the way in which nanocytes are powered."

Curious, Diegert tilted his head, peering at Panzer with a sidelong gaze.

Panzer leaned forward in his chair. "These tiny electronic instruments are powered by body heat. For years, labs have been trying to develop batteries on a sub-nano scale to energize their devices. The sheer size of the batteries rendered the devices useless. The scientists at Creation Labs, inspired by the basic technology by which solar panels turn sunlight into electricity, realized that the heat of the human body could power the nanocytes. Sixty percent of the calories consumed by the body are converted into heat, which the body has to get rid of by releasing it into the environment."

Diegert picked up on this point. "You mean like sweating."

"Yes, the body produces a constant source of energy which we have harnessed to power the tiny devices which now can direct the body's functions through digital communication."

"That's smart."

"Not only smart, but it's also ingenious. Seeing the possibility and then turning the obvious into the practical requires a level of vision that few possess. Creation Labs has made one of the most significant discoveries in the world."

"And you're going to keep all that power for yourself?"

"Not exactly. We're applying this technology to some projects in support of Crepusculous and Omnisphere."

"It sounds selfishly evil," said Diegert.

"It's progressive and revolutionary," replied Panzer.

Diegert defiantly held eye contact with Panzer. The older man shifted his gaze and seemed to soften his demeanor.

"David, I want to be your father and share all this with you."

"Fuck you. I don't even know you, and you have me locked up in here." Diegert jerked on his restraints.

Panzer shook his head. "I will admit to some perplexing emotions as I react to your arrival in my life. It's certain that we got off to a rough start, but I believe the bond of family can heal all wounds, and I look forward to being a good father to you. Do you want a father in your life?"

The sneer on Diegert's face progressed to a snarl as Panzer spoke. The question, though, widened Diegert's eyes and softened the edges of his mouth. *Do you want a father?* The question assumed there was a choice to be made or was it that Panzer was looking for him to open the door? If he said yes, on whose terms would the relationship develop? If he said no, would Panzer get angry and destroy him? Besides these practical points, Diegert had to consider what was missing in his life that the guidance of a man could provide? What aspects of himself would be different if he had the love of a father influencing his life? Did he want a father? More specifically did he want Klaus Panzer as his father?

"Yes, I want a father, but I don't know what that means, and I don't know if you're the man."

"I can understand your doubt and perhaps it is presumptuous of me to assume you are not already satisfied with the man who currently fills that role. How about you tell me all about your dad...Tom Diegert?"

Anger rushed through Diegert, and he scowled. How could he reveal anything but the ugly truth about that awful man? "What do you already know about him?"

"I really know nothing about him."

Diegert considered the differences between these two men and hoped that Panzer had a real intention to be a father. "He's a loser. He hates me because he knows he's not my father. He hates me because of you."

"He couldn't see what an extraordinary young man you are."

Diegert recognized the manipulation, but it was difficult to ignore the emotions such compliments brought in him. "Instead of a father's love, I had only disdain and distrust."

Panzer held his gaze from within the screen. "How did he earn a living?"

"What the fuck do you care? You're just asking because you don't want to discuss your complicity in my shitty life."

"You are suggesting that I am responsible for the quality of your life?"

"Right from the end of your dick."

Panzer shuddered when Diegert spat out his last word.

"Now you want the benefits of a son without having to have been there when I was growing up through every shitty part of my childhood. The guy laying here in this bed is a product of your absence, not your influence."

Panzer reacted, "My father, your grandfather, always made me earn everything I wanted. He was a strict man and enforced very structured rules within the family."

"Oh yeah, did use a gun to enforce his rules?"

"What?"

"You know, point a pistol at your head to get you to do whatever he wanted? Did he keep a loaded gun handy for resolving domestic disputes?"

"No, but that doesn't mean there weren't high expectations of behavior and achievement."

"It's hardly the same. Poor people have to earn stuff or else they go without. Rich people get things granted to them from those who already have so much. You may think you earned something because your dad made you do some work at home, but try being a kid and knowing that your father won't give you anything. You have to get what you need from outside the home. It's totally different, and you have no idea what it's like."

Panzer contemplated the severity of that level of poverty.

"I can see I have much to learn from you, David. I hope you will grant me the opportunity to become significant in your life.

"Oh I'm sure you're going to be significant, but I don't know if we'll ever be close."

"I want to be... close," said Panzer awkwardly.

From a scowl of doubt, Diegert said, "A man who pays to have people killed was never what I hoped for in a father. Your power has corrupted both of us. I have killed in your name and hardened my heart to do so. You have made your son a murderer."

Panzer looked around the room he was in. His gaze fell everywhere but on the face of his son. Diegert could see the consternation in Panzer's contemplation. Diegert was getting mad as he wanted his "father" to acknowledge the consequences of his actions.

"Tactical actions are often necessary to achieve strategic objectives," said Panzer as he flexed his fingers to inspect his nails. "I believe you will come to understand this as we move forward." Bringing his hands together, leaning forward and looking directly into the screen, Panzer pressed on, "David, there is much for us to overcome, and I expect you to realize this if you are going to be anything more than just a hitman in my organization. You will have to show me that you are more than a lonely, sad man who snivels about every decisive action he has ever taken."

Diegert was gobsmacked to have Panzer shift his tone so severely. He had no reply as Panzer expounded. "If you want to be something more to me than just an embarrassing bastard, you'll have to demonstrate your value and succeed with me or cease to be. Soon I will have Avery Forsythe visit you. He is a special operations trainer who will begin your transition here at LPU. Good day, my son."

The screen went black, leaving Diegert shocked and dismayed. Another threat to his life if he didn't comply. This time from the man who claimed him as his son, a bastard son! Diegert grew angry, and the sense of wanting to attack Panzer heated up within him. How dare that fucker threaten him and call him a bastard, the label he hated the most and had to bear because of Panzer. If they were in the same room, he'd show him how dangerous it was to have an assassin for a son. This man had so much to offer, but would they ever be able to connect on an emotional level? Did it matter? Should he just play the role of a dutiful son and take advantage of all the riches, or should he force this man to acknowledge the pain he created by abandoning him and later turning him into an assassin? Diegert realized he was stuck in a love/ hate relationship with Panzer. Well, not really love, but curiously hopeful crossed with hate. Could he have the paternal bond with this man that he longed for, or was he going to kill him the first chance he got?

CHAPTER 4

Carolyn Fuller did not appreciate having to meet the Head of the CIA British office in her hospital-issued pajamas. Lying in her bed, with IV tubes in her arms and drains out of her chest, she felt vulnerable, or at least not very professional. The fact that she was here, involved in an operation, without even notifying the British office, was a breach of protocol for which she would be held accountable. Carolyn was someone who understood protocol and had a long history of adhering to it. This situation made her afraid her behavior was going to seem erratic, a stark departure from normal, a key flag for the agency to believe an agent had been compromised. She considered taking the tranquilizers the doctor had suggested so she would be unconscious when Richard Ramsey arrived, but she wasn't one to shy away from her problems.

The CIA had posted a guard outside her room, and it was he who opened the door allowing Mr. Richard Ramsey to enter. Ramsey had an appearance the agency handbook would refer to as "non-descript." He was just shy of six feet, and a little over 200 pounds. His brown hair had receded past the crown of his cranium, and his eyes were the color of mud. Carolyn knew that, in his career, he had some success as an agent, but the allure of bureaucracy with its lack of physical activity and danger had an early appeal for Ramsey. She had watched him play his politics well, and she knew that being the head of a foreign office was an important stepping-stone up the agency's mountainous career path.

"You're looking good," he began.

"Thanks, I wish I could say I picked out the pajamas myself."

With a polite chuckle, Ramsey replied, "Are you being treated well?"

"Yes the staff is very attentive, and the doctors are top-notch."

"I understand you'll be out in a week or so."

"They're telling me they want the lungs to heal enough so that movement won't undo the surgery."

"Well, that certainly makes sense."

Carolyn smiled and nodded, but she was afraid her anxiety was beginning to show.

Ramsey squared his shoulders as he narrowed his gaze before saying, "I'm sorry if I seem blunt, but I have to say something here."

Carolyn's smile faded.

"What the hell are you doing here? With all the shit going down in the US, how is it that you're here in London having been shot and lying in a hospital bed?"

Carolyn regretted not taking the tranquilizers. "I know it seems surprising and a little out of protocol, but I can explain."

Ramsey pulled a chair to the side of the bed and sat down.

Carolyn's dry throat made it uncomfortable to swallow as she started to say, "I met David Diegert at a CIA safe house in Detroit. He had been brought there by an FBI agent, a professional colleague of mine, Jim Donovan."

"Diegert? The guy who assassinated the president five days ago?"

"He wasn't the shooter."

"An accomplice then?" said Ramsey, raising his voice.

"Not exactly."

"Then what was he... exactly?"

Carolyn's mind raced for the right term to convey Diegert's innocence in spite of his complicity with everything that led to the assassination of Peter Carson, President of the United States. "Diegert was a fall guy. He was set up to take the blame for the assassination. The real force behind the attack is far bigger and more powerful than he is."

"A great big conspiracy theory. I look forward to seeing the evidence for that."

"Have you ever heard of Crepusculous?" asked Carolyn.

Ramsey frowned as he turned his head. "Is that something I'm going to catch while I'm here?"

"It's not a disease, it's an elite organization of very wealthy and powerful businessmen. I told MI5 about them, and I think they're probably questioning them."

"You think businessman, not terrorists, are behind the assassination?"

Carolyn nodded. "I believe it warrants further investigation."

"Was it a businessman who shot you?"

"It was dark," snapped Carolyn sharply. "The attack was sudden, and the shooter's face was obscured by a large hood. This isn't a fucking joke. This is real, and it doesn't end with the president's death, it's way bigger than you realize."

Ramsey snorted. "Height, weight, approximate age, male, female, the color of clothing? Your powers of observation must have picked up something. How are we ever going to find a suspect?"

"I gave all that information to the police at the scene. Finding that suspect is their job, ours is to protect the United States."

Forcing a smile as he leaned forward in his chair, Ramsey said, "Thanks for the reminder, but I see the two issues as intertwined. My real dilemma is what do I charge you with?"

"Charge me? I didn't do anything that I could be charged with." Alarms went off in her room and at the nurse's desk as her heart raced.

"Oh no? Not aiding and abetting a suspect, not obstruction of justice, not collusion with perpetrators of an act of terrorism? There are several charges I could level at you."

"I'm innocent of all of that," said Carolyn trembling in her bed.

Ramsey stood up, leaned over and said, "No problem, we'll just get a polygraph in here and have you answer my questions."

Dr. Gibson knocked on the doorjamb as he entered the room. "Excuse me, but my patient is not to have any visitors."

Ramsey faced the younger man. "Don't worry, Doc, Carolyn and I are professional colleagues. She doesn't mind if I'm here."

"She may not, but I do. You've upset her, and I want you to leave."

"Just a few more questions."

"In the hospital, I am the authority, and I decide what is in the best interest of my patients. Now I believe I have made myself clear. Please leave now."

Ramsey glared at the taller man but yielded to his authority. "All right," he said, throwing up his hands as he walked to the door. "We'll talk some more when you're feeling better." With a hand on the shoulder of the big guard at the door, Ramsey said, "Officer Weiss here will guarantee your security while in custody." Turning and standing so he filled the doorway. "I hope you're feeling better soon." Tipping two fingers forward off his forehead in a poor facsimile of a military salute, Ramsey turned and walked away.

"You all right?" asked Dr. Gibson.

"Yeah, I'm fine," said Carolyn.

"Your vitals were going crazy. Who was that guy?"

"It's OK, it's just business."

"Yeah, well when your business is the CIA that can be some deadly stress."

Carolyn spun her gaze to look directly at the young doctor. She felt as exposed as when she walked the hall in her open-backed hospital pajamas. "How do you know who my employer is?"

"As a doctor, I'm concerned about everything that could affect my patient's health. It's my job to know."

"OK," said Carolyn giving the doctor a wan smile.

Sliding a chair up next to the bed, Dr. Gibson sat down. "Carolyn, I have something more to discuss with you."

Carolyn's smile faded as she sat up and leaned forward in her bed. "What?"

"We perform full blood diagnostics on every patient admitted to the hospital."

"Yeah so?"

"So, a portion of your results reveal that you are pregnant."

Carolyn brought her hands to her face and rubbed her eyes with her fists as she laid her head on her pillow staring up at the ceiling.

"We will be monitoring your condition and providing appropriate treatment while you're an inpatient. Do you have any questions?" asked the doctor.

"No," Carolyn said softly.

"OK, then, I'll let you get some rest."

"Thanks, Doc," came her muted reply.

The threat of arrest, the implosion of her career, the destruction of the United States, all dissipated in her mind as the horror of sharing parenthood with David Diegert pierced her soul. This had to be a mistake. She wasn't in for an obstetrics appointment. The results must have gotten mixed with up someone who wanted a child, was ready for a child and had nothing but love to give a child. She wasn't that person. This couldn't be happening to her.

CHAPTER 5

By Panzer's order, Dr. Zeidler removed Diegert's restraints. He shaved, showered, put on a pair of gray sweatpants and a black t-shirt. He got to eat with both hands which made the food taste better even though he had mastered one-handed eating. Laying on his bed with his legs crossed at the ankles, arms stretched out with his hands interlocked behind his head. Diegert smiled to himself and thought of how the little victories are what help you endure captivity. Barney Pinsdale, Captain of the *Sue Ellen* sailboat, taught him that when they first met. Diegert recalled how he and Barney sailed across the Indian Ocean, the Red Sea and the Mediterranean, from Mogadishu to Alexandropoulos. That was real freedom. He now understood why Barney preferred life at sea, even if his boat was financed by transporting assassins from one job to another, leaving dead bodies in the wake.

Patience and endurance; Diegert figured he'd need a lot of both before he was going to get on the other side of this ordeal. As he contemplated his place in life, a distinguished looking man of African descent stood at his door waiting to be acknowledged. He and Diegert made eye contact and silently considered one another. The man was tall, maybe 6' 2". He was lean and fit looking although his clothing made body assessment difficult. He was dressed in a loose-fitting cotton shirt covered by a dark green tunic, sashed at the waist and draping his lower body like a skirt. The drapes were open on both sides revealing black canvas pants and black boots. His ensemble looked to Diegert like he'd just walked out of Tatooine.

"Well you gonna come in or what?" asked Diegert.

The man crossed the threshold, offering his hand. "Hello, I'm Avery Forsythe."

Diegert shook his hand, feeling the strength and the callouses. He also noted that the right hand had a deformity in the first two bones of the palm. They were indented, perhaps having healed incorrectly after being fractured.

"I heard you were coming. You're the trainer who's supposed to get me ready for whatever they have planned for me."

"I prepare my pupils for the path that destiny has laid before them."

Diegert tried not to smirk, but it came through anyway.

"We all follow a path that life has laid out before us," said Avery. "My teaching is to help you recognize the path you are on and maximize your skills and abilities for life's journey."

"I thought this place was going to be a bit more prescriptive in its expectations."

"Expectation is nothing more than a long word for bias. A preconceived notion that can be communicated but is rarely perceived as it was intended."

"Woo… how do you get anything done?"

"Outcomes are achieved by finding the person whose path is aligned with a specific need."

"Sounds like you go through a lot of people before you get what you need."

"We are getting ahead of ourselves, but I'm refreshed by one whose intellect will be as potent as his ability to kill."

Diegert's eyes widened at the last part of the statement. "I guess the mystical stuff is over."

"Oh no, far from it. You and I will travel a path that is filled with betrayal, corruption, violence, and death."

"That's the shit that got me here."

"Precisely, your path led you here. We achieve our objectives and accomplish our goals by finding the right people on the path from which we have a need."

Diegert, with nothing more to say, stared back at Avery Forsythe with curiosity and apprehension.

"You and I will spend time in training, and I hope you will find it meaningful. Right now, though, I have a different mission to complete with you."

"What's that?"

"The drugs you were given at the Ambassador were Benzodiazepines. They're an anesthetic that is memory toxic. I want to discuss some recent events with you to jog your memory and assess it for loss."

"Ok, I feel good. I don't feel like I've lost memory."

"Sometimes we can't know what we've lost."

"Right."

"Can you tell me about your experience in the Army?"

Diegert recalled how his time in the Army did not end well. He was dishonorably discharged for striking his superior officer. Being dishonorably discharged is just one speeding ticket away from being a felon, which reduces your employability to under the table wage work.

"When I think of the Army, I recall the training I received with firearms and defensive tactics. I gained the critical skills required of all soldiers; to fight and kill with efficiency."

"So you're comfortable with killing?"

"I'd say I'm skilled at it, but not really comfortable."

"Do you feel guilty about killing?"

"Yes, but I've learned to compartmentalize it. It's not a resolution for how it makes me feel, but it's a method of coping."

Avery tilted his head, looking at Diegert with a hint of suspicion.

Diegert held eye contact and his tongue on the subject.

"Do you recall shooting the President of the United States?"

"I didn't shoot the president. I pointed the gun, but it was operated remotely, and someone else pulled that trigger."

"You pointed the gun."

"Under duress. I was sent a video on my phone of my mother with a gun to her head. I had to point that gun."

"I see the details of that incident are fresh in your mind."

Diegert shrugged his shoulders and nodded.

Avery went on, "Do you recall how you escaped and made it all the way to London?"

Diegert had been led to a trap.

"Time is of the essence in this process," said Avery. "Please answer the question."

"No, I don't remember. I can't recall what happened."

"You see, the drugs can be toxic. There's no way you could get from Detroit to London without a functioning intellect, but now you can't recall."

Diegert almost smirked while nodding his head. He looked at Avery, ready for the next question.

"Do you recall being helped by anyone? Did you meet anyone?"

Diegert recalled Carolyn Fuller, the CIA agent, who saved his life and made the whole trip to London possible. There was no way though that he was going to share one shred of memory about her.

"No." He shook his head. "I can't recall anyone helping me at all."

Avery arched one eyebrow. "Do you recall fighting with Javier Perez?"

Perhaps against better judgment, but with bravado, Diegert replied, "I kicked that fucker's ass."

"What were you fighting about?"

"He's an asshole and deserved even more than I gave him. When I have the chance to kick ass on a spoiled rich dickhead, I do it."

"Do you remember where the fight took place?"

Diegert did, of course, recall it all, the exchange of Fatima's son Hamni for the detonation device. The fact that Javier was a better fighter than Diegert ever expected. And that Fatima got away with Hamni after shooting Carolyn.

"No I don't remember, but it doesn't matter because I will kick his ass any time, any place."

"One last question," said Avery. "I want you to answer this question immediately after I ask it. Do you understand?"

Diegert nodded, and Avery squared up looking directly into the younger man's eyes.

"Do you know Carolyn Fuller?"

"No, I don't know anyone by that name."

The tell was there. Diegert's eyes flinched to the right for just a fraction of a second. He did not want Carolyn's name to be known to Crepusculous. Diegert wasn't sure that Avery saw it, but going to all this trouble to ask the question, he knew the mystical man was looking for a tell.

"I see," said Avery. "Well, that is all quite enough for now. We covered a lot of ground." As he exited the room, Avery said, "I'll let you get some rest and be back to train with you again."

Just before the door Avery turned to Diegert and said, "Minwaadizi."

After Avery walked away, Diegert's bells were ringing. *That was an Ojibwa word.* He hadn't heard Ojibwa, the native language of his mother, spoken for such a long time. Avery's effort to learn and use an Ojibwa salutation was surprisingly impressive.

CHAPTER 6

Dr. Marie Zeidler, in addition to caring for David
Diegert, also saw his mother, Denise. As the Director
of Medical Services in the underground labyrinth of
Panzer's secret activities section within LPU, Dr.
Zeidler realized that the patients she treated performed
acts of moral turpitude for their common employer.

Ambivalence rumbled inside her as a result of
providing care for people who killed people. It was an
annoying distraction which often made her regret
winning the full academic scholarship to medical
school she was awarded from Klaus Panzer's "Light the
Way" foundation. She was only one year into her five-
years of obligation.

Denise was an oddity that excited the young doctor.
Upon her arrival, Dr. Zeidler had ordered blood work to
be performed on the mother of David Diegert. It was
undoubtedly unprecedented that she would treat an
assassin and his mother. Some of the guys she had
cared for were so tough and cold it was hard to think of
them as even having a loving mother. Here now, she
was examining the results from the lab of the woman
who raised the deadly David Diegert, the assassin of the
President of the United States. At first, Denise Diegert
needed sedation to calm her. Valium did the trick, and
Dr. Zeidler was able to conduct her exam. During her
assessment, she found a healthy, fit 47-year-old woman
with a height of 5 foot 10 inches and a weight of 135
pounds. Her jet black hair, which framed an exotically
beautiful face, was braided into a long ponytail. She

seemed to be someone who was physically active and capable of endurance. The analysis of her blood though revealed a red flag. Now that Denise was comfortable in her quarters and the Valium had worn off, Dr. Zeidler paid her a second visit. The apartment was spacious and well furnished. It was bigger than the entire house in which Denise lived in Minnesota.

"Good afternoon, how are you feeling?" asked the doctor upon entering the suite where Denise was now residing.

"I'm OK. Do you know where my son is?"

"Yes, he's in another room within this facility."

"Is he Ok? Is the room nearby? Can I go see him?" came the rapid-fire questions.

With a gently raised hand and a soothing smile, the doctor sought to calm the nervous mother. Dr. Zeidler was impressed with Denise's maternal instincts. "He's OK, I've been taking care of him. He's a very strong guy who's on his way to a full recovery."

"Is he conscious?"

"Yes."

"Oh good, when I last saw him, he was helpless and defenseless."

Dr. Zeidler raised an eyebrow. "I can tell you he's awake now and quite able to represent himself."

Denise let out a big sigh.

"I'd like to discuss some of the results from your bloodwork."

"OK."

"Have you ever seen an oncologist?"

Quizzically Denise replied, "What kind of a doctor is that?"

"An oncologist specializes in cancer."

"No."

Taken aback, Dr. Zeidler said, "Oh… Ok. I have results here that indicate an elevated level of CA-125."

Denise remained impassive, but the doctor could see tension in her expression.

"When we find these elevated levels, they indicate that we should do more investigation. I want to ask you some questions about your family health history."

Denise gave a slight nod.

"Has your mother or other family members ever been diagnosed with cancer?"

"My mother died before she was thirty years old."

"Oh, I'm sorry to hear that. What was the cause of death?"

"Suicide."

Now the doctor felt like she'd intruded. She began to feel like Denise's family history may reveal more than she was hoping to find.

"That's unfortunate. It must have been very hard. How old were you at the time?"

"Twelve," said Denise harshly.

In spite of having rubbed a sore, the doctor persevered, "How about your father?"

"My mother was raped by a white man. I never knew who he was."

The doctor had stepped into a minefield and from where she stood her next question could very well trigger an explosion. She shifted her focus. "We're going to have to do some additional testing."

"Like what? My insurance probably won't pay for any of this."

"Don't worry about the costs, Herr Panzer will cover the expenses."

"What's it like... working for him?"

"Working for Herr Panzer?" clarified Dr. Zeidler.

"Yes," replied Denise. "How well do you know him? How much do you know about the kind of man he is?"

A quick look at Denise preceded the doctor's reply. "I work for him, I really don't know him personally," she said with a stiff smile. "Now I'm going to order a CT scan and a sonography study of your abdomen."

"He seems to always get whatever he wants," said Denise wistfully.

"Herr Panzer is a very powerful man."

"Yes. From where does a man get so much power? How can one person live so much better than everyone else? Even though life is not fair, he reminds us every day how unfair it really is."

"Mrs. Diegert…" The doctor sat in a chair next to her. "May I call you Denise?"

A polite smile and nod granted permission.

"I understand your question. I too am at times both amazed and annoyed at the attitude of Herr Panzer. His wealth affords him privileges that most people will never experience. But right now, you are going to receive the benefit of his generosity by undergoing a thorough medical exam free of charge."

The doctor gave Denise a reassuring smile.

"Thank you, I appreciate your kindness. What if these tests show I have cancer?"

"LPU has a full medical school. Cancer studies are one of the biggest areas of research. If cancer is detected, you will receive treatment. Herr Panzer has already authorized all expenses."

"Do you ask yourself why he would do that for me?"

"No, I serve the medical needs of all the patients in my care."

"Yeah but why me?"

"For a man who has so much, generosity is easy," said the doctor reassuringly.

Denise fell silent. She dropped her head in her hands as tears welled up in her eyes. Sobs escaped from her as gasps. Convulsions rippled through her as the force she struggled to repress burst forth. Her cries drew the doctor closer. Marie Zeidler recalled that counseling was one of her least favorite parts of medical school. She was hesitant to engage even though her patient was obviously going through an emotional upheaval.

"Are you all right?" asked Dr. Zeidler with the timidity of a dormouse.

Denise raised her tear-streaked face. "Do you know what he is capable of?"

Zeidler swallowed hard, grimacing as she leaned back from Denise.

"As my doctor, you are obligated to keep information private aren't you?" blurted Denise.

"Yes."

"What I'm about to tell you stays between you and me."

The squeamish doctor looked at her patient with both hesitation and anticipation.

Denise stretched her sleeve as she used it to dry her eyes. "You know that I am David's mother, and I want you to know that Klaus Panzer is David's father."

The doctor, practiced in keeping emotions in check, dropped her jaw, repeatedly blinked her eyes and couldn't find her words.

Denise pounced on the doctor's shocked surprise. "I will tell you how it happened, but you must keep it secret."

Dr. Zeidler nodded. "As your doctor, all our conversations are confidential."

Denise's trepidation retreated as she began, "I was a waitress at the Deerfield Lodge in Kitsak Minnesota over twenty-five years ago. The Lodge was a hunting club that catered to millionaires. Klaus Panzer was there demonstrating his company's hunting rifles. After we had served dinner, I was working with the kitchen staff cleaning up and getting things ready for breakfast when my manager came and asked me to deliver a tray of fruit, biscuits, and cognac to Klaus Panzer's room. He looked me right in the eye and told me to make sure Mr. Panzer was completely satisfied… completely."

Dr. Zeidler's look conveyed the dread, which accompanied any woman's recognition that she was being forced into a compromised situation.

"When I got to his room, he ushered me in and told me to place the tray on the side table. Once I was in the room, he began talking to me, small talk. Having read my name off my badge, he used it repeatedly. I listened but did not engage. As I moved to the door, I followed my training and asked him if there was anything more I could do for him."

The edge of the doctor's lip rose into a sneer.

"He said there was something more. He proceeded to tell me that he had made love to almost all of the exotic women in the world. Asians, Africans, Arabic, Nordic and Latinas, but he had never had sex with a Native American. He told me I was beautiful, and he approached me with his hand reaching for mine. I pulled my hand away and told him I wanted to leave. He looked irritated. I moved to the door, and he blocked my way. You know he's a big man, but twenty-six years ago he was way more muscular. He was imposing and entitled. I will never forget what he said, "You aren't going anywhere. You will submit, and it will be better for both of us."

The doctor closed her eyes and tilted her head away. Re-opening her eyes, she returned her gaze to Denise.

"He unbuttoned his shirt, undid his pants, and removed his underwear." Denise started to tremble; moisture filling her eye lids. "Standing there in the nude-" a gasp escaped her throat. "He pulled me into his arms and began kissing me. He undressed me, laid me on the bed and fucked me. He was hard for so long, it hurt." Clutching her chest as she dropped her head, Denise sobbed as tears fell into her lap. "He didn't notice or care. I screamed out in pain, he just covered my mouth and kept at it. It was humiliating and degrading." Denise fell into guttural gasps as she used a Kleenex to soak up the tears draining from her nose. Crushing the tissue in her fist she said, "I was forced into having sex with this man because of his position of power. As I got dressed, the demeaning fucker told me my manager would include extra compensation in my next paycheck. That never happened."

"You were raped."

Denise nodded as a frown forced her lips into a curve of sadness. "Within a month, I was pregnant. I was so distraught, I hadn't had sex with my husband since before that night. He was upset and suspicious, but I was broken and confused." Another spasm of anguished tears enveloped her as she sobbed with more force than the doctor had ever witnessed. Possessed by her need to cry, she was inconsolable until her voice, stricken with grief, re-emerged. "When the pregnancy was obvious, Tom beat me until I told him what happened." Running her hand through her hair and pulling her ponytail in front of her she said, "About that same time, the town gossip, generated by my co-workers who saw me enter and leave his room, spread the story all over town. I thought Tom was going to beat the baby out of me, but I refused to let a life within me die. David was born on May twentieth. In spite of being unwillingly conceived, he received all the best of a mother's love."

Wiping tears off her cheeks, Denise looked at Dr. Zeidler with reddened eyes full of despair.

"That's a painful story." With her chin quivering, Dr. Zeidler said, "I don't know what to say."

Sniffing, Denise said, "There's nothing to be said, just be aware of what that monster is capable of. I want you to see a rapist every time you look at him."

Despite the fatigue of her grief, Denise bore a look of determination the doctor hadn't seen before. The strength of this woman to persevere through all that was thrust upon her was now visible in the set of her jaw and the glare in her crimson tinged eyes.

Doctor Zeidler overcame her halting emotions to say, "I'll look upon him with refreshed eyes. I'm going to go order your tests now. I hope you find peace."

"Thanks a lot," said Denise "but I don't think I'm going to see peace in my future."

CHAPTER 7

Diegert laid in his bed. It was 5:30 a.m. He was awake but had no intention of getting up.

"Good morning," said Avery Forsythe with a cheerful tone as he walked into Diegert's room wheeling a device which he parked in the space typically occupied by a second bed. He locked the brakes on the wheels and looked at Diegert with a big smile. Diegert remained in his bed, wiping sleep from his eyes.

"You've been physically inactive now for six days including more than twenty-four hours unconscious," Avery stated in a matter of fact tone. "You're going to be in medical a few more days so I brought you this gym on wheels so you can get your strength back."

Diegert swung his legs out of bed and sat at the edge looking at the contraption.

Avery was excited, "First it's important to recognize that with all four wheels locked this thing is solid. You've got dumbbells, and kettlebells, ten pounds through forty pounds and the dumbbells can be adjusted through five-pound increments with these add-on plates." Avery pointed out the black discs with a slot down the middle, and the little lever which secured them in place.

Diegert, having not yet said a word, gave a nod to the obvious.

Pressing a button on the shaft of the upright cylinder on the right side of the rolling base, Avery extruded three feet of steel tubing. He flexed the tube at the hinge, attaching the open end to the upright cylinder on the opposite side of the base. With the crossbar in place, he pulled on a cable, telescoping the vertical support sections until the crossbar was seven feet high. Turning the twist lock on the base shaft solidified the supports. Stepping back, Avery said, "Give it a try."

Diegert slid his feet to the floor and stood under the crossbar. He reached up, grabbed the steel tube with both hands, and slowly did a pull-up. He struggled four more times and, after completing five, let go of the bar, dropping to his feet, toiling for breath.

Unable to mask his disappointment, Avery said, "It looks like this device has arrived just in time."

Sitting back on his bed, Diegert pledged, "Let me get some breakfast, and I'll get on it."

When Avery returned the following afternoon, he asked Diegert, "How do you like the gym?"

"Yeah, I like working out," said Diegert.

"Which is more important," asked Avery, "strength or quickness?"

"For what?"

"Fighting."

"I dunno, aren't they both important?"

Avery shot his right hand out, instantly touching the backside of his fingers to Diegert's cheek. He pulled his hand back before Diegert could blink. The younger man's startled reaction occurred after Avery had already returned his hand back to its folded position.

The contact was a touch, not a slap. There was no harmful force delivered to Diegert's face. His defenses, however, had been breached without him even realizing or reacting.

Avery began, "Quickness is the speed of interchange between the sensory, central and motor components of your nervous system."

"Central?" Diegert asked.

"That's your brain and spinal cord. The sensory and motor make up the input and output networks of your peripheral nervous system."

Central is my brain and spinal cord, and peripheral is the rest of the nerves in my body?" stated Diegert seeking clarity.

"Precisely. When you're quick, you can sense what's happening and react to it appropriately."

"So you think quickness is more important than strength."

"Strength is the generation of force. Is great force always necessary to defend yourself or defeat an opponent?"

"All right, so there both important, so what?"

"So gaining strength will not increase your quickness. You must train both."

"Well, you brought me a whole cart there for building strength."

"And now I have some drills to make you quicker. Move that chair into the corner and sit down."

Diegert moved the sturdy chair, so it faced the corner of the room. The floor and both walls were covered in aquamarine tile. Sitting in the chair, Diegert turned his head to look over his shoulder at Avery, who held a tennis ball in his hand. Raising his hand, Avery twirled his extended index finger indicating that Diegert should turn around. Now facing the corner, Diegert heard Avery say, "Catch the ball."

Immediately, the tennis ball bounced into the corner, first contacting the floor and then ricocheting off the right wall. Diegert reached, but his reaction was too slow, and the ball shot past him.

"Ok, I get it now," said an agitated Diegert. "Throw it again."

This time, Avery threw it at the right wall, sending it down to the floor where it bounced to the left. Diegert's reaction was again too slow, and the ball got away from him.

"Hey, it's supposed to hit the floor first," shouted Diegert as he turned to face Avery.

"There are no such rules. Turn around."

Diegert swung around to face the corner again. He leaned forward in his seat with both hands ready. He turned his head slightly to the left and then the right anticipating the coming of the ball from either direction.

Avery lobbed the ball over Diegert such that it fell right in front of the tense young man. The ball bounced up, and Diegert grabbed for it, first with the right and an instant later the left, neither of which contacted the ball as it fell to the floor and rolled under Diegert's chair.

Avery picked up the ball as it rolled to him. Diegert stood up from his chair to face his tormentor. "Hey, this is not fair. I don't have a chance. How can you expect me to know where the ball is coming from?"

"David, there are no rules, it is not fair. It is a game of skill. It is a test of your ability to react to visual stimuli, generate appropriate neural signals, and allow your muscles to be guided by them."

"Well, that makes it sound so simple."

"I believe it is. The real test is whether or not you are going to let the simple thing happen, or whether you're going to clutter your mind with unnecessary and conflicting information which interrupts the simplicity."

"Fuck you, let me try again."

"OK, but you are filling your mind with anticipation. Creating visual cues in your imagination trying to predict where the ball is going to come from, rather than allowing your eyes and your visual cortex to relax and accurately interpret what comes before it, without all the extraneous data created by your imagination."

Diegert looked at Avery. He felt like a jack lighted buck just before being shot.

Avery smiled. "Relaxation isn't just time off to watch TV. It's a state of conscious presence during which we must still the mind, allowing it to absorb and interpret what is before it, without bias or judgment. In a truly relaxed state, we can see with eyes that are fresh, and gain insight that is not prejudiced by all that has come before it. While relaxed, we can see a simple truth and follow the path of something as basic as a bouncing ball. You ready to try again?"

Diegert let out a big sigh as he turned and sat back down in the chair.

The ball came from the right, struck the floor and ricocheted off the left wall. Diegert could see the ball moving, going high and to the right. His whole body lurched forward, coming out of the chair. Both hands shot forward toward the ball. His right hand contacted the fuzzy yellow sphere which bounced off the base of his thumb. The ball went high, Diegert's left hand grasped at it striking the ball, sending it higher and farther to the right. Diegert moved his right hand below the path through which the ball was now falling. He brought his left hand down and trapped the ball between them. Falling to his knees, he rolled onto his back until he lay on the floor. Raising the ball in his right hand like a triumphant outfielder, Diegert looked up at Avery with a smile.

"Better, but let's see if you can do it while remaining in the chair," said the lesson master.

Seated again, Diegert looked into the corner. This time the ball again came from the right. Its trajectory, though, was much steeper, hitting the floor hard and bouncing high off the left wall. It must have had a lot of spin on it because it went sharply to the right, striking the right wall. From there the ball went low and to the left. Tracking the movement with his eyes and letting the images in his brain guide his muscles, Diegert simply opened his left hand, slid it forward into the path of the ball, and closed his fingers around it when it touched his palm.

"That's more like it," Avery said.

Diegert was stunned. How simple this had been. Without reacting to all the distraction of the bouncing ball or preoccupying himself with anticipation, he had just let his brain interpret the visual signals, and the action was obvious and easy. Too easy, he thought. And maybe that's the problem. If things are too easy, we often complicate them, so they feel like more of an accomplishment. From now on, he would just try to accept easy as appropriate.

Diegert tossed the ball back to Avery, and they continued the drill for another fifteen minutes during which Diegert's success climbed to ninety-five percent.

"All right, so you're teaching me about being in the zone," said Diegert.

Avery looked at him with an inquisitive tilt to his head.

"On the wrestling team, we were taught to chill out before our matches. Coach didn't want us psyching ourselves out. Like you said, you just have to let your nervous system react and do what's necessary."

"The zone sounds very much like the state of the empty self. In this state, you detach from your judgments and prejudices and simply perform the act that is required of you."

Diegert turned his head to look at Avery, eager to hear more.

The trainer of men continued, "The empty self does not mean there is nothing within you. It means you are free of the baggage of being human. When wrestling, how can a man succeed in doing something which takes rapid neural integration when his mind is completely pre-occupied imagining the outcome of the event?"

Avery looked at David, indicating his question was not rhetorical.

"I don't know," said Diegert.

"Then you will know as our training progresses."

Avery leaned forward, getting uncomfortably close to Diegert. "You will know so that assassinating people will be something you do with an empty self."

Diegert drew back from Avery keeping his eyes fixed on the man. Avery's eyes never blinked or shifted.

"You want me to continue to be an assassin?"

"David, you are an assassin whether I want you to be or not. It is the path your life has chosen. You are a unique individual with skills and abilities possessed by few others. You are what you are, and that is a killer of men."

The assessment left Diegert feeling dejected and confused. He didn't feel like a killer sitting in this medical room in his cotton t-shirt and sweatpants. He still felt bad about all the people he had killed. Carolyn made him define a lethal code, which he had stuck to, but he also had to admit that when he was on a mission, he found himself in the Zone. His purpose was clear, and he was always capable of making the kill. Like when the wrestling match was over, he felt lost after a mission. He didn't know what his purpose was except to escape. He may have skills and abilities that few others possessed, but those who did were either in jail or dead.

"Shouldn't my mission in life be something more than just killing people?"

"You mustn't confuse the act that you perform with the mission of your life."

"Why not?"

"Your mission is to serve Crepusculous. The mission of Crepusculous is to provide goods and services to the entire planet to sustain and enhance human life." Avery intensified his gaze to elicit a response.

"OK, that sounds big."

"It is an all-encompassing mission which requires tremendous resources, extensive human effort, and substantial security to maintain the capacity to achieve this goal." Avery took a few steps away from Diegert, then turned to face him from a stable, solid stance before continuing. "When threatened, it is requisite that we eliminate such threats before they interrupt the mission."

"Boy, you sure drank the Kool-Aid on that one."

"That's certainly a dated reference, but if you're implying that I am a true believer, you are correct."

"I don't believe in it," said Diegert. "In fact, I think Panzer's crazy and it's dangerous to have so much power in the hands of a man like him."

Avery drew several breaths. "What would you propose?"

"I'd burn it down. Fucking Crepusculous should be revealed, indicted, the four of them arrested and the Board destroyed. They've made themselves rich while the rest of the planet suffers."

The strain in Avery's words was palpable, "You don't believe they've helped people?"

"They're criminals, the worst kind because there is no accountability for the damage they do. I'm going to destroy them and take over."

Avery's movement was so swift and powerful that Diegert was on the floor gasping for breath with the dark man's hand exerting a vice-like pressure on his trachea.

"My life," Avery shouted, "has been dedicated to the mission of Crepusculous. Anyone who has access as deep inside as you do must be trustworthy."

With both of his hands on Avery's arm, Diegert could not budge the grip. The mentor's arm was as solid as a tree trunk, and his hand was closing Diegert's throat. Nodding his head was the only movement Diegert could make. Avery watched as the nodding intensified. He took his time deciding if he should let Diegert breathe.

The rush of air swept into Diegert's lungs, making him wheeze through his indented windpipe.

"Fuck man."

"That's not right," admonished Avery. "It's DON'T Fuck with this man."

Taking deeper breaths, Diegert coughed in a painful spasm.

"You will come to realize that protecting the mission of Crepusculous is the most important job in the world. Killing the enemies of Crepusculous ensures the safety and prosperity of the world's markets. As a dedicated assassin, you must embrace your role as the honor it is, or you will be eliminated like a malignant cell."

Diegert let out a sigh and looked at the floor while running his fingers through his hair. From his kneeling position, he saw Avery in a martial arts stance ready to strike.

Diegert coughed again as he slowly started rising to his feet. From his crouched position, he struck out with a rotating kick that drove his heel into Avery's knee. The mentor's leg buckled as he fell backward. Placing his hand on the ground, Avery spun on his palm while flipping his legs under himself like a dropped cat. Diegert, now standing, could see his adversary was not disabled. Wasting no time, he applied a flash front kick to Avery's unprotected thorax. The concussion knocked the wind out of the mentor's ribcage as audible cracks ricocheted off the tile walls.

Diegert's primal sense was kicking in. He saw his opponent's vulnerabilities like a hedge fund manager examining the books of a struggling business.

Avery's eyes could not hide the fear. He had unleashed a killer the likes of which he had never faced. He regained his defensive stance, but the tremble in his hands revealed his misgivings.

Like a bull in a Mexican ring, Diegert exhaled with force as he circled the helpless matador.

Avery, as water taking the shape of a vessel, desperately tried a different approach.

"David, you are obviously a formidable adversary." Avery raised his shaking hands and stepped out of his stance. "You are physically superior, and I relinquish this battle to you. Please don't hit me again."

Diegert saw red, he saw black, he saw pain, but now he saw blue and a waving white flag. He saw Avery asking for mercy. Targets usually only asked when it was way too late. Avery was seeking to preserve himself and perhaps the relationship they were forming.

Diegert opened his fists, relaxed his shoulders and stood up straight. His hardened face relaxed into an expression of stoic, cynicism. Avery's movements revealed the damage to his ribcage. Diegert remembered how it took three long months for his broken ribs to heal.

Raising his hands, Diegert said, "Ok, let's talk."

The teacher's hands fell, and he carefully walked over to a chair.

Diegert sat on the edge of the bed facing his flustered mentor. He watched as the man struggled to regain his composure before speaking. "You occupy a very unique position within this organization, David. Your opportunity to take over Crepusculous and Omnisphere will come to you, but not if you seek to destroy it first."

David raised his chin but kept his eyes on Avery who said, "There are too many layers that you can't cut through. You will be prevented from hitting the heart of the beast."

"It is a beast," agreed Diegert. "The Board is unconcerned with anything but power. Providing for the world is just to gain profit and power, with all the power going to Klaus Panzer."

The mentor raised his hand. "Perhaps you are right, and there is too much power concentrated at the top. Destroying the Board though, will only create more problems and lead to an economic collapse that would engulf the entire world." Avery winced as he shifted in his chair. "Omnisphere's success supports the global economy. If you destroy it, everyone and I mean every man, woman, and child on earth will suffer. If you want to do any good in this world, you have to work within the structure to which you now have access."

Diegert felt the flip. Avery had turned the argument around. The teacher didn't deny that change had to be made, he just didn't support violent revolution, especially within the ranks of the Crepusculous family.

"What do you suggest I do?" asked Diegert.

"Good luck is when preparation meets opportunity. You must be prepared, David, for opportunities that are going to come your way. Bad luck is when an opportunity arises, and you are unprepared. Are you ready to run the world's largest multinational, global corporation?"

The sobering sense of that question left David with a hollow feeling of doubt.

"So I should just wait."

"Absolutely not. You should begin preparing. You will inherit an empire. You won't have to build it. You will have to defend it. It will be under constant attack, so the path you are on now is the right one to prepare you for your eventual ascendancy. As a killer of men, you will have the instinct necessary to protect the empire and preserve the mission of Omnisphere as it provides for the world."

How is it that Avery always seems to be able to turn the message back to where he began?

"What I need from you now, David," asked the aching mentor, "is your word that you are committed to the mission of Crepusculous and that you are not seeking to destroy Omnisphere?"

"You have my word that I won't destroy Omnisphere," replied David.

"And the Crepusculous Board?"

"They should remain vigilant and be advised that the world's best assassin is watching them."

"Very well, David." Avery shook his head. "I accept your word. Words are indications, but actions are demonstrations. You will be tested to assess your skills and abilities, as well as your loyalty. I look forward to working with you."

Diegert didn't know what to say, but he did remember learning martial arts at the YMCA as a kid, so he rose and bowed before his sensei. Avery winced as he rose and returned the bow with a gentle smile. "I will leave you to your morning workout and your breakfast. You have a good day."

Diegert stretched his back, bending from side to side. *A killer of men is what you are and will always be.* His code not to kill women and children remained intact, but this thought kept rattling around his brain, *and will always be.* Its nagging persistence prevented him from finding the empty self. Constant preoccupation with assessing the righteousness of his role was taxing but planning to one day direct the fortunes of Omnisphere brought a smile to Diegert's face. He jumped up, grabbed the crossbar on the gym, and started pumping out pull-ups while waiting for his morning meal.

CHAPTER 8

Two days out of restraints, able to move around the room, gave Diegert a small sense of freedom. The armed guard outside his door kept that feeling small.

A day after his visit from Avery, Diegert was taken aback when Klaus Panzer appeared at the door of his room. Leaping off his bed, dressed in gray sweatpants and a black t-shirt, Diegert stood with defiance. Facing his father, who had last referred to him as an embarrassing bastard, Diegert didn't know what to say and asked only, "What are you doing here?"

Panzer replied, "I've come to see to it that you get out of that bed and get yourself back in shape." Panzer leaned out the door and dismissed the guard, who turned and walked down the hall. This action surprised Diegert as well as raised his suspicions.

"It's good to see you out of bed. I don't want you getting soft. You're using the equipment Avery has provided?"

Diegert nodded, feeling no other reply necessary.

"I want you to keep your hard edge. I want you to get ready for more assignments. Having the world's best assassin at my disposal is something of which I am going to take full advantage."

Diegert grew tense. Instead of a son, he felt like an obligated servant.

Panzer's smile broadened. "You know you haven't killed anyone in quite a while. Do you feel the need? Is the itch to kill getting annoying?"

Diegert felt a sick kind of vicariousness as he imagined how Panzer got off on killing, but only through the hands of others. He peered at the man through narrowed eyelids.

"Nitaage (Nit-ah-gay)," said Panzer with an exaggerated tone. "I almost sound like an Indian, don't I," he said with a self-amused chuckle.

Diegert tilted his head, intensifying his glare at the sound of the unusual, yet strangely familiar word.

"That's what you are," declared Panzer. "I thought you'd recognize the Ojibwa word for a killer. Hey, you could turn it into a little chant before your next mission. Nitaage, Nitaage, Nitaage," he chanted sounding like a complete imbecile.

Diegert's disgusted glare left no doubt about his opinion of Panzer having learned one Ojibwa word.

"Your mom taught me the word. She wants to know if you're still wearing your *"special"* amulet." Panzer peered to see the thin strip of leather from which a circular amulet with an Ojibwa inscription hung around Diegert's neck.

"She said it says something about walking through the dark to turn on the light."

"One must pass through darkness to find the light."

"Yeah, that's it," said Panzer derisively. "Pretty corny bullshit if you ask me, but Indians believe in spirits and living ancestors and all sorts of dopey shit."

Diegert grew silent as insolent disrespect poured from his father's mouth.

"Do you feel like the Indian part of you drags you down?" Panzer did not allow for an answer before continuing. "Mixing my genes with the weird world genetics of the Ojibwa seems like it might produce a confused bastard of a child."

Diegert's scowl turned to a menacing grimace as his shoulders tensed.

"You know just because I'm the one who fucked your mom doesn't mean you aren't a bastard."

How dare he come in here and spew this kind of shit. And that word; BASTARD. All his life he wore that label because of this man. As Diegert's anger heated up, the muscles in his cheeks knotted into rippling bulges.

"Fucking your mother so long ago was good, but last night was even better," said Panzer with a chuckle and a slight thrust of his hips.

Diegert sprang at him like a mountain lion, hitting Panzer hard, driving him into the wall and to the floor. The tall gray man laid on his back as he pounded on Diegert's shoulders and head, his blows having no effect on the younger, much stronger man. From his position straddling Panzer on the floor, Diegert grabbed the older man's neck, encircling the throat with his thumbs and forefingers. With maniacal force, Diegert crushed the airway of the man responsible for all the shit in his life. Panzer's face turned red as Diegert tightened his grip allowing no air to pass. Panzer desperately struggled in spite of his declining strength.

What a fucker. Diegert never realized how much he hated this man until right now. He unleashed his anger, not only about the last few days but the years of dejection he felt ever since he learned how his mother became pregnant. The irresponsibility of this man left him to be a bastard child.

Diegert could see the blood vessels in Panzer's eyes enlarging and deepening their red color. He felt the moment of expiration coming. *How dare he rape my mother again?*

Diegert's fury exploded, and he lifted Panzer's head off the floor and smacked it back down hard. He did this again and again until a bloody smear appeared on the floor. The blood grew into a puddle from which a ring of droplets sprayed each time Panzer's head was driven into the crimson pool.

Diegert kept pounding Panzer's head until he heard the cracking of the skull and felt the tension slip away from the muscles in his father's neck. The head felt like a crushed melon slung in a canvas sack. The striking gray-blue eyes were vacant, staring through open lids. Diegert's fingers, embedded in the flesh, disobeyed the signals to relax as he struggled to release his grip. Straddling the limp body, he realized the only breathing in the room was his own.

Diegert fell forward on the body as he burst into tears. He cried with anguished grief for the loss of the opportunity to ever have a father. He cried with anger at the thoughtlessness of Panzer's words. He cried for his mother who suffered mightily at this fucker's hands. He felt like a failure for not protecting her. He cried and cried and cried, without the warmth of a woman, but for the suffering of his mother and the fact that he would never have a father.

His crying intensified until his breathing was nothing but guttural spasms from a tortured soul. The exorcism of his pain felt as though his heart had been ripped from his chest. He opened himself to the realization that the man he hoped would love and guide him now lay dead beneath him. The victim of violence similar to that which he had perpetrated on others.

Alone, confused and exhausted Diegert rolled off Panzer, collapsing on his back next to the body. With his eyes closed, he felt his whole world spinning, turning and twisting out of control. How could he have done this, and what if he had not? Panzer was an evil man, but Diegert carried half of his genes. He felt disgusted by his own evil.

Feeling a change of light on his lids, he opened his eyes. Towering above him, dressed in impeccable gray was a man of distinction. Peering down on him were the ice blue eyes of Klaus Panzer. Diegert was in an acute emotional crisis, but this felt like a psychotic hallucination. He blinked several times, but the same vision continued to re-appear. He shot his hand out and took hold of one of the legs. It was real. He felt the fine worsted wool of the suit and the stability of the man. Spinning around into a seated position, he looked up. "Panzer?"

"Yes my son," came the reply, "It is I."

With a blank look of disbelief and uncertainty as to what was real, he failed to form words. From above him, he heard, "I will explain all of this to you."

Squatting down, Panzer examined the damage done to the head which was identical to his. The pool of gooey blood and brain matter fascinated him as he carefully inspected the splintered cranium. Grasping the nose, he turned the head side to side. Satisfied, Panzer rose to his feet.

Diegert, sitting against the wall, observed a two-man team enter and place the corpse into a large black bag and zip it up. Grasping the handles, the two men carried the bag away. A young woman wheeled a bucket and mop into the room, quickly cleaning the blood from the wall and floor.

Diegert looked up to hear, "You certainly did give'm a thrashing."

Coughing and clearing his throat Diegert asked, "Are you a ghost?"

"No, I assure you I am quite real. It is the man you killed who is an apparition, a cipher, a doppelgänger."

The big words rattled around Diegert's head, providing no clarity.

The Panzer figure smirked. "Do you remember when I told you about Creation Labs and the capacity to restructure amino acids by manipulating DNA with nanocytes?"

Diegert remembered hearing about this but did not understand it. He nodded.

"With wireless nanocytes, controlled by a photo-specific app, we can directly reconfigure proteins into the exact appearance of someone else's face."

"You mean the dude was not you but had his face made to look like yours?"

"Yes."

"And you did this with nanocytes?"

"Along with very sophisticated software but, David, I did this to see if I could trust you. To see how you really felt about me, and now I know that you harbored a great deal of anger toward me."

If Diegert was confused before, he now became further removed from reality. Had he killed Panzer or not?

"The violence I witnessed convinces me that you are conflicted about me being your father. I want you to know that this experience was, for you, as real as any could be. The anger you felt, and your catharsis was a true expulsion of the painful feelings you carried within you."

Panzer stopped talking and held his gaze upon Diegert, who looked back and shrugged his shoulders.

"I hope we move forward now," said Panzer.

"What?"

"Move forward and leave those feelings behind."

"What do you mean? Nothing's changed," shouted Diegert.

"On the contrary, everything's changed. You have released the disquieting feelings you had for me. We can start anew."

"Are you fucking kidding? You're still here. You're the same, and I killed an innocent man."

"Don't let the facts negate your feelings. I gave you an opportunity to indulge your feelings of hate and anger, fulfilling your primal need to kill. Now we should be able to move beyond such feelings."

"Feelings?! When you have me assassinate someone, that's not just to express your feelings, is it?"

"An assassination is a killing to fulfill a strategic objective. Murder is killing someone out of hate, anger and boiling emotions. You did not assassinate me just now, you murdered me."

"But what good is it if you're still here?"

"With your feelings expunged, I'm confident we can forge a brand-new relationship."

Diegert was thunderstruck. He was overwhelmed with the audacity of this man to define human relationships so distinctly in his own terms and then expect others to feel the same. The whole use of technology to change the other man's face was fascinating, but the fact that he arranged for that man to be killed just so his son could express himself was repugnant. Diegert had been duped into murder and then was encouraged to accept it as relationship therapy. This man was crazy in a perilous way, and Diegert knew he had to take from him the power of Crepusculous.

Panzer stepped to the door and looked back before exiting. "Move beyond your trite feelings. You and I have much to accomplish."

Stunned and confused Diegert struggled to get a handle on his feelings, but what was clear was that he did not love his father, Klaus Panzer.

CHAPTER 9

Three months after the release of Digival, the world was responding. This cryptocurrency, unlike all the others, had wealth behind it that gave people faith to use it as money. Javier's assertion that the best way to undermine the dollar was to steal away the customers was having an impact. More and more people were using Digival for purchases in Omnisphere businesses. Enterprises outside the enormous corporate umbrella were accepting it as well. Panzer was very pleased. He excitedly anticipated the results of a meeting his CEO of Omnisphere was having that day.

In Washington DC, Abaya Patel arrived at the K Street address of the Federal Reserve. A security officer escorted her to the office of the Head of the Reserve, Janet Steiner. Entering the executive suite, Abaya relaxed at the sight of the soft cream upholstered furniture and the textured beige of the walls. The Head of the Federal Reserve came from behind her desk to greet the CEO of Omnisphere. As they shook hands, Abaya said, "It is such an honor and a privilege to meet with you." The smiles were pleasant, but they both knew they were girding for battle.

"Likewise Abaya," replied Janet, "thanks for coming. I hope you don't mind, I also invited Andrew to join us."

Andrew Elliot, the Secretary of the Treasury, entered from a side door and strode toward Abaya.

"I don't believe you two have met," stated Janet.

"No I don't believe we have," said Abaya in a somewhat guarded tone.

"How do you do?" offered Mr. Elliot as he shook hands with Abaya.

"I'm sorry if I've caught you by surprise but I feel as though the issues we will be discussing may be clearer with Andrew here. Shall we?" said the Fed Chair as Abaya and Mr. Elliot sat side by side in front of the desk, and she sat down behind her expanse of polished Cherry. Getting right to the point Ms. Steiner asked, "What are Omnisphere's intentions for Digival?"

With an adroit smile, Abaya began, "Digival is a means of showing our customers that we appreciate them and wish them well in the economy. As a large and diverse corporation, we realize our success depends on our customers' satisfaction. By providing goods and services that people need and desire, we seek to make their lives happy and whole. Digival is a means for us to share the wealth of the corporation with the customers who create it."

"Well then why is there a Digival account for nearly every person in the United States?" asked Ms. Steiner with a raised eyebrow.

"Accounts simply let us manage the value to which each customer is entitled."

"Yes, of course, but every resident of the United States?"

"As a large and diverse corporation, there are many entities under our umbrella. Omnisphere associated companies touch the lives of almost every person on the planet, not just the US."

Choosing now to speak, Andrew Elliot said, "The Department of the Treasury's concern is that Digival is becoming a de facto currency and Omnisphere is operating an unregulated bank."

"Omnisphere already has extensive operations in the banking industry. Digival can be used for purchases of goods and services within the Omnisphere network. The credit is good within the corporate environment, it is not legal tender for all debts, public charges, taxes, and dues."

"It precisely is not," stammered Elliot. "But it is being used as such."

"How so?"

"I understand that you provide interest on these Digival accounts."

"Yes, that's true. Digival held in a person's account can earn an interest rate of six percent."

"Six percent! That's outrageous. How can you afford that kind of payment?"

"Omnisphere has sufficient resources. Providing interest on a Digival account demonstrates our desire to keep our customers engaged with us. How is this a problem? How much interest has your Digival account accrued?"

Janet Steiner piped up, "Tell her."

Elliot hesitated, but went on to say, "The other day my son revealed that he had sold his old game system."

"Yes?"

"Well, I keep very tight controls on his accounts. I know when he deposits or withdraws any money. So I asked him if he had the cash and when was he going to deposit it. He said the whole transaction was in Digival and there was no cash."

Reacting to Elliot's aggravation Abaya asked, "And this upsets you?"

"It concerns me. Digival is extending beyond Omnisphere to become a counterfeit currency."

Abaya turned to look at the Fed, who stared back with a furrowed brow. Looking back to Mr. Elliot, Abaya said, "I appreciate you asking me to meet with you, but clearly, the purpose of this meeting has to be more than the consternation you feel because your son chooses to transact business in something other than US dollars."

The Fed said, "We are concerned that the way in which you are conducting business in Digival creates an impression that it is legal tender, and it is extending to areas of the economy in which it was not intended. We would like to know what restrictions you intend to put in place to prevent the use of this currency outside of Omnisphere?"

Abaya gave a confident smile. "So now I see that you feel that Digival is a threat."

Drumming his fingers on his knee Mr. Elliot said, "We feel your corporation is perpetuating a counterfeit currency."

"Now that's surprising. Omnisphere is not issuing coins or notes. There is no use of any of the symbols, slogans or likenesses of US money. Digival is a number in an account which represents value within Omnisphere. It is not a physical entity seeking to deceive one into believing it is something other than what it is. On what do you base your charge of forgery?"

The two representatives of US monetary policy sat quietly for a moment.

Elliot broke the silence. "People are using it as money."

"Legally, you know very well that people can transact business in whatever form of value they wish. Dollars hold no exclusivity on value."

"Yes but this Digival is completely worthless. It does not even exist in any physical form."

"Digival is backed by the wealth of Omnisphere. A corporate entity with assets, products, and services used by people all over the world. The assets alone carry a worth that is unparalleled in the world. The units of value represent the success of this company to provide the things that turn people into customers. I believe it is your money that is backed by nothing but faith."

"The full faith and credit of the United States Government have maintained the US monetary system for decades," declared Elliot.

"True, but that belief system has begun to wear thin since the US has not paid back what it owes for decades. Honestly, the US monetary system is a sham. How do you explain it to your son?"

Elliot retreated into silence.

Steiner replied, "Our friends over at the IRS may be very interested to know if you are collecting any taxes on these Digival transactions."

"Omnisphere complies with all tax obligations. I am happy to discuss the tax implications of Digival with the IRS."

"You'd be willing to pay taxes?!"

"Any tax on Digival would be paid in Digival."

Silence once again cloaked the room.

Abaya cleared her throat. "Just like all inhabitants of the earth, the US Government is invited to open a Digival account and experience the benefits of the wealth shared by Omnisphere with all its customers."

Elliot scratched his ear while adjusting his glasses. Steiner looked deflated as the threat of taxes only seemed to embolden the executive.

"With an appropriate rate of taxation, the treasury would accrue a sizable amount of credit with Omnisphere. The value could be used in numerous beneficial ways. To whom should I direct my inquiry at Internal Revenue?"

Steiner and Elliot looked to one another sheepishly. Their hope of cowing Patel into restricting Digival was turning into an offer of revenue. Like water to a thirsty man, these two money managers were powerless to resist an opportunity to acquire more revenue, no matter what the source.

Elliot took a deep breath and let out a long sigh. "John Koskinen is the Commissioner of the IRS. I can set up a meeting with his team and your people."

"Excellent," Abaya said with a nod and a smile. "Omnisphere looks forward to contributing to the welfare of the United States. I appreciate your time in meeting with me, and I look forward to the next steps."

Abaya rose from her seat, shook the hands of both of the somewhat stunned and subdued officials, before walking out of the meeting.

CHAPTER 10

Having been released from Medical, Diegert now had a small apartment within the subterranean network below LPU. The apartment had comfortable accommodations including a kitchen and a living room separated by a raised bar. The bedroom had a queen-sized bed, and a large closet with sliding mirrored doors, the bathroom was adjoined. Furnishings in the living room included a couch and table upon which Diegert had placed the laptop he was given. Adhered to the wall was a large screen smart TV. Two stools provided seating at the counter bar.

A knock on the door surprised Diegert, who tensed up as he peered through the peephole to see Klaus Panzer standing outside his door. Diegert's hesitation produced a more insistent knock. As the door opened, Panzer entered the room.

Even though Diegert thought of this apartment as his personal space, he suddenly realized such was not the case when Panzer said, "I'm here to hold a meeting with you right now." It was the first time they'd met since Diegert killed him, or rather, killed a guy who had Panzer's face. Panzer intimidated Diegert, not physically, but intellectually. The guy was so smart, and he always seemed to be enacting some kind of a scheme. Diegert regressed into silence as this clever, manipulative and dangerous man occupied in his new abode.

"I hope you are well, my son. I wanted to meet with you now, under less stressful circumstances."

"You mean I don't get to kill you this time."

"Do you feel the need to do that again?" Panzer replied.

"Maybe later."

"Very well. I want to speak with you about physiology," stated Panzer in a professorial tone, "The human body is the most amazing structure and its functions are absolutely astounding. Its complexity and ability to adapt represent the world's most intricate biological network."

From his slightly downcast gaze, Diegert shifted his eyes up and nodded at Panzer.

"Did you study biology in school?" asked Panzer.

"Yeah," replied Diegert. "I liked biology." Diegert liked learning about the natural world, it appealed to his comfort in the outdoors and his curiosity about animals.

"The study of life has held the fascination of many a great mind. From it has grown, medicine, agriculture, and psychology. Lately, I've been interested in the body's immune system. Do you recall learning about immunity?"

After a brief pause, Diegert nodded. He remembered there are red blood cells for carrying oxygen and white blood cells for fighting infections.

"Do you remember the leukocytes?"

Diegert mulled the question. The word, *'Lukosights'* was ringing bells, but he could not come up with a reply, and he did not want to say no.

Panzer impatiently tapped his foot before interjecting, "They are the white blood cells, the ones which make up your immune system. Leukocytes fight the microbial pathogens that invade your body. As a resource, human beings are constantly attacked by bacteria, viruses, parasites, and mutated cells. The immune system protects us against certain death every day. Without a properly functioning immune system, you would succumb to the microbes within a matter of weeks, if not days. The war is constant, and the adaptations of the leukocytes are requisite for survival. It is an absolutely fascinating system that I have scientists in Creation Labs working to better understand."

To this Diegert only nodded.

"Of all the leukocytes, the ones that fascinate me the most are the NK cells."

The gleeful look on Panzer's face revealed his gleaming white teeth through a broad smile. Diegert reacted with a similar smile, which he tempered as soon as he realized he was mimicking his father's arrogance.

"The NK cells are part of our first line of defense. They identify pathogens and attack them with an array of lethal responses that destroy the invaders and prevent infection. Every day you avoid getting sick because the NK cells assassinate intruders before they do you harm."

Diegert couldn't help but smile again.

"The NK cells, work with the rest of the immune system to make sure invaders are identified and a specific defense is set up to keep the microbe from re-infecting the body. Meanwhile, the NK cells go right back to work looking for trouble and stopping it before it becomes a problem. Their dedication to the protection of the body is absolute and indefatigable."

Diegert didn't quite get that last word, but he realized these '*Enkay*' cells had impressed Panzer with their aggression. Throwing his hands up and shrugging his shoulders, Diegert said, "Why are you telling me all this?"

"Do you know what NK stands for?" asked Panzer.

Diegert shook his head.

"NK stands for Natural Killer."

The two words instantly clarified Panzer's earlier phrase.

"Natural Killer cells use biologic toxins to bring death to pathogenic microbes, just like an assassin uses physical violence to protect the people and assets of Crepusculous."

Diegert snapped a look at Panzer's face, which was now set in a stoic glare.

"You, my son, are a Natural Killer."

The lesson in biology shifted to a personal assessment.

"You are a unique person, with a biological trait shared with only one percent of the population."

Diegert's gaze intensified as he tilted his head. Panzer remained silent.

Feeling manipulated, Diegert kept his eyes on the older man, who seemed like he was waiting to be asked.

Diegert bit. "What's the trait?"

"Fifty percent of your white blood cells are Natural Killers. Most people have between ten to fifteen percent NK's, but you have five times the average."

"So what?"

"So, you don't get sick, do you?"

Diegert shrugged.

"When was the last time you had a cold?"

Diegert couldn't remember the last time he was sick. He was always healthy even when others all around him were sick. He shrugged his shoulders again.

"When you're injured, you heal quickly."

Diegert recognized that this was also true, and even more so since being given Healix.

"These are traits you would expect from a strong front-line defense. The fact that you have this trait is no accident. I too possess Natural Killer cells as fifty percent of my leukocytes. You have inherited a trait of the Panzer family that has helped us survive the plague, the flu epidemic of 1918 and the advent of antibiotic-resistant bacteria. We are survivors, and I am glad to see that this valuable trait is being carried forward by my son."

"Is this another engineered thing from Creation Lab? Did you inject these into me?"

"Absolutely not. We are not yet that sophisticated. The concentration of NK cells is a genetic trait passed on from me to you. There is no other way for you to get this powerful advantage except through my genes."

"How do you really know I have these?"

"We've done the blood work," said Panzer pointing out the obvious. "Your NK cell count measured at 150,000 per microliter. A value that's five times more than the average person. You're a killer, and it comes to you naturally."

Diegert's eyes narrowed into a steely glare as he fixed his gaze on Panzer.

Pointing his finger Panzer said, "See I can see it in you now. Anger is rising up in you, and you are getting ready to kill."

Diegert leaned back and softened his expression.

"What did it feel like when you first killed a man?" asked Panzer with intense curiosity. "Was it exhilarating? Did the adrenaline rush take over? And what about the sense of triumph, was it not the best feeling you've ever had?"

Diegert sheepishly turned away.

"Aha, see I know this. I know you felt the power of the kill. You know I'm right."

Diegert spoke, "You're so happy about it, but I think it's a curse."

"It's definitely a burden, but it's a blessing, not a curse."

Diegert's eyebrows posed the question.

Panzer said, "Just like the rich resources of the human body, the wealth of Crepusculous is under constant attack. The holdings are so vast and the value so great that invaders and pathogens are always seeking advantage and parasitizing what is ours. Like the immune system, the Crepusculous and Omnisphere security operations are complex, adaptable and very effective. At times we need to aggressively eliminate an intruder that will do us great harm if allowed to create an infection. It is then that I assign an assassin to strategically remove an enemy."

During the pause, Diegert looked to see a broad smile slowly spread across Panzer's face, as warmth filled his icy blue eyes and a rosy color percolated through his tan skin.

With an expression of fondness, Panzer said, "I then need a man to be my NK cell. To have the best man to ever do that job be my own son fills me with pride like I've never felt before."

As unaccustomed to compliments as Diegert was, he couldn't help but feel a bit of… hope, or camaraderie, or appreciation, or… he didn't know what to call the feeling he was having, and he sure wasn't going to use the word love, yet there was something inside him that reacted to Panzer's kind but twisted words.

Snapping out of his emotional moment Diegert asked, "Was the president really invading and infecting Crepusculous? Was he really your enemy?"

The ice in Panzer's eyes returned as slivers of gray streaked through the blue irises.

"We all know the best defense is a good offense. The sanction against the president was part of a larger plan to adjust the world's economy."

"Destroy the world's economy is more like it."

"Oh really, did you study macro world economics at Broward County High School? Can you inform me about international trade deficits, the fluctuations in global currency markets or the third world consequences of the dominant US dollar? Can you share your opinion of default dependent hedge funds or credit requisite leveraged borrowing? Certainly, you can tell me how the impact of municipal debt influences the value of local real estate."

Intellectual intimidation returned, but Diegert was not going let this asshole silence him again.

"You can say what you like and think what you will, but killing the president was unnecessary, and now I have to live with that for the rest of my life," said Diegert thumping his chest with his extended fingers.

"Do you think the NK cell feels bad each time it kills a pathogen? Or is the health of the entire body much more important than the emotions of one single cell?"

"This cellular analogy is stupid. You can't really expect people to act as simply as a cell. It's idiotic to believe people are going to act on your behalf and have no reactions to the violence you order up."

"I can see your point," said Panzer calmly. "But your vision limits actions to only those things that feel good at the moment. Often the greater good requires emotional sacrifices where we give up feeling good to change the balance of power that surrounds us."

"That's bullshit."

"Really?" said Panzer snapping his head as he drew back his gaze. "Son, I do believe you need to expand your vision. You need to see what really lies before you and how economic power is truly balanced in this world."

Panzer pulled a remote from his pocket, clicked the device, and brought the giant screen of Diegert's smart TV to life. He manipulated the device until the screen revealed a number of brightly colored pie charts. Diegert liked math, and these charts were divided into wedges representing different percentages of the pies.

"Let's look at this first one," said Panzer as he clicked on a single pie chart, which then filled the screen.

The circle was divided into two sections, the blue one representing ninety percent of the pie, the red one ten percent. Graphics on the pie indicated that the ninety percent was the wealth held by one percent of the population and the ten percent represented the wealth held by ninety-nine percent of the population.

Panzer began, "Certainly by now you've heard of this statistic, but what you might not be aware of is this." Panzer clicked his remote, and a green pie section now appeared representing seventy-five percent of the circle. The graphic read, Holdings of Omnisphere. Panzer turned his head to see Diegert's reaction.

Diegert was nonplussed and simply said, "I've already been told this, but am I included in the 'We'?"

"Yes," said an ebullient Panzer, nodding his head, smiling with pride. "You are my son. You are my heir. You own the world, but I have more to show you."

Panzer clicked up the next pie chart, which revealed a breakdown of the world's reserve currency.

"A world currency is a monetary denomination from one country that will be accepted by other countries for the payment of goods and services. Many commodities that are traded all over the world are priced in US dollars." Panzer paused to make sure Diegert was listening.

Reluctantly Diegert nodded, and Panzer went on. "This fact makes the dollar the world's dominant money even though the US is basically bankrupt. The whole monetary system is based on the faith in a government that is incapable of tying its own shoes, let alone pay its bills, and leave the system better than they found it."

Diegert scratched his head.

"We will remove the US dollar as the world's reserve currency and replace it with a corporate based currency backed by the true wealth of Omnisphere."

Panzer was as proud as a Peacock with feathers in full fan. Diegert looked at him as if he was a drunken bum preaching in the subway.

Panzer furrowed his brow. "Come now, son, I can see you are having trouble grasping the plan. I realize your recent actions delayed things, but I'm quite certain there will be a role for you to play as we move forward."

"Don't be so sure, I'll be your trigger man."

"Indeed. Anyway, I want you to know that by replacing the dollar, we relieve the world of the uneven burden of fluctuating currencies. The Omnisphere currency will be worth the same all over the world."

Diegert smirked a contemplative frown while nodding his head.

"With control of the world's money, we will have unprecedented power that'll allow us to influence almost every economic transaction in the world. From bread to bananas, to bullets, it will all be purchased with our currency."

The grandiosity of such an idea was something Diegert could hardly imagine, but the inevitability with which his father spoke of the plan gave the younger man all the more reason to doubt the sanity of his paternal sire.

"You're already aware of how powerful we are."
Diegert looked to see Panzer gently nodding his head as he tried to extract the doubt from his son. "We're going to make this happen, and it will be the greatest economic accomplishment in the history of the world."

Diegert's skepticism and Panzer's certainty collided in the room as they both projected their beliefs into the air between them.

Panzer's mobile buzzed softly. Extracting it from his pocket, he said, "I'm sorry, son, I have another appointment, and I'm afraid I must go now, but I want you to contemplate what we've discussed. Soon I will need to know if you are a useful asset or an unfortunate liability. Do choose wisely my son," insinuated Panzer as he reached out and patted Diegert on the shoulder.

Do or die, thought Diegert.

CHAPTER 11

After Carolyn was attacked by Fatima Hussain, Diegert waited with her until an ambulance arrived. He took her phone with him as the ambulance took her to the hospital. Now, having convinced one of the medical orderlies that he needed the phone from his personal effects to complete an assignment from Klaus Panzer, Diegert checked the incoming history. He could see that the phone had been called three times from the same number at about 6:00 a.m. So he was ready the next morning when the phone rang at 6:03 a.m.

"Hello."

"David?"

Diegert recognized her voice but suddenly realized he had no idea who else might be listening or influencing her on the other end. Having disabled the GPS signal, he knew tracking the device would be nearly impossible.

"Yes," he replied.

"Are you okay?"

"Give me some assurance this call is secure."

During the pause, Carolyn exhaled with a snort of indignation. "I suppose it hasn't occurred to you that I'm in some really deep trouble as well. My boss thinks I'm in collusion with you and is looking for evidence. Plus my ribs, where I was shot, hurt like hell!"

Gaining her perspective, Diegert felt like a real jerk, but he couldn't ignore the risk involved in communicating with her. "I'm sorry you're in pain."

"I'm on some pretty strong drugs. The bullet was surgically removed, but I'm going to have a scar on my chest that'll ruin the look of any plunging necklines."

"That's unfortunate. What is your boss doing to investigate?"

Diegert heard that snort again. When Carolyn spoke, he sensed her tone had shifted such that she was detaching herself from her feelings and just stating facts.

"He's doing what I would do. Checking financials, seeing if I'm in debt. Reviewing communications to establish our history. The fact that you have my phone makes that one pretty difficult. But not getting answers only makes him more suspicious."

"How is it that you're calling me?"

"I coerced a medic into getting me a burner, and I'm in the bathroom during my guard's shift change. This situation won't last but keep this number, and we'll be able to communicate. David, I need actionable intel on the people who directed Strakov to kill the president. I need you to give me evidence from inside Crepusculous, or I'm toast, and the hunt for you goes into overdrive."

"Are you in the hospital or jail?"

"Both, they've got guards stationed 24/7 right outside my hospital room. I'm in real trouble." Carolyn's voice rose in pitch, and Diegert could sense her anger and frustration. "I had a clean solid career, an impeccable reputation, and an unblemished record. Now I'm under investigation, my colleagues suspect me of treason, and no one trusts me. Plus, I'm hiding in the bathroom talking on a burner to the man who actually did shoot the president."

"You know I didn't shoot him."

"Fuck it, I'm the only one who knows that. My only way out of this is to produce some evidence that confirms the lie you set up and everyone wants to believe. Without evidence, the obvious story of Strakov is still under suspicion. Get me some proof, David, or you and I will both be fucking toast!"

Diegert had to help Carolyn convince the world that Strakov was the assassin of the President of the United States.

"Ok, I'm on it. I'll get that intel to clear you and get people to forget about me."

Diegert heard her sigh of relief as she replied with a softened tone. "Thank you, we need to do this as quickly as possible but, David, I must tell you I will not be the only one who isn't going to forget about you. Please be careful."

While the last part of her message was both reassuring and chilling, Diegert relished the camaraderie, and perhaps something more, that he felt for Carolyn.

"I will be. I'll text you."

"Yeah, that'll be best."

Diegert didn't want the call to end or go on. Carolyn was next to speak. "Ok then, I'm out."

"Right."

Diegert held the now silent phone to his ear realizing that his only connection to Carolyn was a cold piece of electronic plastic.

Wasting no time, Diegert called Klaus Panzer. "Hallo," came the German-accented greeting.

"This is David, I need your help with something."

"Oh really, and what is your need?"

"I need evidence that indicates that Alexi Strakov was the man who assassinated the president."

"And you believe I can help you with this?"

"I know you can. You control enough media outlets that you can generate any message you want the world to believe."

"You're assuming a great deal of gullibility on the part of the general public."

"Maybe, but this is something they want to believe, so we just have to give them a plausible story and evidence to back it up."

"So what's your story?"

111

Diegert was caught flat-footed. He assumed Panzer would assign someone to figure out all the details. Instead, he had to come up with something clever to make the blame stick to Strakov. Diegert knew that people would accept information, presented as fact that confirmed ideas they already believed, therefore Islamic terrorists would be at the center of the story.

Diegert began, "We need evidence that Strakov was acting on behalf of Abu Jihad. Let's fashion intercepted texts between Strakov and an associate of Nassar Irbil Mohammed. Have the texts direct Strakov to acquire the gun I planted on him. Create a video which shows Strakov arriving in Detroit and doctor a grainy video which captures the moment of the shot."

Panzer smiled with a sense of pride, the kind most dads have when their sons jog back to the dugout having caught the inning-ending pop fly.

"What about payment?" the tyrant asked gently.

"Oh yeah, right. There has to be a price. Shift the focus on how much the life of the president was worth."

"A million, ten million, maybe 100 million dollars?" suggested Panzer.

"How much could Abu Jihad afford before authorities get suspicious?" asked Diegert.

"Of course, I say ten million then. It's an attention-grabbing number for which most people could imagine themselves being coerced into taking this action."

Diegert frowned. "I don't know if most people could imagine themselves shooting the president for ten million dollars, but they can believe that a Russian assassin would."

"Very well. I do have media people I can get to work on this story. We'll broadcast it worldwide."

"It also has to be leaked to the authorities for independent verification," added Diegert.

Panzer asked, "What authorities do you have in mind?"

Diegert felt that Panzer was now testing him. "They should be American. They should already be working on the case, and they should have the international scope to verify the evidence we create."

Diegert hesitated to see if he could get Panzer to suggest an agency that fit the criterion, instead, Panzer asked, "Why does it have to be American?"

"The Americans have to be seen as solving the assassination of their own president."

"Very well. We'll operate through the CIA."

Diegert pumped his fist. "Thank you. This misdirection will buy us a lot of room in which to operate."

"I'm glad to see you taking this kind of initiative. I'm beginning to see new potential in you, son."

There it was again, the ambivalent feeling that shook him each time Panzer called him son. The feeling of hatred for the past, mixed with the hope for the future made his stomach turn.

Panzer broke the pause. "Look, I have another appointment coming, but I will instruct the media department to expedite this story. Is there anything else?"

"No," replied Diegert. "Thanks for doing this."

"You are most welcome."

His own statement of gratitude caught Diegert off guard. He felt thankful for a father who could help him solve a problem. It was a truly unprecedented experience.

Panzer's next appointment was a video conference with Abaya Patel. "Guten Morgen Abaya, how are you?"

"I'm fine, Klaus, thanks for asking and you?"

"If I was doing any better, I'm sure I would be arrested." Panzer chuckled at his own joke.

Abaya smiled ruefully, while thinking, *He should be arrested for a hundred crimes.* "I believe I have a way for Digival to replace the dollar."

"Well there's no need for suspense, what is it?" asked Panzer.

"What is the one expense that everyone is subject to that no one wants to pay, but must?"

"Aw, you come with a riddle. Is the answer healthcare?"

"No, but that's a good one."

"Food?"

"People are happy to spend money on food. Come on, think like an economist… A government economist."

"Oh, taxes."

"Right, no one wants to pay them, everyone must, and people spend money figuring out ways to not pay them."

"So how does this help us?"

"Taxes are vital government revenue. All government spending is through taxes, except in the US where they borrow more money than they collect."

"OK, Econ 101. What's your plan?" asked the curious German.

"I'm proposing that we encourage the US Government to tax Digival." Patel fell silent, giving her last statement a moment to sink into Panzer's diabolical brain. Over the video feed, she observed him lean back in his chair, gaze off to the left and bring his hand to his chin. The contemplation was absolutely palpable, and Abaya was so pleased for the video image.

"Would the taxes only be collected on purchases?"

"At first, yes."

"What would the government do with the Digival it collected?"

"I hope they would spend it. Use it for entitlement payments. Give it to poor people, or soldiers in the military. They would be able to purchase whatever they want from Omnisphere vendors."

"This would raise the validation of Digival by getting the government to use it as revenue."

"Precisely. Once they are comfortable with this arrangement, we can allow regular people to pay their taxes with Digival."

Panzer cast a suspicious eye across the screen at Patel.

She explained further, "When a purchase is made, we pay the taxes in Digival. We pay the government a higher rate than what it usually charges. Say instead of eight percent, we give ten. At the same time, we put ten percent into the customer's Digival account. They are making money every time they spend money, and they're doing it tax-free."

The concern showed across Panzer's face as the math became apparent to him. "That's twenty percent of every purchase!"

"Yes," said Patel, "but it's twenty percent of nothing. We just put more numbers in an account. When they go to spend them, they give the numbers right back to us."

"And they get products and services for those nothing numbers."

"Well, that will be the result of this whole plan. If you are going to control the world's money, you are going to control nothing but faith and belief in perceived value."

Abaya looked at the screen to see Panzer, who was aware of all this, struggling with the reality of his plan.

In a softer voice, she spoke. "We are working to get people to believe in a digital currency. But we are also seeking to gain their trust that Omnisphere will always be there to finance their lives and share the wealth."

Panzer slowly turned to look directly into the screen. "But with that faith comes the power."

"Only if you are successful in getting people to believe in Digival."

After a short pause, Panzer said, "We can do this. We can make this happen. We can get people to believe, and we will actually improve the economy."

"You will sacrifice all of your wealth which is held in current money."

Panzer nodded slowly. "When my grandfather lived through the hyperinflation of the Deutsch marc he came out of it realizing that assets were more important than money. He had his factory and all the parts necessary to make tractors. Even without money, he still made the tractors, and they tilled the fields so that food could be grown. People survived."

Abaya looked at the screen, eager for Panzer to continue.

"We now possess so many more assets than he did. We can fuel the world's economy by providing both the goods and the services necessary to make people's lives better."

"I detect a hint of altruism."

With a wry smile, Panzer replied, "You know me better than that. What's our next step?"

"Our finance people are meeting with officials from the IRS to review the process of approving Digival for taxation."

Panzer nodded.

Abaya went on, "This step is crucial. The IRS has to see that Digival is a valid and reliable entity that will benefit the US Treasury. Our department of finance is preparing a presentation which will highlight the scope of Omnisphere and the assets upon which the value of Digival is based. We are lifting the veil on Omnisphere's reach into the world's economy. This is unprecedented for us, but it will be kept confidential."

"Surely you won't show them everything?"

"Only that which is legal."

Panzer's smile was slow and deliberate.

"By convincing the IRS that we can pull this off," said Abaya. "We are taking on a huge tax burden, or so it seems. The truth of the matter is that we are establishing credibility with the US Treasury, which will expand the presence of Digival in the market. We will set up the tax payments; the market will do the rest."

Panzer's lips lifted farther, "Excellent, thank you. I look forward to your report on the meeting with the

IRS. Who would have thought, taxes would be the way in which we replace the mighty dollar."

It was Abaya Patel's turn to smile as she and Panzer both exited the meeting.

Abaya reviewed the plan with her finance team. As a result of the agreement with Omnisphere, the IRS will implement a plan to tax transactions made with Digival. The tax rate will be eight percent. Omnisphere pays eight percent to the US Government and also places ten percent in the Digival account of the customer. For US customers the impact of sales taxes is eliminated. Digival accounts grow with purchases, and Omnisphere pays an interest rate on the accounts of five percent annually. For many people, their Digival accounts will become large enough to pay their annual income tax bill. The government accepts the revenue and uses the resources to fund entitlements. Medicaid, SNAP food allocations, housing assistance, all will be provided to needy people through the corporate currency, Digival.

Once the US Government accepts Digival as revenue, Omnisphere will break the hold of the dollar on the price of oil. The Saudis will lead the way by pricing their oil in Digival and accepting it as payment. Agricultural commodities will also be traded in Digival. Most of these companies are owned by Omnisphere so the transition to Digival will be easy and smooth. Since Digival's value is independent of the dollar, international businesses will be able to conduct transactions without having to determine exchange rates. Digival will eliminate the need for currency exchange.

Within a month, as the dollar's value drops, China which is the largest foreign holder of US debt requests payment of twenty-five percent of the debt. China's Ministry of Finance requires the payment in Digival, in order to hedge its losses against the dollar's decline.

As the role of Digival becomes more evident, media broadcasts start reporting worst-case scenarios regarding the declining dollar. People begin freaking out. Omnisphere calms the masses promising to "see us through this storm," by offering Digival exchange for dollars at their current value. People start switching, and the dollar's fall accelerates.

****

Avery began, "David, look at this man." Avery handed Diegert his phone with a picture of a handsome man with olive skin, dark hair, and a stubbly beard. Like himself, his ethnicity was difficult to identify. From a photo alone it was hard to tell if he was Arabic, Hispanic, Greek, or possibly Italian? He looked tough, he looked mean, but that was pretty much all Diegert could tell about him.

Handing the phone back he said, "So?"

"This man is a member of Cerberus."

Even though Avery said the name like Diegert should know what it meant, he did not. "What's Sir-ber-us?"

"Cerberus is a character in Greek Mythology. A ferocious three-headed dog that guards the gates of hell."

"So what's the meaning?"

"Omnisphere security operations are extensive. They coordinate with affiliate corporate security teams to maintain a secure environment for the worldwide functions of all of our businesses."

Avery paused, and Diegert nodded.

"Separate from Omnisphere security, I maintain a paramilitary force of special service operators that can be deployed when threats require an immediate response."

Diegert said, "You've got your own private army."

Avery nodded as he peered at Diegert with a narrow glare, "The force is stationed in different facilities around the world, like the one you visited in Romania."

Diegert snorted, "Yeah, I sure had a great time 'visiting.'"

Ignoring the comment, Avery said, "In addition to Romania there are four other facilities strategically distributed around the globe. Each facility has between twenty to thirty soldiers. They can be deployed at a moment's notice to protect the mission of Crepusculous."

"And you call all this, Cerberus?"

"No, Cerberus is a specific set of operators that conduct extrajudicial covert missions under my direct supervision."

"They are your assassins."

"The mission profile of Cerberus does include assassinations, as well as sabotage and abductions. The operators are highly skilled, keenly motivated and absolutely discreet."

"And how many of these guys do you have?"

"Three, of course, but they're not all guys."

Diegert remembered the three-headed dog, but he was intrigued by the inclusion of a female. "So now that I know all this secret stuff, am I to be part of this team?"

"Only if you earn your place."

Diegert's brow wrinkled as he realized he would always be tested by this organization and that no matter what he'd already done, each day was brand new. "What do you want me to do?"

"The picture I showed you, that man's name is Jarod Masoni. He is very strong and exceptionally quick. He is smart and extremely cunning. He is also confused and following a wayward path."

The last statement raised Diegert's eyebrows. "Wayward?"

"Yes, he has overlooked the fact that membership in Cerberus is the highest calling for a lethal operator. It requires absolute loyalty and is a lifelong vocation."

"He's gone rogue on ya."

"He has."

"So now you want me to kill him."

"No. I want you to abduct him and deliver him to me. He is an excellent operator, and I believe if I could speak with him, he would realize the true value of his place within Cerberus."

"Catching this guy and bringing him in alive is going to be a lot harder than killing him. Why don't you call him up?"

Avery grimaced at Diegert, "We're beyond phone calls. This mission will not be easy, but you know we have chemical agents which can render him unconscious."

"Yeah."

"To your phone, I have sent a dossier with all the pertinent information you will need to know about the target. In the packet, you will find videos of Masoni's recent movements and the locations he frequents. Plan your actions carefully and remember that absolute discretion is the expectation of a Cerberus mission."

Turning to look at Avery, Diegert asked, "Does this mean I'm in?"

"The mission is being conducted under the authority of Cerberus, but you are not yet a member. Study the dossier, including the maps. Later today I will bring your kit. Good day, David."

"Wait, you say this dossier has everything I need to know but does it tell me why he's gone rogue?"

"You have everything you need to know. You don't need to know what you're asking about."

Disappointed, Diegert slowly turned and held his eyes on Avery, "What if I don't want to be part of Cerberus?"

"David, you are an assassin. It is your path, and there is no greater calling for you than to serve Crepusculous through this elite organization."

Diegert remained ambivalent, but Avery did not acknowledge it. The mentor walked out of the room leaving the student with his conflicted thoughts.

Sitting on his bed, Diegert picked up his phone and looked at the picture of Jarod Masoni. Did he really want to earn his way into Cerberus? What could he learn from this guy when he found him? How would he transport him, especially if he was unconscious? He had to admit that being on a mission had a lot more appeal than being trapped in his little apartment. He kind of felt good about not having to kill the guy. Swiping the screen, he began reviewing the file.

CHAPTER 12

After leaving Diegert, Avery went to a section of the labyrinth controlled by, not only an access card but also, biometric eye and hand scanners. Solid steel doors swung forward after Avery completed the scans. He moved down the hall past several rooms fronted by closed doors. Taking a right-hand turn, he continued in an easterly direction. This hall ended at a set of double doors, which required him to scan his eye and hand again. Both doors slid into wall pockets as Avery entered and stood still, having arrived at the facility he built for the training of his soldiers of Cerberus.

Today was a critical step in the selection process for a new Cerberus operator.

Avery stepped to the glass and looked down into a tiled room. There was a single entrance on the opposite wall. LED lighting on the ceiling cast diffuse light against the white ceramic floor and walls. To the left and right, slots occupied positions on the wall at the height of ankles and wrists. As Avery surveyed the enclosure, he pressed a red button on a control panel mounted at the windowsill.

The door to the room opened, and two men were escorted in by Omnisphere security agents. Each man had a black cloth bag over his head. They were both dressed in black combat pants and a gray Under Armour sleeveless shirt. On their feet, they wore black tactical boots.

Led to opposite sides of the room, they were positioned by the slots. Avery pushed another button and metal bands extended from the slots, encircling the wrists and ankles of each man, securely fastening them to the wall. The guards pulled off the cloth bags, and both men squinted in the blinding whiteness of the room. From where Avery stood, he could clearly see that both young men were fit and well-muscled. He observed the white man to his right, seeing his red beard and hair framing a determined, stoic-looking face. The black man to the left was cleanly shaven with closely cropped hair. His expression was intense, but his breathing was slow and steady. As the guards exited the room, the last one to leave drew from his belt scabbard a Gough knife, which he threw back into the room where it landed on the circular center drain.

Pressing a green button on the control panel, Avery's voice cast into the room. "The man who survives will be a soldier of Cerberus." Depressing another button retracted the metal binds, unleashing both men. The white guy leapt for the knife, sliding across the tile floor to snatch it from the grate covering the drain. The black guy rubbed his wrist as he strode away from his original position looking down upon his adversary. The bearded man quickly regained his feet with a wickedly triumphant smile. In his hand, he held the world's best-constructed knife. The anodized black blade of hyper-hardened steel tapered into a deadly point. A diamond grinder was used to hone the edge so sharply that the knife must be stored in a carbon-reinforced scabbard. The red-bearded man extended his arm, holding the knife as a menacing threat. Both men moved in a slow clockwise circle. The white guy's smile grew wider, yet a flicker of doubt shimmered in his eyes, because the black guy didn't seem dismayed by the knife, in fact, he had made no attempt to acquire the weapon. The white guy lunged forward, swiping the air where the black guy had been. The six-inch blade made no contact, as the dark man's deft movements made the attack look feeble.

"Is this your first time in here?" asked the black man in a deep calm tone.

"Fuck you," came the Dublin accented response.

The Irishman held the knife out in front of him, sure the weapon gave him an advantage. He looked at his adversary as he stepped forward, ready to end this contest and step into the elite service of Cerberus. As the black man circled, the Irishman cut off his path. The dark man doubled back, but his way was cut off again. The Irishman pressed forward, pushing his target into the corner. Standing just two feet from his opponent, the white guy faked a lunge, then thrust forward aiming the blade for the black man's chest. The forward thrust was fast, but the black man was swift. He moved to the side, grabbing the Irishman's forearm, pulling it hard while shoving his shoulder with his other hand. The move sent the Irishman hurtling forward into the wall without his arms to slow him. His head striking the tile sounded like a coconut. The Irishman's neck snapped, and he crumpled to the floor. The black guy stepped closer, and the Irishman struggled to get his feet underneath him to rise. As soon as he could get balance, the Irishman stabbed out again, and again the black guy avoided the attacks. Stepping into the center of the room, the black man drew the Irishman out of the corner. Resuming the circular process, the two men had a measure of each other and the Irishman's eyes expressed dismay over the calm of his opponent. The black man kicked out with a flash of his right foot striking the Irishman on the elbow. The knife clattered to the floor, as a bolt of pain shot through the Irishman's forearm and hand. The black guy quickly kicked the weapon into the corner, positioning himself to block the pained Irishman, who rubbed his elbow. As the black man assumed a defensive stance, the Irishman settled his shoulders and lifted his fists.

Locked eyes, focused on one another, rather than the knife. The black guy's lips curled into a derisive smile. He started the circular dance as the Irishman moved to the center drain where he rotated, keeping his defenses up. The black guy bounced as he accelerated his movements. He looked for advantage and could see that his lack of fear had disillusioned the Irishman. A lightning-fast punch to the jaw twisted the bearded man's face, his teeth colliding with a sickening crunch. The strike sent the Irishman stumbling, unable to keep his balance. As he wobbled on unsteady feet, he saw a devious smile on his tormentor's lips. The black man front kicked him in the hip sending him toppling into the far corner of the room. Reaching back to pick up the Gough, the black man approached like a butcher about to dress a fresh carcass. He knelt next to the gasping Irishman, ready to slice his throat.

Springing up like a rabid raccoon, the Irishman grabbed the head and neck of his executioner. He swung his legs, wrapping them around the black man's torso as he pulled him to the floor. Using his left hand, the Irishman clasped the black man's right wrist, rendering the knife inert. With his right hand, he gripped the black man's chin, torquing it as hard as he could.

With both hands occupied, the Irishman opened his mouth and bit down hard on the black man's ear. Clamping his jaws shut, he tore the top half of the cartilage from the side of the black man's head. Yowling like an animal, the black man kicked his legs, driving both of them forward. Yanking his right hand free, he drove the Gough into the Irishman's back. Plunging it in again and again, until he hit an artery which pulsed across the floor. The Irishman clung on trying to snap the African's neck. The black man's muscles resisted the weakening force of the Irishman's efforts.

As had been done to him, the black man sunk his teeth into the Irishman's hand. The bite dislocated the knuckle, as it crushed the first metacarpal bone. The disabled hand lost its grasp on the black man's chin. Pulling his head free, the black man rolled the Irishman onto his back. Breaking free from the supine man's grasp, the African positioned the point of the Gough just below the beard in the suprasternal notch. With a hard smack to the butt of the handle, he drove the blade into the Irishman's windpipe. Twisting hard and thrusting upward, the blade ripped open the airway forcing blood into the deepest recesses of the lungs. Several spasmodic gasps erupted as the final breaths left the Irishman's dying body.

The black man dropped the knife and pried open the Irishman's mouth to retrieve his ragged piece of ear. He stood to look in the mirrored window with blood flowing down over his neck and shoulder. Holding the damaged chunk of cartilage, he said, "A little help here." The door opened and the guards led the man away. As he was escorted to Medical, Avery stopped him in the hall, "Very impressive Tiberius. You remain my number one."

"That fucker bit me."

"And I saw you bite him back."

"That's the first time I've ever done that."

"Medical will be able to reconstruct you."

Tiberius Dupre' looked at Avery with menace and contempt as he followed the lead of his guards.

CHAPTER 13

Trevor Cobb was a tech giant who, at the age of twenty-seven, had established one of the fastest growing and most influential start-up companies to ever come out of Silicon Valley. As the founder of Ambient Solutions, he directed the production and distribution of successful apps that everybody had on their phones and used all the time.

Find Me, was an app which used social media to find and locate missing and abducted children. The app was also used by police to find criminals of all sorts. The public's enlistment made it practically impossible for a person being sought to escape detection, especially since there was reward money.

APPostle, was an app that organized all the apps on your phone according to an algorithm which quickly learns your use patterns. Phone manufacturers include the app as a feature, thus Ambient Solutions gets paid for every phone manufactured on planet earth.

The company also developed the technology which enabled phones to project images. Phones offer this technology as an extra feature, but each time a unit included this capability, Ambient Solutions got paid. Soon all phones would have this technology as standard.

Trevor watched the advent of Digival with curiosity and recognition of the "next-gen" concept. He converted all his personal money and promoted the idea that Ambient Solutions should do the same. The accountant's hesitations were not enough to stop the young CEO from convincing the other principles of the value and virtue of Digival. Three months after its release, Ambient Solutions converted all cash into Digival and conducted all monetary transactions including purchases, sales, and payroll in the electronic currency. Ambient Solutions wasn't the first company to do so but it was one of the most notable. Trevor Cobb made the rounds of media interviews and was especially proud of being featured on USPR's 'Shooting the Breeze' with Terry Grover.

Terry: "Trevor, welcome to Shooting the Breeze. You know one of the real pleasures of my job is meeting the young lions of the future. Your Apps are revolutionary and have changed the way people behave."

Trevor: "Thank you, Terry, it is such a pleasure to be here with you. I don't think I've ever been called a "Lion" before. I might have to let my mane grow out a bit more."

(Chuckling) Terry: "Using Carbon-Not last year I reduced my carbon footprint by over a third and made over $500 dollars. I helped the environment while getting paid to do so. It's brilliant."

Trevor: "Thanks. You and 17 million other users all over the world have reduced carbon emissions by twenty five percent since the inception of the app. That's the single greatest reduction in environmental pollution that has ever been recorded and it was achieved by many people changing just a little. Did you find the changes difficult?"

Terry: "No, no they weren't difficult. The app showed me the impact of the choices I was making while providing alternatives which indicated the reduction in my energy consumption. The subtle reminder and the freedom to choose makes the app helpful without being annoying."

Trevor: "No one wants to be forced to do anything. Carbon-Not was founded on the principle that if people knew the impact of their choices and were offered easy alternatives, they would choose the more energy-efficient way of doing things."

Terry: "I don't like being forced."

Trevor: "But if allowed to choose, the reduction in carbon emissions become a side benefit of energy efficiency. Especially in America, where people have habits that use a lot of energy. Carbon-Not addresses those behaviors by providing advice and incentive to change, that's convenient and without judgment."

Terry: "You mentioned incentive to change and I said earlier that I made $ 515.34 last year by being more energy-efficient. Instead of fining, or penalizing people you found a way to pay people for the benefits they provide to the environment. I find that amazing."

Trevor: "That money you were paid reinforced your behavior. The monetary reward makes the inconvenience of changing no longer an annoyance, but a benefit. If you had changed more, you could have made more and if you had done less then you'd make less. This is simple economics applied to a huge global problem. My bet is that you'll find even more ways to be efficient, and next year you will earn even more money."

Terry: "This year I measured my "earnings" in dollars but now I will be incented with Digival. Why are you and Ambient Solutions going whole hog with this cryptocurrency?"

Trevor: "Terry I'm glad you brought this up because you're right, there are many cryptocurrencies out there and of course Bitcoin is the granddaddy of them all. The problem with all those currencies is they are worthless. They are based on nothing and promoted by folks who want you to believe in a value that is supported by nothing but faith. Take Bitcoin, which right now is being used as a speculative investment tool. Its worth is vacillating on an hourly basis as people speculate on what's going to happen to the price in the next few seconds. That's not a currency you can spend. No one buys anything with Bitcoins. It has become an anomaly investment, that I believe will completely tank when people finally realize that Bitcoins are valueless bytes of computer code."

Terry: "Yet Digival is only computer code sitting in an online account. It's not a physical thing."

Trevor: "I'm sorry, I didn't mean to say that Bitcoins were useless because they are code, they're worthless because nothing is backing that code. Digival, on the other hand, is backed by the immense wealth of Omnisphere."

Terry: "Of course, Omnisphere, the world's largest corporation with a gigantic, diverse, global umbrella of subsidiary companies united under one entity."

Trevor: "Wow, you really practiced that promo! You can't go one day without encountering several Omnisphere companies, all of which are seeking to fulfill your daily needs. That kind of reach makes Omnisphere more influential in people's lives than any government.

Terry: "But for most people money has always been issued by the US Government. The US dollar is valued all over the world."

Trevor: "I see your point, Terry. I grew up with George Washington and all the other dead presidents, but the truth is money has taken many forms and been issued by many private entities in the past. The US dollar has dominated for the past 150 years, and there was a time when the money was backed by reserves of gold. Way back in the 1970s that plan was abandoned, and the government started printing money backed only by the 'full faith and credit of the US Government.' We don't have to recount all that has put that into doubt."

Terry: "So if we lose faith in the value of the US dollar, you're suggesting that we should shift our faith to Omnisphere?"

Trevor: "In a global economy, with a planet that is more closely intertwined than it has ever been, national government's influencing the economy are much less relevant and are in fact an impediment to growth, prosperity, and peace as they each seek to retain the power of their currency. It is time for us to move into a post-government economy."

Terry: "A post-government economy?"

Trevor: "Yes. Business is business and should be able to operate as a true economy unencumbered by governmental politics."

Terry: "Whoa, that sounds like it's going back to the 1800s with the robber barons."

Trevor: "I'm aware of the history, and I see the risks, but I also see the impact of technology and accountability of companies to their customers on a first-hand basis. Ambient Solutions is constantly addressing customer service issues, so we remain a highly regarded, well-reviewed and recommended company. If we fail to satisfy our customers, our reputation can be torpedoed, and our success undermined through social media. The robber barons never had to deal with the blogosphere."

Terry: "Earlier you mentioned government currency as an impediment to peace. Care to expand on that?"

Trevor: "Sure, companies compete all the time. They are constantly battling to take customers away from one another. It's competition, but it's not war. Governments conduct war. They fight using violence as a way of competing for dominance. Governments will go to war to protect their currency and maintain its dominance in the world market. Companies can't do that, so they compete instead."

Terry: "Do you think there will be many corporate currencies and will there be a market for exchanging them?"

Trevor: "Great question. Right now Digival is the clear choice for actual currency use, and its success will surely spawn many competitors, but Omnisphere is a huge player. It remains to be seen how the world responds to a currency that needs no exchange since it holds a common value all over the globe."

Terry: "Amazing times. One last question, Trevor. You have been exclusively Digival for three months now, do you have any regrets about switching?"

Trevor: "When I was getting ready to make the switch, I was fine with it. From a logical point of view, I could see what they were doing, and I was totally there. When I was about to push the button and abandon all the money I have always known, I panicked and had a moment of hesitation that left me cold and unsure, but I dove in anyway, and I have not regretted it one bit once the switch was made. My net worth is now higher than when I had only dollars. I wish I had the wealth and vision to have invented Digival."

Terry: "Trevor, I know your R&D department is very active, what can we look forward to from Ambient Solutions?"

Trevor: "We're always looking to make life better, so soon you'll be able to download our newest app, Digiwallet. It's an App that helps you organize your Digival account and easily track all your purchases. For those who've gone totally digital, it's an essential tool for living in the new economy."

Terry: "Is this app authorized by Omnisphere?"

Trevor: "The app is open market, but we believe Omnisphere will embrace what we've done and encourage people to use the App since it simplifies the process of living with a digital currency."

Terry: "Well Trevor, I want to thank you for coming on the show, and I wish you all the best in the new digital economy."

Trevor: "Thank you, Terry, what an honor it is to be on your show. I really appreciate the opportunity to shoot the breeze with you."

CHAPTER 14

The Gulfstream G650 is as good as it gets for private jet aircraft. Diegert recalled his previous flights on the Crepusculous owned airplane. His first was when he was escaping America and flying into the unknown world of covert operations. By the time he had his second flight he had completed his 'training' in Romania and was assigned to protect Fatima Hussain as she carried out an assignment in Frankfurt, Germany. Diegert foiled a double-crossing counter strike designed to kill Fatima after she assassinated her target.

The G650 provided luxury, speed and most importantly, no questions asked when you boarded or exited the craft. Private jet flight made missions possible, convenient and while in the air, the plane provided a place of comfort and safety. Diegert sat in his broad soft leather seat reviewing the dossier on Jarod Masoni. The flight was destined for Italy, to the "Eternal City" of Rome.

From the dossier, Diegert had learned that Mr. Masoni had joined Crepusculous five years ago. Previously he had been an independent hitman picking up work through criminal enterprises operating on the boot-shaped peninsula. One of his jobs went sideways, and he was arrested. Hope that his Mafioso connections would free him faded as his incarceration dragged on. Searching for recruits Aaron Blevinsky, whom Diegert knew well from his training in Romania, bought Masoni's release and sent him to London to be trained under Avery Forsythe. At first, the Italian killer was grateful to have been released from prison. He completed Avery's training, successfully fulfilled seven lethal sanctions and seemed content with his role. Last winter he grew tired of the dreary weather of London. An argument erupted between him and Avery when Masoni insisted he be allowed to vacation in a tropical climate. The dossier, which was put together by Avery, described how he had denied the request for mission and security reasons. There was no clear indication of how the argument was resolved, but Avery listed dissatisfaction with the weather in England as the main reason for Masoni's defection. Diegert found this difficult to believe. He hoped Jarod would enlighten him as to why he left and rejected his membership in Cerberus.

Leonardo Da Vinci never got to fly. He was of course, ahead of his time in imagining and calculating ways in which humans would one day leave the ground and safely return. Now pilots and passengers the world over enjoy the boundless freedom of flight. So it was entirely fitting that the International Airport serving Rome would be named in his honor. The actual terminals were divided into the Fiumicino and Ciampino locations. Private jets used the Ciampino location, and it was here that Diegert exited the G650 and picked up the car that was reserved for him, a Fiat 500. The 500 was an extremely small car, but it surprised Diegert how comfortably it accommodated his 6-foot 2-inch frame.

Before checking into the Hotel Fontana, Diegert spent time looking at the historic Trevi Fountain. The eighteenth-century sculptures, having recently been restored, looked fantastic, especially lit up at night. Even though it was 10 p.m., the throng of tourists was thick. The plaza in front of the fountain was a sea of people moving and changing as much as the constantly flowing water that was pumped over the rocks. Diegert smiled though to see happy couples, families and tourist groups, all wearing the same colored t-shirts, posing in front of the imposing likenesses of Oceanus and his seahorses. The sculpted women on both sides of the king of the water were intriguing. Diegert read a placard which identified them as Abundance and Health, both of which are dependent on water. The whole fountain represented the importance and value of water. The effort, energy, and commitment that went into building and maintaining this massive work of art seemed even more impressive to Diegert when he understood its meaning.

Diegert was grateful his room was in the back of the hotel, it was quieter, and he was looking forward to a good night's sleep since Masoni was an early riser.

Up before sunrise, Diegert checked the belongings he would carry. Euros in his wallet, map of Rome on his phone, a folded knife in his pocket and something Avery gave him to use if necessary. Avery called it a stinger. The device was a one-inch square which looked like a super-strong band-aid. When the backing was peeled, adhering it to the skin delivered a potent dose of benzodiazepine, the anesthetic that incapacitated Diegert at the Ambassador Hotel. The early hour was necessary because that's when Masoni went for a morning run. Diegert was dressed for running in a pair of shorts, an Under Armour t-shirt and his favorite pair of Nikes. He hoped he could convince Masoni to return to London with him, but if that failed the stinger gave him another option. Since he would not be returning to this room, he zipped up his bag, left the key on the stand and headed to his car. The drive to the park, which surrounded the zoo and bordered several museums including the National Gallery of Modern Art took under fifteen minutes at this early hour. Parking his car along Via Strasse, Diegert exited the vehicle just as the sun was starting to rise. The roadway wound through the park to a section flanked by trees beyond, which open fields were used for football, dogs chasing balls, and people having picnics. Right now though, there were only a few healthy people up taking advantage of the coolness of the morning.

Diegert used a park bench to stretch his legs. He moved his joints to the point where muscle tension was not yet pain, and there he held his position allowing his nerves to register the current length of the muscle tissue as the new normal. It was in such a position, with his hip flexed and his knee extended that Diegert saw his target approaching. From the dossier, he knew what to expect but like so many things in life, seeing the actual, startled him for a moment.

Masoni stood just over 6 feet tall, an inch or two shorter than Diegert, but he was a compact man, muscular and formidable. He was dressed in black tights, a gray shirt with black and red trim. His Adidas runners were bright green. Masoni was jogging, slowing down having already completed the more intense part of his workout. Sweat soaked his shirt and beaded on his forehead.

On his approach, he only paid enough attention to Diegert to avoid running into him. As he passed, Diegert surprised him by shouting, "Hey, Jarod."

Masoni brought his jog to a stop and turned back.

"Hey it's good to see you," said Diegert.

Masoni snapped a glare at Diegert. "Do I know you?"

Diegert stepped forward to the polite edge of Masoni's personal space, "No, not really. I'm here on behalf of a friend of yours."

Diegert could see the guy was bracing himself. He figured as an assassin for hire, Masoni was not unfamiliar with being approached in unconventional manners.

"What friend?" asked the Italian cautiously.

"A friend from London."

Diegert could see the tension that the British city's name triggered in the man.

Masoni's eyes darted left and right, scanning for additional threats. "Is this friend from Cerberus?"

"Avery sent me to encourage your return to service."

Masoni chuckled, but it did nothing to lighten the mood. "Avery's an asshole, and there is no way I'm going back to London."

"He told me to tell you he is willing to meet your demands and accommodate your earlier request as well as increase your compensation by thirty percent."

Masoni rolled his eyes as he snorted at this offer. "That sounds like bullshit to me."

Diegert removed his phone from his pocket. "He's willing to speak with you directly."

"No fucking way. I'm not talking to that guy."

"What is your problem with Avery?"

"The guy is the most psychologically manipulative person in the world. He can twist your mind to believe things you shouldn't, to get you to do whatever he wants."

Diegert took a small step closer, "Like killing?"

"No," said Masoni with a shake of his head. "But believing things."

Crestfallen that Masoni dismissed concern about killing people, Diegert pressed him to explain. "Believing what? What do you mean?"

"Look just forget it. Tell Avery whatever the fuck you want, but I'm not going anywhere with you."

"You know I can't just walk away."

"Yeah," said Masoni as he slowly clenched his fists and slid his left foot back, setting his fighting stance.

"You really ought to just talk to Avery."

"You really ought to shut up and get outta here."

It was Diegert who threw the first flurry of punches. He came straight at Masoni, testing his defenses. He kept up the barrage, forcing the other man to give ground but was unable to land a significant strike. This guy was good, effectively defending his center mass. Diegert moved to the left, Masoni pivoted continuing to face him. Diegert kept the attack on, never giving the Italian a moment to attempt a counter. Diegert's movements were strategic. When he lashed out with a front kick to the hip it sent Masoni staggering back to collide with the park bench. The immobile piece of seating caused the man to fling both arms out to the sides. Diegert was right there to shove him in the chest with both hands. The high force combined with the immobility of his legs sent Masoni toppling over the bench.

Masoni turned his fall into a flip landing awkwardly but decidedly on his feet. Rounding the bench, Diegert tackled Masoni, taking him to the ground. All that wrestling as a Minnesota teen made Diegert very comfortable when the fight went to the dirt, and the game became one of joint locks and submission holds. Masoni didn't want to get pinned, and he had no hesitation about using his fists. As Diegert sought to control the man's center mass, Masoni punched him in the head and chopped him on the neck. Diegert drove his feet against the ground plowing Masoni forward, putting the man's back to the ground and his head in the dirt. The punches opened a gash above Diegert's right eye, which bled down his face and onto the Italian. While Diegert struggled to grab Masoni's right wrist, he managed to straddle him with his legs. His hips were positioned on the center of Masoni's abdomen. Once he had Masoni's right arm in his grasp, he pressed it to the ground. Diegert sat up, reached into his pocket to extract the stinger. Panic streaked across Masoni's face as he lashed out with his left arm pounding against

Diegert's body. Ripping open the package with his teeth, Diegert freed the adhesive tranquilizer. Masoni trained his eyes upon the band-aid-like device in Diegert's hand. As the American tried to stick the small patch on the Italian's skin, Masoni used his left arm to block Diegert's right while at the same time rotating his hip to the right causing Diegert to lurch to the side and put his hand on the ground. When the stinger hit the dirt, the adhesive clung to sand, grass and leaf debris. Diegert righted himself, but the tranquilizer could no longer be delivered.

Using his right arm, Diegert grabbed Masoni's left wrist and drove it to the ground as well. Diegert now had both of the Italian's arms pressed to the dirt while sitting on his chest.

Leaning over his pinned opponent, Diegert shifted his head to the right, so his bleeding gash no longer splattered Masoni's face.

"I'm not going back," persisted Masoni.

"Why not? Tell me why not?" insisted Diegert.

Masoni continued to struggle, but Diegert knew just how to exert force at the right time, and in the right place, to counter his efforts. Diegert also kept an eye on Masoni's legs ready to deflect any attempt to use them as weapons.

With a great deal of resignation, Masoni said, "It's a woman. I'm in love with a woman."

Diegert could feel the tension leaving Masoni's body. He held tight though not wanting to be the victim of a ruse. "I don't get it. What's the problem?"

"The problem is, Avery doesn't believe that an assassin should be in love."

Diegert raised his eyebrow in disbelief, forcing blood to ooze towards his nose.

Masoni said, "Avery believes that defending Crepusculous is the highest calling an assassin can have. He thinks it should be your whole life. Not just a job. He sees people you love as a vulnerability. A weakness in the web that protects Crepusculous is unacceptable to him."

"So he threatened her."

"Exactly, so I moved her here, and now you've found me. What are the full parameters of your mission?"

Diegert realized what he was asking. "My mission was to acquire you and return you to London, nothing else."

"Are there other operators on this mission with you?"

"No."

"Did your dossier include the address where I live?"

"No. The plan was to encounter you here."

"I don't trust Avery. If he sees something as a threat to Crepusculous, he won't let it go. There was this journalist who wrote for one of the Omnisphere news blogs. She was investigating the membership of the Board. As she got closer to the truth, Avery had her killed. Not by me, but by one of the other Cerberus operators."

Diegert's thoughts were conflicted. He kind of liked Avery, but now he had to see him in a different light. Was Masoni's story true, or was it emotional manipulation? How could he remain in control and confirm any of what was being said?

"What's your girlfriend's name?"

The muscles in Masoni's cheeks bulged as he clenched his jaw.

"If you can't even tell me her name, why should I believe any of this?"

Diegert could feel the tension return to Masoni's muscles as he blurted out, "If right now, another operator is harming her while we're here in the park, I will kill you both, as well as fucking Avery."

Diegert brought his face closer to Masoni's, dripping blood on his cheek. "I swear I do not know of any plan to harm her. Now, what's her name?"

"You don't need to know her name, besides Avery already knows. He's met her."

Diegert's thoughts were jumbled. *Avery never mentioned a girlfriend. Why would he leave that out? Did working with Avery mean a life without love? Celibate assassins whose only role is to protect Crepusculous. Avery seeking to control all aspects of the lives of those who serve within Cerberus. Could*

Masoni's, girlfriend actually be in trouble as he had him pinned to the ground?

The screech of tires pulled Diegert from his thoughts. A Ford Fiesta stopped in the road opposite the bench. The window went down and a concerned, but striking, face of a young woman with dark blonde hair, peered out to ask, "Jarod? What the hell's going on?"

Masoni lifted his head, and Diegert turned to see the perplexed woman getting out of the car.

Diegert released Masoni and stood up. The Italian quickly got off the ground, stepping to meet the young woman on the other side of the bench.

"What's going on? You've got blood on your face." She reached out to his forehead.

Placing his hands on her shoulders, he said, "It's OK, it's not mine."

She looked to Diegert who stood defiantly on the other side of the bench. "Who is he? What's going on?"

Masoni put his arm around her waist and moved closer to her. "I don't know, but we've got to go."

As he directed her to the car, she kept looking at Diegert.

Diegert realized he must be a sorry sight with the gash above his eye dripping blood all over him.

When she was in the car, Masoni stepped back to Diegert. "If you have any decency, tell Avery you killed me. If another operator comes for me, or anyone

149

harms her, I'll kill them, and then I'll find and kill you too."

As the car sped away, Diegert realized the failure of his mission may have revealed more than he ever expected.

CHAPTER 15

Embezzlement is a crime of greed. It requires only dishonesty and access. Gerald Hempstead oversaw the accounting processes for Exceptional Insurance, a subsidiary of Truststone Management, one of Omnisphere's most substantial financial services companies. Exceptional Insurance underwrote the risks associated with owning luxurious vacation homes, exquisite yachts, exotic sports cars, private jets, all the bells and whistles of the lifestyles enjoyed by the world's wealthiest people.

Gerald was well to do, making more than 250,000 Digival a year, but it was a pittance compared to the money his clients spent on entertaining themselves for a weekend. So it was when Gerald reviewed the monthly receipts he had found a deceptive way of disguising his removal of 10,000 to 20,000 Digival each month. Hiding the money was easy for such an accomplished electronic accounting whiz, he told himself. Gerald created a digital hide for his stolen electronic bits, tucking it into an account that billed in excess of 5 million Digival a year.

Dishonesty was most typically revealed by hubris and arrogance. Unfortunately for Gerald, he practiced both. His dual faults had ripened at the same time so that, what he had been doing for years, blossomed into a flower an audit could not help but stop to savor. Tech Sec had found Gerald's secret slush fund when justifying expenses against an inventory of client assets.

Tech Sec's investigative branch was interested in what Gerald was doing with the money, so they followed it. Gerald, it turned out, was a man who enjoyed a good bottle of wine with a fine meal all on the bare midriff of a lovely lady named Sheila Lamb. They would meet at a chateau, which had a large and well-appointed kitchen. Sheila would cook a substantial meal and open a bottle of fine red wine as she waited for Gerald to arrive with a ravenous, lustful appetite. She would then recline on the dining room table where Gerald would serve himself generous helpings of her gourmet dish directly upon her flat, femininely sculpted abdomen. Her naked body appetized the gastronomic fantasies of the sex-crazed accountant. He would first feast upon her and then of her, ending his meal with food festooned sex. Sheila embellished it all, as women paid to provide for perverted benefactors always do. Dinner theater sex became the norm for her. Gerald paid her well, but he also promised her a future of wealth and abundance even though she was left to clean up the mess after he belched a few times, wiped the wine and beef stroganoff from his mouth, chest, and crotch before exiting the chateau.

Clandestine video captured several of the disgusting rutting and glutting events allowing Tech Sec Director Ken Kindler, to share his findings with Abaya Patel. The gentile and gracious CEO of Omnisphere was so disgusted that still pictures were all she wanted to see. The video was then secretly delivered to Avery Forsythe who saw an opportunity to both put an end to the embezzlement while making an example of what he considered to be reprehensible behavior. From Klaus

Panzer, he received authorization to immediately plan and execute a terminal sanction.

Shelia Lamb arrived at the chateau, grocery bags in hand. As she unlocked the door, a dark form came behind her, shoving her through the entrance. Sheila screamed as she stumbled, dropping the bags of groceries to the floor. The dark form shut the door behind her as she threw off her hood revealing a stern-faced woman a few years younger than thirty-year-old Sheila.

"What are you doing? What do you want?" shouted a frightened Sheila.

The young woman placed a finger over her lips ushering a short, "SHHH."

Sheila grew tense but silent.

The young woman spoke. "I know all about you and Gerald."

"Gerald," screeched Sheila. "The man is not named Gerald."

"Gerry, perhaps," offered the younger woman, whose short dark hair had bleached blonde highlights. Her dark eyes, set in lids edged by dark lashes, projected controlled intensity.

"His name is Christoph," blurted Sheila.

"Of course it is, but your man is actually a thief. He has been stealing from his employer for years."

"He's an artist. He doesn't have an employer."

"He's an artist all right, a con artist."

Sheila knelt to the floor gathering up the groceries.

"I can't believe this. He's shown me his art."

"Where?"

"On his website."

With the food back in the bags, she walked to the kitchen setting them on the counter. Pulling her phone from her pocket, she brought up a website with impressionistic paintings of nude women. Much of the art depicted misogynistic bondage and female mutilation.

The young woman frowned with disgust. "All right," she said pushing the phone away, "that's enough."

"You see, he's an artist."

"He's a liar and a thief, and I'm here for a little justice."

"Justice? You're no cop."

"That's right, and this justice might get a bit rough, but first I'm going to need your help."

"I'm not helping you."

"Let me ask you, what promises has Christoph made?"

Indignantly, Sheila faced the younger woman, who was shorter by at least two inches and lighter by twenty pounds. Sheila removed her jacket, revealed a plunging neckline. The young woman's gaze took in the deep cleavage formed between the massive breasts pressed together by a constricting bra.

"Christoph is a creative genius whose work is in demand all over the world. As his muse, it's my responsibility to preserve his inspiration. We'll get married as soon as his work is installed in the Louvre."

"And when's that?"

"Next year."

"Sheila, I've got a few things to tell you about Christoph."

Hands on her hips, Sheila grew impatient.

"Christoph's real name is Gerald Hempstead, and he's a serial murderer."

"You're crazy, that's impossible. I don't even know you, and now you tell me this crazy thing about a man I have known for six months. Get Out," shouted Sheila as she pointed to the door. "Get Out right now."

The young woman softened her features as she asked, "Would it help if you knew my name?"

Sheila did not relax, but shouted, "Yeah, who the hell are you?"

"I'm Beth Melbrook," lied Fiera Getzler instinctively offering her hand.

As a Crepusculous operator, under the direction of Avery Forsythe, the young woman knew better than to give an unwitting accomplice her real name. Fiera had been tasked with confronting this man, interrogating him and dispatching him as she saw fit. Getting help from Sheila Lamb would just make things easier and hopefully keep the body count to one.

Sheila ignored the outstretched hand as she stepped back toward the counter. The big woman kept her eyes on Fiera. "I don't really care who you are, and I don't believe that's your real name. I just want you to get the hell out of here, Beth." From the angled wooden scabbard on the countertop, Sheila withdrew a long sharp kitchen knife. She pointed it at Fiera shouting, "Get Out, Get Out right now."

Calmly, Fiera turned her body at an angle and, stepping around the island, she placed a barrier between her and Sheila. Fiera lifted her phone, showing Sheila it was not a weapon. She manipulated the screen, bringing up pictures. "Have you ever heard of Feather Fowler or Bovina Cattell?" Fiera spun her phone around showing Sheila the grisly pictures of two brutally murdered women.

Sheila, with her knife firm in hand, said, "Everyone's heard of those girls. Their strange names were clues to the crime."

"A crime that officially remains unsolved."

"So what about them?"

"They were murdered, dismembered and consumed by Gerald Hempstead, the man you call Christoph."

Although her grip on the knife relaxed ever so slightly, Sheila held her doubts, "How do you know this, but the cops don't?"

"I'm much better than the cops. My employer has a lot more money and is not constrained by acts of legislation."

Sheila did not release the knife, but she lowered her hand to the countertop.

"You could see in the pictures that the women were mutilated. Forensic evidence indicates certain body parts were never found. Hempstead pulled the same ruse with them as he is with you, but it seems to me with these two, he took the eating part just a little further."

The etched lines in Sheila's forehead, along with her deep frown, told Fiera she had started to turn.

"Has he ever said he'd like to eat you up?"

"Well yeah, but I didn't think that's what he meant."

"The other girls ended up as courses in a Hungry Man's meal plan. He's a cannibal. You're better off helping me than becoming a helping for him."

Sheila sighed. "What are you going to do?"

"Mr. Hempstead stole money from my employer. He's embezzled hundreds of thousands in Digival and spent them on you and the other girls. I'm putting a stop to that. I want you to go about your whole routine as if nothing was different, except ask him to go upstairs and change into a robe before the meal starts. Will he do that?"

Sheila nodded.

Shooting her a glance Fiera confirmed, "Are you sure you can do that?"

Sheila nodded again. "I can't believe he's been lying to me. All the weird food sex was just leading up to him getting ready to kill and eat me."

"It's going to be OK. We're going to stop him."

Fiera saw a faraway look on Sheila. It seemed as though the realization of her situation was weighing heavily upon her.

"He's going to be here soon isn't he?" asked Fiera.

Pulling Sheila over to the sink Fiera said, "You clean the salad, I'll start cooking the chicken."

A short time later with the chicken in the oven and the salad in a big wooden bowl, Fiera went upstairs to the bedroom to hang a black silk robe on a dressing hook. Returning downstairs, she laid out the plan to Sheila.

"I will be out of sight when he arrives. You greet him as always, except you ask him to go upstairs and change into the robe. Play it up like you're really excited about him in a robe. Men will believe anything."

Sheila smiled wanly at that line.

"When he comes back downstairs, I'll be ready for him."

Fiera extracted from her bag a long leather tube the end of which was securely sewn. She held it by the open end, reached back into her bag to get two golf balls. She dropped the golf balls into the length of the leather tube clutching it closed with her fist. Sheila looked quizzically at the device.

"I call it the scrotum. It's a very effective tool of persuasion. I'm going to step out of sight for now."

Fiera went to the library beyond the kitchen. She perused the titles on the shelves seeing The Freedom Broker she opened up K.J. Howe's novel and was immediately pulled in by the first paragraph. Before she could finish the first chapter, she heard Hempstead arrive.

"Hello Lamb Chop," said the unsuspecting liar and thief.

Fiera listened to hear Sheila tell him to go upstairs. She waited, but then she heard Sheila screaming, "LIAR, you're a Fucking LIAR."

Fiera rounded the corner of the kitchen just as Sheila slashed downward with the kitchen knife, gashing Hempstead's forearm. Shocked by Sheila's attack, the perverted accountant was doubly surprised to see Fiera, who stood still for a moment comprehending the scene. Hempstead bolted for the door, Fiera gave chase, swinging the scrotum. With practiced skill, she timed her strike to hit his right knee with both golf balls. Hempstead's joint crumpled, sending him face first to the floor of the foyer.

Sheila followed the chase, flinging herself at the howling man ready to stab him with the knife. Fiera caught her, and with surprising strength, stopped her from impaling Hempstead with the eight-inch blade.

"I have to interrogate him, then you can finish him off."

"He's a liar. You can't believe what he says," screamed Sheila.

"She's right you know," said Hempstead through short gasps, as he strained to look behind him while lying on his belly. "I'm not going to tell you anything if you're going to kill me." Turning to Sheila, he pleaded, "Lambsy chop, is this some kind of weird role play?"

Fiera whacked him with the scrotum on the middle of his back.

"You're a liar, and a thief and my employer wants to know if there are other accounts," demanded Fiera as she dangled the leather sack with its two heavy bulges in a pendular fashion.

"Like bloody hell, I'm going to tell you."

Fiera bashed him in the side of the face, cracking a tooth out of his lower jaw.

With blood oozing from his mouth, he spat out a chunk of the tooth. Looking up he saw the leather-bound bludgeon descend upon his forehead. The blow created an immediate goose egg and a bleed from the ridge of his brow.

Fiera addressed him matter-of-factly, "If you've got nothing more to say, guess there's no need for delay."

She swung the scrotum several times, building speed. Sheila shouted, "Wait, he's mine."

With a swiftness Fiera did not expect of the bigger woman, Sheila pushed past, straddled the fallen man and dropped onto his chest.

"Get off me you skanky cunt," shouted Hempstead. "I'm going to barbeque your ass and your fat tits."

Raising the knife over her head, Sheila angrily plunged the blade into Gerald Hempstead's throat. She did not repeat the strike, but instead leaned forward on the knife's hilt, rotating the blade as she listened to the gurgling last breaths of the man who would never lie to her again.

As the female member of Avery Forsythe's Cerebrus Corp, Fiera Getzler's missions often had a more cerebral, seductive and relational nature to them than her male counterparts. She was an operator, fully capable as a unit member for a military-style mission, but Avery relied on her ability to develop relationships that could be exploited. She embraced the role and appreciated how Avery recognized her capacity as entirely different than the men while treating her with the utmost respect.

Returning to LPU, she went immediately to Avery's office.

"I'm glad to see you're back from the mission," said Avery.

"Thank you, sir," replied Fiera from the seat in front of his desk.

"What did you learn from Mr. Hempstead?"

"I believe there was only one account, and a deceived lover can very quickly become a killer."

Avery tilted his head as he asked, "How so?"

"The fatal blow that ended the life of Gerald Hempstead was not delivered by me," said Fiera. "Sheila Lamb, the woman we tracked down and who was having an affair with Hempstead, was so enraged at being lied to that she attacked Hempstead killing him with a kitchen knife."

"Is she a problem for us?" asked Avery with an elevated eyebrow.

"No. When I explained how she would have been killed and her flesh eaten by her perverted lover, she agreed that he was better off dead. Subsequently killing him, even though he deserved it, without due process was undeniably murder. As a murderer, I convinced her it was best that she does not report it and she should go off to live a quiet life as a model citizen. I further emphasized that if she did not do that, I would find her and kill her myself."

With a beaming smile of pride, Avery proclaimed, "Excellent work Fiera, very well done. Your additional compensation is in your account. Go enjoy yourself, there are no current mission assignments for you. I'll be in touch as necessary."

"Thank you, sir," said Fiera as she rose, extending her hand over the desk to receive an enthusiastic shake from her pleased employer. When their hands released, Fiera asked, "Sir, permission to voice a question?"

"Go right ahead," said Avery.

"With Jarod no longer serving Cerberus, will there be a replacement?"

"I too am sorry that Jarod no longer works with us, but let me reassure you I am working to make the Cerberus team stronger than ever."

Fiera gave her boss a quick smile as she turned to leave saying, "Thank you, sir."

CHAPTER 16

The flight back to London was swift but anxiety producing for Diegert. He didn't know what to do about his failure to acquire Masoni. He was glad he hadn't done anything more against the man and his girlfriend, but he knew mission failure would not be well received.

Back in his quarters in LPU, Diegert felt stuck. He knew he wasn't free to leave and the sense of freedom he had in Rome made his living situation back here frustratingly oppressive. The knock on his door was a welcome relief from his boredom although he knew exactly who it would be.

Through the open door walked Avery Forsythe. His dark pants and light blue long sleeve shirt were not at all unusual, however, the black trim around the neck of the shirt gave way into a dark black cape with a gold interior draped over his shoulders. The garment extended to the knees and the gold lining shimmered with each movement. Diegert felt like Lando Calrissian had just walked in. He wondered if Avery was only stopping by on his way to a cosplay convention.

"All roads lead to Rome, don't they, David?"

"I guess so, but Jarod Masoni didn't follow them. He wasn't in Rome," said Diegert

"That must have been disappointing."

"I was in the park well before sunrise, and he never showed."

Avery extracted his phone from his pocket, tapped the screen, pointed the device at an area of the blank wall and projected upon it an image of Diegert with his foot on the park bench stretching his leg.

"Well, hopefully, you were able to get a good stretch and go for a nice run since you were already there."

Diegert said nothing but turned to look directly into Avery's eyes, which were intently staring him down. Avery clicked through the series of photos revealing the meeting, the fight, the arrival of Masoni's girlfriend and the eventual departure of the couple in their car.

"Why did you let him go and more importantly, why are you lying to me?"

"Why do you deny a man the opportunity to love a woman?"

"What are you talking about?"

"Masoni said he left because you wouldn't allow him to have a girlfriend."

Avery snorted and shook his head. "Now that was clever of him."

Diegert was confused by this flip of perspective. *Had Masoni duped him or was Avery playing him now?*

"What is your policy about operators of Cerberus having personal relationships?"

"They are free to do so. I have no control over that."

Diegert struggled. *Who's telling the truth, who's lying.*

"Do you even know his girlfriend's name?"

"Joanne?! Sure I met her several times. She's a lovely girl."

Diegert couldn't hide his confusion.

"Why, what did he say?" pressed Avery.

"He said you threatened her. He was afraid you would have her killed."

"Well now that's ridiculous, how could a young woman like that ever be a threat to us? Why would I ever want to harm her?"

"Then why did Masoni leave?"

"I believe it was greed that took him away. Greed can twist the minds of men and make them believe things they shouldn't. Greed blinds you to what you have and shows you only what you don't."

"Well, what are you afraid he's gonna do?"

"Sell information. His position within Cerberus will attract those with whom we compete. They will pay him for what he knows."

"Like what?"

"He really knows nothing, but you now see what an effective liar he is. He got you to believe something about me that is preposterous."

Diegert looked at Avery, whose cape covered one shoulder while draping behind the other revealing a bright shiny section of the lining.

"He will sell lies to people that could still harm us. It's up to each of us to recognize the truth and know when we're being lied to."

Diegert's gaze fell to the floor, his head bowed in contemplation.

Avery admonished, "David I now know that you will lie to me. I now see that trusting you is not something I can do implicitly. You will have to earn your way back into my trust."

Diegert lifted his head, said nothing, looked at Avery and thought, *So fuck'n what.*

"What are you going to do now?" Diegert asked Avery.

"This test was your evaluation for inclusion in Cerberus. You have failed. For all other recruits, this would be your point of exit. You, however, as the son of Klaus Panzer, will be given dispensation to remain within the pool of candidates."

"That's not what I meant."

Avery cast a quizzical look at Diegert.

"I meant what are you going to do about Masoni?"

"Oh… given your position, as I pointed out a moment ago, I'm throwing that back at you. Now that you realize Masoni represents a threat to Crepusculous, what are you going to do? This is a strategic issue."

"So now the next steps are my decision?"

"Yes."

Diegert allowed a smile to lift his lips. He felt a bit of triumph, realizing that Avery was giving him power simply because of his birth. It was an unusual feeling, but one he quite enjoyed.

"I want Masoni left alone. Do not disturb him."

"You feel the threat is to be ignored."

"I think the threat needs to be real. You obviously have observers in Rome. Have them track him, and if there is evidence of an inappropriate act, then we will take action. Continue monitoring his electronic communication and act on any significant intercepts. I require evidence for our actions, not just supposition."

"You sounded like your father there. Expressing an opinion and delivering it as an order."

"You gave me the opportunity."

"So I did, and like him, you seized it."

"Do you like working for my father?" asked Diegert who realized this was the first time he had spoken to anyone referring to Panzer as his father.

"Your father is an exceptional man for whom I have great respect and admiration. His decisiveness and determination have created a business empire, unlike anything the world has ever known. Neither Julius Caesar nor Genghis Khan can match what your father has done to amass wealth and power. I am continually impressed."

"You have not answered my question."

"There are great benefits to working for your father. I'll say it is much better to be aligned with him than to oppose him. In fact, opposing him is foolish, futile and often fatal. I like being on the winning side. He has my loyalty."

Diegert recognized the practical nature of Avery's answer. He had to admit that he and Avery shared the trait of making pragmatic decisions.

"So trust me or not," said Diegert "you and I are going to be working together."

"In spite of your privileged position, you're still my student. As is true of your father, being aligned with me is much better than being in opposition. Good day, David."

Avery spun on his heels. The movement swirled the cape, fanning it out behind him as he opened the door and flowed out of the room.

CHAPTER 17

Diegert was now part of the LPU community, albeit he was limited to remaining in the underground labyrinth. He exercised in the fitness center, practiced shooting on the range, trained in the combative tactics room and ate in the cafeteria.

"So what's your story?" Diegert asked the African man sitting across the table from him at the cafeteria. The man was like Diegert in many ways, twenty-something, athletic, stoic and resigned. Yet he exuded a friendly spirit, his confidence showing in the way he sustained eye contact. The bandage over his right ear became a curiosity to Diegert.

"I come from Nigeria."

"Oh yeah, but I was wondering about your bandaged ear."

Nodding, the man said, "An unfortunate training accident."

"It's gonna heal up?"

"One hundred percent."

"So you said you're from Nigeria, let me guess, a child soldier trained to kill as a young boy who gets plucked from the jungle to serve Crepusculous."

The dark man held Diegert's gaze as his face altered from an engaging smile to a doubtful scowl before replying, "You think you know me because you saw a movie or read an article in a magazine. Your assumptions demonstrate your prejudiced thinking that all black people are alike."

Realizing he'd stepped in dog shit, Diegert raised both hands as he said, "You mean I'm wrong?"

"You're limited. Your vision fits whatever assumptions support your perception of the world. You see what you want to see, and you don't question it. Many white people think as you do."

"Well then, how about you enlighten me."

"I saw you on the shooting range," said the dark man waving his fork as his smile returned. "I was impressed by the push-pull action you used to rack the slide of your Glock." The inquisitor pretended to handle a pistol in the manner he had seen Diegert practicing on the range. "You've got good hands," he said as he pointed at Diegert's hands folded in front of him.

"I shoot to kill."

"Ha ha ha, don't we all. I'll tell you my story, but you must then share yours."

Diegert nodded his head without saying a word.

"No, no, no, you must state your promise," scolded the big man as he wagged his finger at Diegert.

With a snorting chuckle, Diegert agreed, "Fine, I've got nothing to hide, but first are you a member of Cerberus?"

"Oh, that Avery, he has to have a special name for everything. Cerberus! Yes, I am a member of Avery's inner circle. We are the best of the best, and I'm surprised you even know about us."

"Yeah Avery told me about it, but he left me to discover the members on my own."

Leaning forward, the African smiled as he said, "You found one, my name is Tiberius Duprie" he broke into a laugh, which coaxed a smile out of Diegert. As they shook hands, the Cerberus operator said, "You've also found a Nigerian Prince. I am the son of a man from the ruling class."

Diegert was unable to stifle his laughter. "Wait, I'll give you my bank account number so you can deposit a million dollars." Continuing to laugh at his own joke, Diegert could see that Tiberius didn't get it. "It's an American thing," he said laconically.

Moving past this strange diversion, Tiberius said, "My family's history extends back for generations. My father was the Director-General of the Nigerian Military. He was in charge of the entire defense forces. A very powerful position. As his son, I was privileged and respected. I went to private school, had servants to care for me while we lived in a big house. My four brothers and two sisters all enjoyed the best of everything. Life was very good."

"The African elite," summarized Diegert.

"Yes, I suppose so." Tiberius was lost in a wistful memory before tapping the table with his fork and turning his gaze directly on Diegert. "I must tell you though that I learned the hard way about my family's history."

"How so?"

"My great-great-grandfather was a slave trader. He and his father before him were very wealthy. They would raid villages, gather the people and sell them to white men. We are Yoruba and would capture Nupe, Edo and Igbo people and sell them out of Lagos to be taken away as slaves."

"You sound like bad guys."

"I'm afraid many feel the same way. As the market for slaves dissolved, my father used his wealth and position to become a Military Man and eventually became the head of the Army." Tiberius grew silent with a downcast look that seemed sad.

"And then what happened?"

Without raising his eyes, he said, "The rebellion."

With memory came a pool of tears, adding a liquid sheen to the dark eyes of this pained man. He sniffed once as he continued his story.

"My father was killed, but not until after being humiliated and tortured. The video was viewed a million times. I never knew there were so many who hated him. Three of my brothers were killed, the other I do not know where he is. Both of my sisters were abducted, and I shudder to imagine what has become of them, but I do not know. I was taken by some loyal soldiers to a camp, but when my location became known I was kidnapped and held for ransom. Boko Haram beat me and made me fight every day. I was the training fighter for the sad boys they were turning into soldier slaves. They told all the recruits about my family history, even though they were doing the same thing, turning these boys into slaves."

"Was there anyone left to pay the ransom?"

"My mother."

Both men fell into silence as Diegert felt the sting of the other man's pain.

"What was the ransom," Diegert asked softly.

Placing his brow in his hands, Tiberius whispered, "Her life."

A maternal sacrifice thought Diegert. He held his tongue and waited for Tiberius to gather himself.

Tiberius picked up his table knife and twirled the serrated point on the tabletop. "Boko Haram was going to broadcast my execution. They announced it on their website, and they were whipping up the people to watch the *Evil Prince*, as they had named me, die."

Anger and sadness creased the brow of Tiberius's pained face.

"My mother pleaded with the local BH leader, Chibueze Ozinwa, to spare me and sacrifice her. Before she did this, she'd reached out to our friend Gunther Mibuku."

Diegert had to stop his face from reacting when he heard the name *Gunther Mibuku*. His first mission in Europe flashed through his mind. He killed a 'drug dealer,' by the same name, in the Hotel Lambert in Paris. He was helped by a prostitute who betrayed the target, allowing Diegert to enter the room and shoot him. Together they both escaped the scene.

"Uncle Gunther, as we used to call him," said Tiberius with a warm smile. Diegert smiled as well, to hide his reaction. Tiberius went on, "He worked for SSI, Strategic Solutions Incorporated. They were an arms supplier to the army, and my father and he were good friends."

The smile broadened as Tiberius recalled his family friend.

"Uncle Gunther would always bring gifts whenever he visited my father. I had a fine collection of pistols that he would add to every visit. He and my father taught me to shoot and made me practice breaking down and re-assembling my guns. I got very good at it and set records while blindfolded. I loved my gun collection."

Diegert squirmed in his seat.

"I now know that SSI is a dark subsidiary of Omnisphere and through them, Uncle Gunther arranged for a Special Forces team to rescue my mother and me. She gave them the intel on my location, and a team struck early one morning. It happened so very fast, the door to my cell blew open, two men entered, announced they were liberating me and hauled me to a helicopter. I was airborne in minutes. Chibueze Ozinwa was so angry, he immediately slit my mother's throat and posted the video before she could be rescued."

Tiberius's look of denied retribution confirmed Diegert's perception that this man was a formidable foe.

"I was flown out of Africa, brought here to London where I've been serving as an operator ever since. My mother's death haunts me, and I will avenge her sacrifice by killing Chibueze Ozinwa."

"Your mother sounds like she was a brave woman."

"She certainly was. She loved me, and in the end, she did a very brave thing. A mother's love knows no limits."

Diegert hesitated on his next question since he already knew the answer. He recalled, in vivid detail, shooting Gunther Mibuku. Diegert also remembered sassy Shei Leun Wong. She was the one who betrayed Mibuku by helping Diegert pull off the hit. Although he was offered additional money to shoot her, he refused to kill the woman. "Do you still see your uncle?"

Tiberius's head snapped at the question, his gaze on Diegert intensifying. The reaction was unsettling. Tiberius projected a desire for vengeance.

"Gunther was murdered by a whore."

Tiberius drew silent as the loss softened his features. "Gunther was a lady's man. He would say, *'I've always got one waiting.'* Well, this one shot him, robbed him and left him dead on a hotel bed. I was so sad. He was all I had left of a family. He would take me out on the town and show me a great time in London and in Paris. He was generous with his money and treated me like a member of his family."

As Tiberius spoke about Mibuku, tears formed in his eyes. His voice wavered as his nose began to run. He used a napkin to blow his nose and wipe the droplets off his cheek. Here was a man, whose physicality and demeanor impressed David Diegert as being *one tough hombre*, crying in public over the death of another man. Diegert felt an immediate kinship with this man. He was coping with the emotions of death and loss, a very painful part of an assassin's life. At the same time, Diegert felt a sense of embarrassment as the man before him wasn't covering up his emotions. Right here in the cafeteria, he was revealing his weakness, his need to cry, his feelings of love, tenderness and concern for another. All the things Diegert consistently kept clamped down and hidden within him, until they burst out in the warm embrace of a loving woman. Diegert was confused and impressed. When Tiberius's napkin was saturated, he handed him another.

Desperate to move the conversation forward without acknowledging the crying, Diegert asked, "Did they catch the girl?"

Tiberius suddenly changed back to an ominous, dangerous man as he pounded his fist on the table. His bloodshot eyes revealing his violent tendencies. "I caught her, I killed her, and I dumped her in the Seine. That whore's lifeless body floated right through the middle of Paris. She was a thief and a junkie and a murderous bitch. I took her life for Uncle Gunther. She deserved to die as she did."

Diegert sat in silence, recalling the actual events surrounding Mibuku's death. He could see Tiberius's anger and grief. He saw how the man channeled his anger into misguided beliefs which led to a violent death Shei Leun Wong didn't deserve. Diegert was to blame, and Shei Leun paid the price.

"Did your revenge feel good?" asked Diegert.

Tiberius looked at him strangely. "What?"

"You seem really angry. Did you feel better after killing her?"

"When someone you love is violently killed, the only thing that makes you whole again is to see the person responsible completely destroyed. This is why I am an assassin for Crepusculous. Vengeance for the rest of my family will be achieved when I return to Nigeria. It is a need more powerful than forgiveness."

The guilt for each of the deaths for which Diegert was responsible weighed heavily on his shoulders. Not killing Shei Leun initiated the formation of his code. Tiberius seemed to be free of this weight. He expressed such certainty of purpose and determination to carry out more violence in the name of revenge. He also seemed to have no qualms about killing women. Diegert realized that Tiberius was someone with whom he would try to build an alliance, but like so many other people in his life, he would be reluctant to trust or be completely honest with him.

Was it so difficult to justify killing when you are not committed to what you are doing, versus fully embracing the role and feeling as if it is a fulfilling purpose in life? Diegert's perception that Tiberius had this all figured out left him thinking that maybe he should more fully accept his plight as a killer of men. He should admit that he was good at it and strive to become better. He should cast off concerns that he was a sinner and a wrongful murderer and instead embrace the fact that he was adjusting the balance of power in the world in a way that has been a fact of human life for millennia. These abstractions were always wrestling in Diegert's thoughts, but seeing the ease with which Tiberius described himself as an *assassin for Crepusculous*, with such pride and assurance, made Diegert once again mull over the consequences of the choices he'd already made.

Tiberius's voice broke Diegert's thoughts. "So I am a hired gun, a killer for payment, a private contractor of assigned death. It's a dangerous job, but I have a dark heart," with his fist, Tiberius thumped the middle of his chest, "under my dark skin. I am what I am and will continue to be. I will die by the bullet, but not until I have taken the life of my enemy," he extended two fingers from his fist like a gun, "with the power of explosive propulsion fired from my hand." He suddenly extended his arm, pointing his finger at Diegert while flexing his thumb and audibly emitting the sound of a suppressed pistol, "pfft, pfft, pfft." He then flexed his elbow, retracting his arm as he burst out in laughter.

A slow smile crept across Diegert's face as he looked at the perplexing man laughing out loud with a winning smile full of perfectly aligned gleaming white teeth. This man's mirth was infectious, and soon Diegert was also laughing as he hadn't done for quite some time. Anyone who can make you laugh with such abandon is someone whom you would be wise to make a lifelong friend.

When the laughter subsided Tiberius made his request, "Now you tell me your story."

Diegert nodded. "I'm from Northern Minnesota, my father is a tow truck driver, my mother is a waitress, and my brother is a low life drug dealer. I got kicked out of the Army and then framed for murder by the Russian mafia. I had to run for my life, and I escaped into the arms of Crepusculous, for whom I have become the… the assassin that I am. I'm not so sure I embrace the role with the assurance you do, but I don't deny it."

Tiberius sat in silence with a look that expressed disbelief in what Diegert was sharing. Diegert reacted to his doubt with, "What?"

"I told you the truth, the whole truth and nothing but the truth."

"Yeah, well everything I've said is true."

"Perhaps, but it is not the whole truth. Rumor has it that you are a far more important person than you are telling me."

"What rumor?"

"The one that says you are the son of Klaus Panzer."

Diegert was non-responsive. The turmoil in his mind kept him from finding his voice. This was the first time his status as Panzer's son had been revealed to him by someone who had heard it from an unknown source. At the moment he was still struggling with a "father" who drugged him and kidnapped both he and his mother. A man who was holding him against his will, considering him a guest but treating him like a prisoner. He knew Panzer was powerful, but he felt like a victim, not a son.

Tiberius grew impatient. "Did you not know your father was the most powerful man on the planet? Which makes you the heir to his empire. You are not only wealthy beyond measure, but you will possess the power to rule the world."

Diegert was well aware of the power of Crepusculous, and he had heard these grand statements before, but they always created in him a sense of righteous indignation. From his position as a servant, he felt like that much power, outside the confines of a government, was improper, primarily since it was maintained through lawless violence. Carolyn, and the threat to blow up the United States, both pointed Diegert's mind toward using his position within the organization to disable it, dismantle it, destroy it. Now he was being challenged to consider that all that Panzer had built could be his. The possibility of inheriting Crepusculous was still beyond Diegert's comprehension. Yet here he was being asked to react to that very scenario.

"I know that I am his biological son. He and my mother confirmed that, but I am not so certain he has any plans to groom me to be his heir. So far I feel more like a prisoner."

Tiberius's smile brightened the room as his lips revealed his dazzling teeth. "Do you know the story from the Bible about the prodigal son?"

"Is that the one about the son who comes back, and they kill the fatted calf?"

"Yes of course," laughed Tiberius, "The fatted calf. Do you know the meaning of the story?"

"What?"

"It is the tale of the love a man has for his children no matter what they do. The prodigal son did not leave his father on good terms, and he did not act honorably while he was away. But when he was desperate and returned destitute to his father, the older man was overjoyed and given to celebration. He loved his son, forgave him and shared his abundance. That son grew to love and honor his father for the rest of his life. It's a parable about God and sinners, but it's also an allegory of your life."

Diegert began his protest, "But-"

Tiberius interrupted, raising his hand for silence, "I know there are differences. It is not what is different that is important but what is similar." He smiled at Diegert as he lowered his hand, palm up inviting a reply.

Shifting from protest to acceptance was straining Diegert. He dropped his head and scratched his temple.

"Do you mean that as the son he never knew he had, I will be given a place of prominence in his life?"

"Yes, of course! Why is it that the obvious is always so hard to see? Has he not said this to you?"

Diegert sat quietly as his perspective shifted. He could be the wealthiest, most powerful man in the world. What a contrast to the rest of his life. Did he want that? Could he handle that? Could he trust Panzer to really follow through on this promise? He looked at Tiberius who seemed so happy to have enlightened him to what was right in front of him.

"I'll have to think about it."

"Of course you will, how can you think of anything else? Your future is coming at you either way, but I can tell you as the son of a formerly powerful man, life is better with the strength and privileges that power grants."

Tiberius's gaze turned inquisitive.

Diegert felt his features being inspected by the dark man's eyes. "What now?"

"You look like you could be Arabian or Argentinian or maybe even Italian. What was your mother?"

"My mother is Ojibwa. It's a Native American tribe."

Tiberius's face lit up. "You have a tribe then. Are the Ojibwa a powerful people?"

Diegert felt Tiberius's sense of belonging that he associated with tribal membership, but he did not feel that way about the Ojibwa. "I don't know."

Tiberius's brow furrowed and his gaze projected his disappointment. "What do you mean you don't know? How can you not know the status of your tribe?"

Diegert's reply was a sullen shrug of his shoulders.

Tiberius sat silent for a moment seemingly letting Diegert's perplexing response percolate in his mind.

"See, my man, tribe is everything. I am from Nigeria, but that just describes a geographic location, I am Yoruba. In Africa, your tribe is your identity, your history, your culture, your purpose, and meaning. Your mission in life is to protect, preserve and advance your tribe. People see you, and they can tell which tribe you are from by your appearance and your bearing."

Diegert thought about how all the kids in school knew he was Ojibwa, but he didn't know any of their backgrounds, they were just white.

Tiberius said, "When I first came to London, I learned that no one had a tribe. They are just lost sheep herded together with no common goal. Each of them struggling to become a millionaire. There is no unity of purpose. If they got rich, they would just spend the money on themselves. No sense of community, it's stifling and oh so limiting."

Diegert cocked his head, crossed his arms over his chest and leaned back in his chair.

"Your tribe is your source of power in Africa. I am so very much a Yoruba and will always be for the rest of my life. When I think of my tribe's history, I walk with pride. When I enter a room in Africa, they all look and say, there is a powerful Yoruba man and they know that I have self-respect and confidence. What does it say when an Ojibwa man walks into a room in America?"

Diegert struggled with the question, self-respect and confidence were clearly not what he felt when walking into a room full of Minnesotans. Shame, derision and a wish to be pale white or invisible is what came to mind. He realized he had subsumed everything negative that the people of Broward believed about his Native heritage without questioning the value, strength, and purpose that he may have found by embracing his Ojibwa culture. His mom had tried, but it was too little too late, and besides, she definitely was ashamed and accepted the ostracism that she got from people who judged her for being a half-breed. Wow, to feel like Tiberius does about his tribe struck Diegert as a great source of pride while for him tribal membership was just a great big disappointment.

"I was on a wrestling team," Diegert replied.

The remark drew a stinging sidelong glance and raised eyebrow fromTiberius.

Diegert dropped his gaze. "I am a very good wrestler. I won the Minnesota State Championship in high school. Our team had won the local, county and sectional titles my senior year and everybody was so proud of that team. When we were winning, people would congratulate us wherever we went. People in school encouraged us to win, and they would come and watch, cheering on the guys. I pulled from the crowd's adoration. I performed for them, taking pride in my victories, they cheered and applauded each take-down, point, and pin. At the State tournament in Minneapolis, I carried their hopes on to the mat and delivered to them a hard-fought victory as I pinned my opponent. It was the greatest moment of my life."

Diegert's pride had risen while he spoke. He was glad to see Tiberius smiling, but as he recalled that time in his life he also felt disappointed.

"When we got back to Broward, the pride, the happiness, the acceptance lasted about two weeks. Then my dad got in a bar fight. He hurt another guy real bad, hitting him with a broken bottle. When he came home, he started beating my mom. The police came, and I was in the middle of it trying to stop him. The local media reported the domestic mess, and I was once again a halvsy from a trash heap of a family."

Tiberius sat quietly, patiently waiting for Diegert to conclude.

"So you see there is no tribe for me. There is just a family and a pretty lousy one at that."

Tiberius offered, "I can see that the wrestling team was important to you. And I can see how the championship earned you respect, but it's focused on a limited event. It fills the mind and the heart that is otherwise empty. The true person that you are and the true value that you hold is not reflected in a single or even a season of performances."

Diegert looked at Tiberius with a furrowed brow, seeking understanding.

The proud African proclaimed, "Tying your value as a person to your ability to perform in sports is to limit yourself to the fleeting power of youth, which will leave you no matter how well you train. Your school, your community, your tribe should embrace you and value you regardless of the outcome of a performance because your greatest value is in being a member of the tribe. I fear that your people cannot even comprehend the importance of that belief."

"You're right, but isn't Crepusculous doing the same thing?"

"Crepusculous provides us with a whole lot more than your wrestling team ever did. We are on a mission that transcends the world. We protect the provision of all the products and services that Omnisphere-"

"Yeah, yeah, yeah," Diegert jumped in, "Avery already gave me all that we feed the world stuff. But we also kill people with complete disregard for the law. Do you really believe that's right?"

"In Nigeria, there were violent times when killing was a matter of survival."

Diegert jumped in again, speaking sharply. "In times of war and when you are under attack, it is totally right to defend yourself. But Crepusculous attacks pre-emptively. They are the ones killing people before they've committed a crime. I want to know if you really think that's all right?"

187

"The decision to mark someone for death is not ours to make. When we are assigned, a whole lot of work went into designating that target for elimination."

"I know you want to believe that," Diegert leaned forward, "but do you really?"

"Do I really what?" asked Tiberius.

"Do you really trust Avery, Panzer, and Crepusculous that every kill mission is absolutely necessary?"

Now Tiberius leaned in, drawing close to Diegert as he said, "I am a servant and will carry out my role." Pointing at Diegert he went on, "You will one day be the man ordering the assassinations, then I hope you will carefully consider if every mission to kill is absolutely necessary."

Tiberius piled his silverware atop his dishes, wiped his mouth with a napkin and stood with his tray in his hands, smiling broadly as he said, "I'm glad we'll be working together."

Watching the big man walk away Diegert knew no one wanted to confront the reality of killing for Crepusculous. He wondered if he too shouldn't think so deeply about being a man of violence and start thinking about being a man of power.

CHAPTER 18

With her surgical wounds sufficiently healed, Carolyn's hospitalization concluded. This meant she was out of Dr. Gibson's care and into the exclusive custody of the CIA. The guard, who'd been outside her room, now pushed her wheelchair to the patient discharge exit. As final papers were signed, he motioned for the black Chevy Tahoe to pull forward. Carolyn looked at the vehicle, which screamed America, and wondered if there could be any easier target than an oversized SUV with diplomatic plates.

"Where are we going," asked Carolyn suspiciously.

"We'll be transporting you to a secure residence."

"Yeah but, where?"

"The location is monitored by the agency, so your security is assured."

Carolyn recognized the language and knew this agent wasn't going to divulge anything more. She shot him a glance of mistrust as she slowly climbed into the back passenger seat, her ribs still smarting.

They had not driven far before the big truck pulled up to a garage door, which automatically opened, allowing the Tahoe to enter. When the vehicle was parked, the guard opened Carolyn's door and escorted her to the elevator. Inside the cabin she observed the guard press the button for the seventh floor. *Lucky*, she thought.

Exiting the elevator, she was led to room 721. The apartment door opened into a large area, which combined the living room and kitchen. There was a bathroom at the end of the hall. On either side of the hall was a bedroom. The one on the north side had its own bathroom and a window, which looked out onto the street. After surveying each room, Carolyn stood facing the guard.

"Ma'am, the entire floor is secure. There will be a guard posted in the hallway at all times. The director will contact us when he needs to see you. In the meantime, you will remain here."

Not really meaning it, but at a loss for anything else to say, she muttered, "Thank you."

The snap of the lock after the door closed made the apartment feel all the more confining. The kitchen though was well stocked with eggs, cheese, fresh greens for a salad, a nice loaf of bread and cold cuts. For drinks, there was orange juice, bottled water, a six-pack of Stella-Artois and even a bottle of Cabernet-Sauvignon. In the north side bedroom, the clothes in the closet were the right size. The shirts and pants were very utilitarian, but they were brand new, and Carolyn was happy to exchange her blue scrubs for a pair of jeans, a heather T-shirt and a light blue oxford, which she buttoned partway and left untucked.

The bathroom cupboard had lots of thick, soft towels, several choices of shampoo, skin lotion, and requisite feminine hygiene products. To Carolyn's shocked surprise, she also found a home pregnancy test kit. The presence of this last item struck her as if someone was watching. Setting the box back on the shelf, she looked around expecting someone to have seen her. She saw no cameras, but she had no faith in the coincidence. She couldn't shake the feeling of her privacy having been violated.

The box, with its picture of a positive red plus on the plastic device, brought back the news she'd been given at the hospital. One night, one fucking moment of human lust and she was now linked to the world's worst assassin forever.

All the actions for which she was guilty could be explained. Her choices could be justified as critical to the mission. Given what she was now aware of, her conduct could be seen as brave, decisive and significant. All of it sensible and effective at protecting the United States. All of it, except fucking the asset and carrying his child.

Carolyn slammed the cupboard door, walked to the bed, and flung herself upon it. The drop hurt like hell, and she groaned as the pain in her ribcage spread through her abdomen. She stared up at the textured stucco ceiling wondering how much trouble she would be in when Director Ramsey realized she was pregnant. How would she explain it, since the only man she was with, within the timeframe of conception, was Diegert? She had to keep Ramsey focused on the bombs and Strakov's guilt so that he didn't take notice or make mention of her eventual belly. She had to get back Stateside before her condition could not be denied.

The thought of an abortion ran through her head, but the immediate wrenching of her gut told her she could never go through with it. Even though it made a lot of sense in this case, Carolyn could never kill a baby no matter what her circumstances. Diegert's genes may be flawed, and the baby may even grow to be a violent killer, but Carolyn felt that the life within her was a sacred priority to protect.

She carefully rolled to her side, tucking the pillow under her head, softly crying as she fell into a fitful sleep.

****

The shooting range was one of Diegert's favorite places to be. The power of the guns, the variable targets and the opportunity to improve a skill upon which his life might depend, always made him feel good. Diegert realized he was sharing the range with a female operator. The young woman was practicing with pistols. Diegert was impressed with the speed and accuracy with which she was filling the silhouettes with fatal holes.

Using a stall two spots away from her, he practiced using a submachine gun. Firing three-round bursts took a steady hand and an ability to scan the field for targets. Diegert positioned the silhouettes, so they rotated randomly. He was using up a lot of ammo but was becoming more lethal with each magazine of bullets.

When he stopped firing, he realized the other stall was now quiet. Looking behind him, he was surprised by the woman with whom he was sharing the range.

She was cute, with a broad smile and soft brown eyes. Her dark hair was short with blonde highlights. She was about 5 foot 7 with an athletic build, a confident demeanor and a Glock 17 holstered on her hip.

"Hi, I'm Fiera."

Diegert took her hand and was pleased by the strength of her grip.

"I'm David, David Diegert."

Their mutual smiles ushered in a friendly mood.

"You like the MP5?" Fiera asked.

"Yeah, I like the way the bullet stays true as the barrel heats up." With a nod at her holster, Diegert said, "You use the Glock."

"Simple and reliable. If all my family and friends were as reliable as my 17, life would be a whole lot easier."

"What's that?" Diegert indicated the semicircular device surrounding Fiera's neck.

Removing the mechanism, Fiera folded it at its two hinges, reducing it to one third its original size. "This is my Ear Shield, it's the most convenient set of earplugs I've ever used."

Diegert nodded as he placed his much larger earmuffs on their storage hook.

"What's that around your neck?" she asked as she gazed at the rawhide emerging from Diegert's collar.

With a bit of hesitancy, Diegert pulled on the thin leather string and revealed his amulet. Fiera immediately leaned forward inspecting the leather circle divided into a dark bottom half, white top half with a foot crossing over both.

"Hmmm… how very interesting." As she took a step closer, she asked, "Can I touch it?"

Diegert nodded, and she held the warm leather circle between her thumb and forefinger. She turned it around and attempted to read the inscription. She cocked her head to the side, like a curious dog. "This is not in English, or any other language I speak."

"It's Ojibwa. It says *A man must travel through darkness to find the light.*"

"Just men, or women too?"

"Yeah, I suppose women too. It's an ancient saying, but I guess it needs updating for gender neutrality."

"Sounds like a universal human statement. So you're an Indian?"

"Native American actually, one quarter."

"You Americans, always dividing yourselves into halves, quarters, thirds," she said with disdain for the cultural habit of sharing one's mixed heritage.

"My mother is half Ojibwa. The tribe lives in what is now Minnesota and Wisconsin as well as parts of Canada. She gave me the necklace and wanted me to embrace my heritage."

"And do you?"

"What?"

"Embrace your heritage?"

"I'm wearing the necklace, aren't I?"

She gave him a sidelong glance. "What's the meaning of the foot?"

Diegert shrugged. "Travel… movement, I guess."

"It's a left foot," observed Fiera.

Diegert was surprised and immediately looked at the amulet to confirm her observation. Recognizing for the very first time that it was, in fact, a left foot, Diegert said, "I never realized that."

"Well you're right-handed aren't you?"

"Yeah."

"So you're probably right-footed too."

"What?"

"Stand straight with your feet shoulder width apart and even."

Diegert did as directed while Fiera took a couple of steps back from him.

"Ok now step forward towards me."

Diegert instinctively began to move by raising his right foot as he stepped towards her.

"See you're right footed. You took your first step with your right foot."

Diegert smirked and nodded.

"Most people are. Their dominant hand and their dominant foot are the same," instructed Fiera.

"So what does that say about my amulet?"

"Ojibwa is not your dominant spirit."

Diegert's brow furrowed in contemplation as he considered the depth of this young lady's statement. Fiera stepped closer once again taking the amulet in her hand. "This is a spiritual symbol, but the non-dominant foot symbolizes it's not your strongest spiritual force."

Diegert passed his hand between them separating her hold on the amulet as he turned and walked a few steps to look down the range. Fiera stood still, watching him gaze at the targets she began, "Have you ever tried to write with your left hand?"

Without turning to face her, Diegert responded, "Yeah, it doesn't work."

"How about shooting baskets or firing your gun, are you any good with your left?"

"Not as good." Diegert stepped towards her. He could see the tension in her as she stood her ground.

Looking up at him she said, "Imagine having to do everything with your left hand. Would you find that comfortable?"

Diegert looked down at his open palms. "No." He curled his fingers into soft fists.

"You would never give up your left hand. It's useful, necessary, and… meaningful, but it's not your dominant, go to hand."

Diegert looked her right in the eyes.

Fiera spoke softly, but directly, "Ojibwa is important and meaningful, but it is not your dominant spirit."

Diegert felt lost for a moment. Like he had just lost his way and his beliefs. He also felt Fiera's words rang true. He was beginning to embrace Ojibwa principles because he didn't have any others. His mom was exerting more and more influence over him, but was it really coming from within him? Or was it like trying to do a combination lock with your left hand? Awkward, uncomfortable and kind of stupid.

Fiera said, "I'm sorry, I didn't mean to upset you."

Looking at her, confused and a bit annoyed, Diegert said, "Look I know you weren't trying to hurt me, but this part of my life is really frustrating, and you put me into a tailspin with just one idea. What kind of a spiritual base do I have if I can be so easily toppled by the words of someone I just met?"

Holding his eyes with hers, Fiera offered, "Don't be too hard on yourself. Spiritual balance is far more labile than standing your ground. Being too rigid with your spiritual life will damn you to the constant dissonance between your beliefs and the realities you face every day. Especially with the kind of work we do."

"Well, that's exactly it. How can we have any spiritual peace when we kill people for a living, for money, so others can have more power? I can't find spiritual peace with that."

"I struggle with the same thing, but I've found there is a warrior inside of me. Not taking on the fight and not using my skills is just as dissonant as always expecting peace and harmony. You and I live in balance by being right on the knife's edge between life and death."

Diegert looked at her while the words gave voice to feelings he held, but never expressed. Life could be balanced, if by killing someone you helped someone else. This was the dilemma with which soldiers must live all the time. Diegert just had to believe that killing for Crepusculous was worthwhile. He asked Fiera, "Do you think Crepusculous is on the right side?"

She smiled as she tilted her head back while holding her gaze on his eyes. "If only it were that simple. This is the difference between you being a man and me a woman. There is no 'Right Side.' Men possess all the power in this world, and no matter what I do I will always be in service to them. There is no freedom from that fact, so whatever I do, it is overshadowed by the reality that I am a servant. My willingness, my ability, and my perspective are a blessing and a curse, which allow me to kill in service to this world. I would be a warrior no matter whose side I was on. Crepusculous found me and gave me the opportunity to be the woman I was destined to be. With all that is stacked against women in this world, I am going to embrace my role and live on that sharp edge of an assassin's blade. I gotta believe that's true for you too."

"Don't forget we are servants to the powerful." Pierre Lebeau's words came back to him. They were delivered just before he tranquilized Diegert in Panzer's penthouse of the Ambassador Hotel. They were of no comfort then, but they were clarifying now. Diegert grated against authority. He longed to be free and independent, he didn't want to take orders from anyone.

What does it mean to have no alliances, no associations, no back-up? Could he survive without Crepusculous? They would no doubt, seek to hunt him down, and kill him. Survival required remaining in service to Panzer and Crepusculous. Scylla and Charybdis.

"Yeah, I guess it's different for guys."

Fiera rolled her eyes and turned her smirk to a frown.

Diegert asked, "How long have you been a member of Cerberus?"

Fiera's eyes snapped at the mention of Avery's secret force.

Diegert said, "Avery told me Cerberus wasn't made up of just men. Shooting like you did, I figured you might be a member."

"Cerberus is a privilege and obligation, like so much of our business. Being Avery's special ones has its benefits but the cost is killing whenever called upon."

"How do you usually contact your targets?" asked Diegert while gazing at the floor.

"Sex. Or more typically the illusion that they're going to get to have sex with me."

Diegert's head raised in her direction. She met his eyes as she said, "It's the arrogance that burns me up. They always think I'm the fortunate one who's going to get to have sex with them. They're so easily swayed and so conceited."

Diegert saw her pretty face harden into creases of hate and derision.

"When they tell me how lucky I am, I have no hesitation to drive that dagger deep into their hearts." Fiera struck her hand with her fist. Diegert flinched as the smack shot across the room.

"Every mission they send me on I achieve two objectives, theirs and mine."

"You enjoy killing men."

"The arrogant, philandering misogynists, yes. And there are a lot of them."

Diegert replied, "I don't feel anything for my targets. No hate, or anger… or sympathy. I won't kill women though. Have you killed a woman?"

"I have yet to be assigned."

"Would you?"

"I don't want to. They're already subjugated. I wouldn't want to do the bidding of a man who wants someone naturally subservient to him killed."

"You've submerged yourself into the assassin's dilemma, inserting your values and judgment into the assignment. Doing that can drive you crazy and get you killed."

After a quiet pause, in which they exchanged glances Fiera said, "I imagine I will succumb to the latter." Her wistful expression gave way as she said, "Live by the sword, die by...," picking up the Glock 17 she held it up between them, "whatever weapon is in the other's hand."

Diegert turned to the shooting shelf, released the magazine from his MP5, placed it and the gun into their foam cradles before snapping the case shut. Turning to Fiera, whose mischievous smile had returned, he said, "You're all right Fiera. I'll see you down here again sometime."

Fiera rolled her eyes, watching Diegert leave, but she couldn't drop her smile.

CHAPTER 19

At 7:15 am Diegert received a text message from Klaus Panzer.

Son, please prepare yourself to accompany me on a mission of indeterminate length and undisclosed objectives. We will depart at 4:00 this afternoon. A kit with all mission-critical items will be provided for you. KP

Why does he put his initials at the end of a text message. Nobody does that. He was surprised though that Panzer had included himself in a mission. There was little for Diegert to do to prepare, packing some clothes and other essentials, he was ready to go.

Diegert's request to have a story in the media further implicating Alexi Strakov as the assassin of the president began to appear on television and YouTube. The story was gaining traction as it was re-broadcast throughout social media. The account described Strakov's background in the Russian military and his role as a private mercenary. He was depicted as a capable killer with skills, abilities and a cold heart. The grim portrait, from which his scowling face threatened the viewer, only made the impression that he was a bad man, a murdering criminal, easier to accept. Diegert was shocked by the conclusion of the story where his picture appeared on the screen. The voice-over stated that the search for him as an accomplice was ongoing. His face and name, and the face and name of Matthew

Wilcox, his alias when undercover within the presidential security detail, were presented as open investigations. Analysis of the photo, which depicted him as dead, had determined it a fake. Of course, it was a fake. Carolyn Fuller had photoshopped the image to buy them time, but they both knew its falsehood would eventually be revealed.

Diegert was confused, and he was also pissed. He had asked that the Strakov story be doctored to take the heat off him. This story only made his plight more problematic. Locked away down in LPU he was safe, or so he hoped. Outside, his picture was on everyone's mobile. He was a wanted man with a bounty on his head and heroism for anyone who apprehended him. Shit, this was not the plan!

He reached out to Carolyn. She answered his call from her apartment controlled by the CIA. Although her personal quarters were private, her access to the outside was controlled and she was afraid her communication would be monitored. The CIA was not aware of the burner phone she was using.

She began, "David, we can't talk for long."

"Ok, did you see the Strakov story?"

"Yeah, the one which ends with your picture and a web address where people can leave their tips and claim their reward."

"I know. I thought Panzer had better control over the media. He agreed he would have his people create a story furthering the blame on Strakov, but now my head is right in the noose."

"The CIA needs more than just a story in the media."

"Apparently. I plan to find incriminating documents and leak them to the CIA. Should I pass them to you?"

"Hell no. I'm stuck in a safe house. I'm in custody, held as a material witness, a prisoner. That would be seen as collusion, don't send them to me. I'm still in deep shit."

"What can I do to help?"

"Turn yourself in."

"I'm not doing that."

"Don't I know it."

"Later today I'm being sent on a mission."

"Who are you killing?"

"I don't know... I don't know if it's an assassination."

"Well, what else do you do?"

"Once, I rescued a kidnapped kid."

"Once. Every other mission you killed someone."

Diegert saw no value in continuing this line of discussion, he redirected the conversation. "At least we can talk."

"We've got to stay brief. I'll let you know if anything surfaces regarding the Strakov documents."

"Ok, hang in there," said Diegert.

"I don't like the mention of hanging, but I'm hanging up on you."

CHAPTER 20

Denise felt trapped in her gilded apartment. She was comfortable and had everything she needed, but she knew she was not free. One of the features that fascinated her was the room with three jumbo screen walls. All she had to do was select a location on Google earth, and the images on the wall would be that place. She could go anywhere without leaving her apartment. The technology was amazing, and it entertained her for a while, but she grew tired of seeing places she'd never been. Most of the time she had the walls project her favorite view of Burntside Lake in Minnesota.

Dr. Zeidler called in to hold a video conference with Denise on the TV in the apartment.

"Denise, I want to let you know we've scheduled your CT scan and ultrasound exam for tomorrow."

"Ok."

"How are you doing?"

"I'm fine. I can't go anywhere, but I don't need anything. I'd like to see David."

"I don't have that authority, but I can ask. It would probably be over video like we're doing."

"If that's the best you can do, then OK."

"Anything else?"

"Does Panzer have any other children?"

"Yes, he has two daughters. Gretchen is thirty-five. She's a forceful woman who oversees quite a bit of the business of Omnisphere. Her mother was German but died in a skiing accident when Gretchen was young."

"Oh. That's terrible. How old was Gretchen when her mother died?"

"I believe she was eight years old."

"You said he had two daughters."

"Correct. Sashi is a bit younger than David, she's twenty-two. Her mother was Taiwanese, and she's also deceased. Died in a car accident."

"My God, two dead mothers?"

Dr. Zeidler shook her head with a frown.

"I just wanted to let you know about the CT and ultrasound tomorrow. I'll stop by your apartment at 10:00 a.m., and we'll go to the facility. I'll make your request for a visit with David to Herr Panzer. Bye for now."

Denise sat quietly thinking of how cancer might change her life. She was strong, but she had seen how cancer had ravaged the life out of other people. Its slow, insidious weakening turning people into ghosts of their former selves.

The doctor submitted the request directly to Panzer. She indicated it was "medically" necessary for Denise to see David.

Panzer's reply included Dr. Zeidler, David, and Denise:

Video conference between Denise and David Diegert to commence at 2:00 p.m. today.

Two hours past noon. David and Denise looked at each other on large video screens. They realized their conversation was not private, but they were so glad to see each other that they didn't care who else was listening.

"Mom, are you OK? Are you comfortable?"

"Yes, David. I'm so glad to see you. Are you OK?"

"Yes, I am. We've got to figure out how to get you home."

"And I want you to come home with me."

The lack of a reaction to that suggestion revealed Diegert's reluctance.

"You first, Mom. Let's get you set. You do want to go back to Broward, don't you?"

"I guess so, where else would I go?"

"If you wanted to go somewhere else, where would that be?"

"I don't know, I never thought about living somewhere else."

"Well you think about it, and then we'll make a plan."

"Oh David, I love it when you make things seem possible."

"Mom I gotta tell you I was really surprised to find out Klaus Panzer is my father."

Denise expressed her embarrassment with a bowed head held in trembling hands.

Diegert said, "Mom I don't want to make you uncomfortable, but I'm kind of lost as to why you never told me. You knew all along who he was."

Keeping her head down, Denise said, "I'm so ashamed. A mother shouldn't have to share such things with her child."

"Mom, I'm not like, so innocent that I wouldn't understand."

"But you are to me. Your innocence is the only thing that's clean and pure in my life. Now I don't even have that."

Denise shook her head back and forth. Diegert watched, but he was compelled to probe further.

"Mom, didn't you think I deserved to know?"

Denise lifted her head and, through tear stained eyes, she said, "I thought I would never see that man again. I wanted my encounter with him to be erased from my life." She raised her voice as she pounded her fist on the arm of the chair. "When I discovered I was pregnant, at first I thought about ending it, for both of us. Then just you. I couldn't kill myself or you. I just had to suffer through it all."

Diegert sat in silence. When she looked at him, he nodded, quietly waiting for her to go on.

"David, it was so difficult with Tom wanting me to get an abortion and everyone in town finding out. There was a lot of pressure to end the pregnancy, and it would have been a whole lot easier, but I just couldn't. Being pregnant isn't about the mother," she said clutching her fist to her chest, "it's about the new life being created."

A deep breath preceded Diegert's contemplation of her perspective. He was lucky to be alive, and she'd weathered some difficult circumstances to make his birth possible.

Diegert began, "When my idiot brother Jake told me Tom was not my father and that you had an affair, I was crushed, but it suddenly made sense. All the shit those two threw at me. All the stuff they wouldn't let me do. I understood then why they hated me." Tears welled up in Diegert's eyes. The feeling of vulnerability shook him as he choked back a surge of emotion. "Once I knew why, it made sense. When you don't know why you're being treated so badly, you can't figure out how to make things better. Once I knew, I realized it wasn't anything I did. It was out of my control. It still sucked, but at least I knew why." Diegert squeezed his lids and wiped the tears from his cheek.

Denise said, "David I'm so sorry. I wish I could have been braver and told you the truth. I always hoped Tom would come to love you and treat you like Jake. You were such a great kid... smart, polite, athletic, what father wouldn't want a son like that?"

"Apparently we found one."

They both chuckled. The light-hearted relief brought subtle smiles to their strained faces.

"David, I don't know what's going to happen, and I don't know if I want to go back to Tom and Jake. I just know that I want you to be safe and I have trouble trusting Klaus Panzer."

"I don't trust him either. He wants to be my father now. He wants to have the son he never did, and he seems to think that the past shouldn't matter."

"What do you mean?"

"The talks I've had with him, he is always looking toward the future. Anything that happened in the past, he just looks beyond it and doesn't really care. It's kind of weird; he doesn't seem to be able to connect how you feel about something from the past with how you feel about it in the present."

"I bet he has a lot in the past he'd rather ignore," said Denise with a rumble of anger in her voice.

"If we can do something for him that'll help his future, I think he'll be fine with that," countered David. "Otherwise I don't think he will bother keeping us around."

"You think he'll let us go?"

Diegert was now speaking to Panzer, who he assumed to be listening in.

"I think the effort and expense of keeping us here will prove wasteful since we have nothing to offer."

"Oh good, I hope so because even though this apartment is nice, I'm trapped in it."

"I'm sure he's going to let you go."

"And you too, right, David?"

"He may have plans for me, but once you're free, you can go wherever you want."

"I want to go with you."

"I'll join you later, Mom, I'm glad you reminded me about what a brave woman you are. I now know that I'm alive because you were strong enough to persevere when everyone said you shouldn't."

"David, I love you so much. No matter what I went through, it was all worth it. Will we get to talk like this again?"

"I'm sure we will and hopefully next time I'll get to see you for a real hug."

"I hope so too. You be safe until then," came the instinctive maternal concern.

"Ok, I love you, Mom."

"I love you too."

The video screen went blank, leaving Diegert hoping his message to Panzer was received. He also felt guilty for needing to be reminded of how difficult it had been for his mother to keep her illegitimate pregnancy and raise her bastard son.

In his office, Panzer folded his hands, contemplating the value of Denise and David. The newfound son, who was an excellent assassin, could not be let go. The mother was of little value except to manipulate the son. It worked so well in Detroit, the erudite tyrant felt he had to hold on to her as well. No one was going back to Minnesota. Besides Panzer already had travel plans for David.

At 4:00 p.m. Diegert was escorted to the motor pool, where he met Panzer and Tiberius Duprie.

"Excellent David," said an ebullient Panzer. "You, me and Tiberius will be traveling together to complete a mission."

Doubtfully Diegert said, "I'm a bit surprised you're going on a mission."

Poorly feigning surprise Panzer replied, "It's good to keep you guessing. I don't want to be predictable."

Tiberius spoke up addressing David, "I'm surprised you're on this mission."

Catching the sense that he was the least informed, Diegert asked, "What don't I know?"

Panzer interjected, "Let's get in the vehicle, we'll brief you on the way." Extending his hand toward the Mercedes van's open sliding door, the tall, gray-haired Alpha directed the two younger men to enter the luxurious interior.

As they sped down the highway, each seated in overstuffed leather chairs, which swiveled so they could turn and face each other, Panzer began, "David, we're on our way to Africa. Our mission takes us to a compound not far from Lagos, Nigeria."

"What are we doing there and don't give me any of that Need to Know bullshit, and what about my mother? Are you going to let her go?"

Panzer's smile was faint.

"For now your mother will remain in London. You will get to see her upon our return and the two of you can decide what's best for her. Is that satisfactory?"

Diegert's steely glare never flinched. He slowly nodded as he said, "Ok, but she better be just fine when we return."

"You have my full assurance; she will be in the best of health. Now, the purpose of the mission is to fulfill an objective for Tiberius."

Both sets of eyes focused on the man sitting quietly between them. Diegert hadn't seen him since their meeting in the cafeteria, Tiberius sported a trim beard, and he had shaved his head. His ear was unbandaged and looked totally fine. There was a slight line of scar tissue about an inch below the top curve, but if you didn't know to look, the damage would go unnoticed.

Tiberius's words were calm and measured, as well as absolutely clear. "We are going so I can kill Chibueze Ozinwa," he said nothing more, letting the statement sink in.

Diegert held an inquisitive gaze, as he slowly raised his chin. Panzer glanced from man to man.

Uncharacteristically Diegert broke the silence. "I remember you telling me about him. He was cruel to your family."

Tiberius nodded his head. "That cruelty's coming back to him, and he's going to die."

215

Diegert observed the faint smile on Panzer and thought about the older man's fascination with killers, assassins, men capable of extreme violence. He wondered if Panzer considered himself a collector of deadly men. Assembling and rearranging his pieces according to the mission, or to see how different acquisitions looked or worked together. A shiver ran through Diegert as he considered that, in spite of being offspring, he was just another component of the set, who would be included or excluded according to his father's imperceptible preferences.

"Is there anything more to this mission other than revenge?" asked Diegert.

Tiberius sat stone-faced, Panzer shook his head as they pulled into the airport, parking on the tarmac. Tiberius exited the van first. Panzer delayed, allowing Tiberius to put some distance between them. Turning to David, he said, "You and I will continue this trip after we conclude our business in Lagos." The resolute German strode away, his long strides quickly relocating him to the boarding stairs of the Gulfstream G650.

Once airborne, seated again in wide leather chairs whose anchorage allowed for swiveling movement, the three men rotated to face one another. The flight attendant was Amber, the same young woman who had served Diegert during his trans-Atlantic trip last year. Her striking beauty beguiled Diegert, plus she was the first woman with whom he had cried. Seeing her again, Diegert recalled making love to her in the sleeping cabin. To look at her now, he couldn't believe it had really happened. Such a gorgeous woman, who was also kind, gentle and so very thoughtful, he felt lucky to have had such an opportunity. Embarrassment and delight bubbled up in him when she gave him a devious smile. He also felt foolish about his habit of venting all the emotional pain, guilt and anguish he held inside following a series of killings by crying uncontrollably in the arms of a loving woman. What a fucking baby he was. How pathetic that a woman who chose to sleep with him, attracted perhaps by his outward masculinity, would then be subjected to the hunk of a man turning into a blubbering baby full of guilt, pain, regret, and recrimination. She was looking for love and hopefully some good sex, and he had provided her a man in need of therapy through a torturous expulsion of tears.

The realization of this dependent process of emotional balancing had begun with Amber and was re-experienced with different women including Carolyn Fuller. It was a burden Diegert thrust upon these unsuspecting women, yet it surprised him how accepting and understanding they were. They seemed to understand it better than he did. Women he'd been with welcomed his release of emotions buried under layers of toughness. They wanted to help him find peace within his soul. Crying out your emotions was more revealing than stripping naked and having sex.

Diegert was jolted from his reverie by Amber's soft voice. "Would you like something to drink?"

Looking at her, he sought some further acknowledgment of their past, while at the same time clamping down on any expression of his feelings. "Just water, thanks."

Glancing past Amber, Diegert saw Tiberius's eyes widen as a lascivious smile crossed his lips while he ogled her ass. *No fucking way,* thought Diegert, was he going let this guy do anything to Amber.

She turned to face the man, who now wore his biggest brightest smile full of gleaming white teeth.

"What can I get you to drink?"

"First, let me say that you are the most beautiful woman I have ever seen."

"Well thank you, but it must have been very uncomfortable living under that rock all your life."

Tiberius burst into a big infectious laugh. Amber couldn't contain herself as she giggled at his reaction.

"Beautiful and also funny. You are a rare prize."

"Thank you. I am here to serve you, what would you like?"

"How much for a lap dance?"

"More than you could possibly afford, but for you, I am only serving drinks."

Laughing again Tiberius said, "Very well, we will start with a drink. Do you have rum and pineapple juice?"

"Yes."

"One third and two thirds please."

Amber nodded as she turned her attention to Klaus Panzer. With a smolderingly sensual look upon her exotic Asioeuropean, face Amber asked Panzer, "Anything other than the usual?"

"No," came the curt response, sending Amber retreating to the galley.

After letting his eyes linger on her departure, Tiberius turned to Diegert like a junior high schooler, "Did you see her ass? Doesn't she have the hottest body you've ever seen? There's a bed in the back of this plane isn't there?"

Diegert did not mince words. "Don't you even think about touching her."

The surprise on Tiberius's face drew an even more sinister warning.

"Don't you fucking touch her."

"What are you, her big brother? She is not your woman."

Locking his dark eyes on the furrowed and bewildered face of the bearded man Diegert said, "I'm only saying this one more time. Don't mess with her."

"PFFT" spat from between Tiberius's lips as his face went from bewildered to annoyed. He turned to look at Panzer who had been quietly observing the confrontation. When their eyes met, Panzer lingered for a moment before looking down at his phone's screen.

Returning with the drinks, Amber found the mood had changed. Each man quietly thanked her, but Tiberius's happy smile was gone. His jovial nature having grown sullen. Holding her tray flat against her chest, she returned forward to the service quarters of the plane.

Breaking the petulant silence, Diegert asked, "Can we discuss the mission?"

Panzer began, "Tiberius has a personal vendetta against Chibueze Ozinwa, the radical leader of a branch of Boku Haram. He is seeking revenge for the rape and murder of his sisters and mother as well as the ruination of his father who was murdered along with his brothers. Furthermore, Ozinwa has been re-selling arms, which he purchased on credit from us while ignoring several requests for payment. Such disregard for his debts cannot go unaddressed. We too have a dog in this fight so we will be assisting Tiberius in his assault on Ozinwa."

"This guy sounds like someone who has his own Army. What's the plan, since there are only two of us," said Diegert, gesturing to himself and Tiberius with a dismissive wave of his hand.

"We are three," clarified Panzer.

"You're going active?"

"It seems to have surprised you, but I am a veteran of many missions."

With a perturbed look, Diegert said, "This sounds like a very physical altercation with lots of weapons and men who are not easily going to die. Are you up for that kind of fight?"

Tiberius snickered at the question. Diegert shot him a glare.

Panzer replied, "Let me assure you I am fully prepared. My advanced age has allowed me to amass valuable experience. Healthy living and the assistance of Creation Labs has sustained my body's capabilities such that I will lead the fight."

"What has Creation Labs done to you?"

"Metabolic functional enhancement. Biosynthesized endocrine mimetics that stave off the degradation of aging, so my systems continue to operate at the rate of a man in his early thirties."

Tiberius said, "The OG is one tough dude. I've seen him sparring in the gym, I've got no reservations about going in hot with him in my crew. It's you I'm not so sure about."

Diegert re-directed, "I want to hear more about Ozinwa's compound."

"We've got aerial surveillance," said Panzer reassuringly. "As well as schematics of the interior of his buildings from people who've delivered shipments of weapons. If you lift the armrest of your chair, you can pull up a tablet, and the data is in the file marked BH Nigeria."

The armchair's cushion was hinged laterally. Lifting the cover, Diegert reached into the compartment to extract a tablet computer. Touching the file marked BH Nigeria, an aerialimage appeared of a multi-building compound surrounded by dense forest and serviced by red dirt roads. Tapping on the largest building brought a schematic of the building's interior. A large storage facility occupied the majority of the space, but along the west wall were four distinct rooms.

Panzer shared, "The first room is an office, which houses all that's necessary to keep the business of Ozinwa's Boku Haram running."

"And the next two look like they're connected," observed Diegert.

"Very good," said Panzer. "They are Ozinwa's residences, which are connected by that inner door."

"What about the last room?" asked Diegert. "It looks like it has extra thick walls."

Panzer hesitated, seemingly looking for the right words. "That room is used for interrogations. It is a room in which acts of human cruelty are committed. Boko Haram enforces compliance with its beliefs with brutal beatings and the torture of local leaders to intimidate the people they have subjugated."

"So how do we get in the compound?"

"I have already arranged for a meeting with Mr. Ozinwa to discuss re-negotiation of his debts to Strategic Solutions Inc. He does not know that it is I who is coming, nor do we believe he will recognize the bald and bearded prince. You are just another white guy who happens to be a member of our party. When the true nature of our visit becomes apparent, we will need assistance. The help will come in the form of armed aerial drones, equipped with DOTS, Dark Operation Technology System. These devices will create diversions, attack the guards and eliminate the defenses, creating distraction and confusion."

Tiberius spoke up, "I'll be the one to kill Ozinwa with all the violence he deserves. He will suffer as much as all my family members combined."

"And how do we get out?"

Panzer smiled as he swiped his fingers across his screen, transferring a file to the screens of Diegert and Tiberius. Opening the file revealed a computer-generated image of a drone quad with a rotor in each corner surrounding an open center circle.

"Gentlemen, you are looking at the PAT, Personal Aerial Transport, they're the drones I mentioned a moment ago. It's a remotely operated drone with ground and obstacle sensing capacity very similar to the technology used in self-driving cars. The controls allow remote operators to direct the drones into desired areas, while the drones themselves react to the specifics of the area avoiding obstacles and remaining aloft. They are powerful machines that can be fitted with," Panzer tapped his screen, and the screens of the other two men revealed, "munitions, high-grade video recording equipment and in the center of the device, a passenger." Diegert watched as the computer-generated image of a man positioned in the center of the drone morphed into a live action video. The image displayed a drone, loaded with equipment and a man, lift off the ground, fly a pattern in which it avoided collision with tree branches while releasing a fuselage of missiles at a junk car. The old Ford Taurus was reduced to scrap metal before the PAT successfully landed on the spot from which it had taken off, allowing the man to exit the vehicle completely unharmed.

With both sets of astonished eyes upon him, Panzer smiled. "That's how we're going to get out."

"Have you flown this thing before?" asked Diegert suspiciously.

Panzer nodded. "I have."

"In a combat situation?"

No longer nodding, Panzer said, "I have full faith that these devices will work."

"But you haven't used them under fire?"

The older man leaned forward. "You will be very happy when we need them."

"Extraction from an extremely violent encounter is always a great relief. But escaping on a flying machine upon which I have no experience sounds as dangerous as staying and fighting to the last bullet."

"The plan is set, and your flight will be assisted by experienced drone pilots, so it will definitely be better than last man standing in a failing fight."

Diegert held his gaze on Panzer as the elder statesman reclined into the cushioned leather back of his chair.

Tiberius said, "I think flying the drones will be fun."

Panzer looked out the window. "Down below, we're flying over Paris."

Diegert, seated on the opposite side of the plane, glanced out the window. Tiberius unsnapped his seatbelt and went to the window next to Panzer. With his nose practically against the glass, he said, "I love Paris. The women are the most beautiful and the city is Europe's most exciting."

As Tiberius returned to his seat, Panzer asked, "Did you fulfill a sanction in Paris?"

"Yes. I killed the whore who murdered my Uncle Gunther."

"Gunther Mibuku was quite a wily man," stated Panzer.

"He sure was. He played it fast and loose, but he did not deserve to be shot in the head by a whore." With an agitated grimace Tiberius said, "Right up to the end, she denied it, saying a man came in the room and shot him. What horseshit."

"You were close to your uncle weren't you?"

"He saved my life. Thanks to him I am the only survivor from my family. He was a hero to me."

Panzer directed his questioning across the aisle. "David, did you ever operate in Paris?"

Diegert couldn't fucking believe it. This asshole, his father, was setting up a collision between him and Tiberius. Panzer knew full well it was Diegert who shot Gunther Mibuku. Shei Leu Wong was an accomplice and a prostitute, but she did not deserve to be executed for Mibuku's death. Tiberius's revenge was misplaced but resolved. Now Panzer was tearing the skin off a scar. Diegert thought quickly before speaking. "No."

"Are you sure?"

"Perhaps you are confusing the operation in Frankfurt."

"When you arrived in Europe, did you not land in Paris?"

"I did, but the next day I flew to Athens and then to Mogadishu."

"You've been to Africa?" asked Tiberius excitedly.

"Yes, I have."

"You performed an operation there, didn't you?" questioned Panzer.

Uncomfortable with discussing his missions Diegert said, "I was taught that talking about missions after the fact with people who were uninvolved is a bad habit that can get you killed."

Chuckling, Panzer replied, "That may be true elsewhere, but up here just the three of us at 35,000 feet. I think your secrets are safe."

Defiantly Diegert replied, "Well I think not. How about we have an after action discussion when we've all been drone flown out of the cluster fuck you're taking us into?"

Tiberius tried to deflect the tension. "How did you like the Great Continent?"

Diegert shifted his gaze to the bearded man, "The small part of the continent where I was is poor, dirty, broken and violent. Of course, when you're inserted to kill someone, tourism is not part of the plan. The bad guy I was assigned to take out deserved his death. But I'll tell ya, getting out of Mogadishu was way worse than getting in. I have no plans for a return visit."

"Africa is the most beautiful place on earth," said a dreamy-eyed Tiberius.

"I'm sure parts of it are," said Diegert sarcastically.

"Africa is the birthplace of the human species," said Panzer thoughtfully. "We can all trace our ancestry to the magic of the dark continent, the cradle of life."

"And to that cradle, we bring the certainty of death," said Diegert scanning the eyes of his two companions. Panzer held Diegert's gaze just long enough so that the younger man saw him press a button on the armrest of his chair. A soft buzz emitted from the forward service area. Amber left the front of the plane, passed through the cabin, and entered the aft bedroom. Panzer rose from his seat. "If you gentleman will excuse me," before he too entered the bedroom locking the door behind him.

Diegert's skin turned red as his jaw muscles nearly cracked his teeth.

Tiberius leaned over. "Looks like your Old Man's got your woman." He pulled back quickly, throwing his arms up in defense as Diegert lunged at him, casting a lethal glare.

Back in his seat, Diegert's anger boiled for having been usurped by power again. He and Amber were not in any kind of a relationship, but it was the arrogance with which Panzer flaunted his position of superiority that pissed him off. Could he have pressed a button to get her to service him? Would he have done that to her, if he could? She was special to him, but he realized now the feeling was his alone.

After about fifteen tense minutes, "Aah, Aah, Aah!" came the rhythmic grunts from the bedroom. Tiberius giggled while Diegert wanted to jump out of the plane. The auditory sex went on for much longer than Diegert imagined it would. There were no sounds from her, just the forceful grunts of the Old Man.

CHAPTER 21

The deep voice of Captain Edward James reverberated through the speakers as he disturbed his slumbering passengers with the announcement that they would soon be landing at Murtala Muhammed International Airport in Lagos Nigeria.

Panzer and Amber exited the bedroom to return to their seats. Panzer made a point of tucking in his shirt as he passed the seat of his son. Buckling up his pants, he strapped into his seat for the landing.

The wheels of the G650 were engineered to already be rolling before touching down, which made for a very smooth and gentle landing. Captain James taxied the powerful luxury jet to the Ikeja Air Service terminal. Private jet customers entered the country with a minimum of inspection. The man who owned and operated the jet service was also a certified customs inspector. He made certain his customers were never delayed or inconvenienced with intrusive inspections or insistent questions. In fact, they were regularly welcomed with broad smiles and the utmost hospitable cooperation. After using the bathroom, the three passengers found that their baggage had already been unloaded and transferred to a dark red Toyota Sienna minivan. Standing next to the driver's door, a tall thin young man with an eager smile stood ready to assist his new guests. Pressing the button to automatically open the sliding door brought a beam of pride to his already happy face. Shaking the hands of each of his esteemed passengers as they entered and took a seat, he introduced himself as Felix. They began the thirty-mile drive west along the Lagos-Badagry Expressway. The divided lane road was paved, but that was where comparisons to American and European expressways stopped. L-B, as it was referred to, bore no paint stripes, guardrails or controlled entrances and exits. People's homes were mere yards from the edge of the road, which was shared with pedestrians, donkey carts and bicycles. The center median was flat dirt, which could be crossed at any point.

Police were on patrol, which the group witnessed when a thirty-minute traffic delay held them sitting still due to an accident between a truck and a passenger bus. The crash blocked both lanes of traffic as the drivers argued and the police struggled to reach the scene.

Looking out the window at the homes along the highway, Diegert felt like these people lived within the same economic conditions in which he was raised. The houses were sturdy but dirty and in need of paint. Old cars, in various states of disrepair, occupied many of the front and side yards. Kids played amongst cast off debris and odd collections of junk. Further back from the expressway Diegert glimpsed homes, which seemed much more refined and well kept. For sure, the better off people lived farther from the edge of the expressway. Diegert realized if he grew up outside Lagos, he would have been a roadside resident.

When the lanes were finally cleared, the traffic flow returned, and Felix was not shy about using speed to make up for lost time.

The ebullient and informative Felix told them Ozinwa's compound was five miles south of Ado Odo and about a half mile east of the Yewa River. After the traffic delay, it took sixty minutes to reach the one-mile dirt road, which led to the facility. As they turned, Panzer pulled out a satellite phone and sent a text message. Diegert's curiosity was easy to see. Panzer said, "As the crow flies it'll only take forty-five minutes. Time for them to fly."

Entering the compound, the van traversed the single red dirt road, which they had seen on the map. Total drive time, including the delay, two hours and forty-five minutes.

Felix leapt from the driver's seat having activated both automatic doors as he exited. Panzer was first out, and he strode straight over to the largest building. A group of four young women approached the van. Carrying baskets of fruit and bottled water, they cautiously came forward. As they neared, Diegert sensed their apprehension. They seemed frightened, hesitant and fatigued. They did not speak or smile. In spite of her dark skin, the tallest of the group bore the bruising from a black eye. Diegert was hungry, but he couldn't ignore the condition of these women and the suspicion they were not being treated well. Pressing Felix he asked, "What's with these women? They don't seem very happy."

Felix's normal high wattage smile dimmed. Reluctant to comment, he withered under Diegert's insistent glare. Looking left then right he whispered, "Under Ozinwa, the women suffer."

The large building, which Panzer was approaching, looked like an airplane hangar with a wide overhead door across the front and a normal entrance door to the right. With twenty yards to go, the overhead door began to retract. The wide metal panels bent at their hinges as they rose from the ground. Like a mechanical curtain on a workshop stage, the door revealed Chibueze Ozinwa, dressed in black boots, olive green khaki pants and a short waisted military jacket festooned with medals, ribbons and gold braided sashes encircling his shoulders, which were topped by embroidered epaulets. Panzer could see it was all fake. The mix of military insignia and awards made no sense and signified no actual accomplishments. Ozinwa's long hair, braided into locks, fell beyond his shoulders while a maroon beret sat atop his head. Upon his hip, a 357 Magnum occupied his holster. In spite of the warrants for his arrest, this self-proclaimed man of military might had no hesitation about appearing before his guests.

As outrageous as Ozinwa's appearance was, Panzer couldn't help but feel satisfied to see the absolute look of fearful astonishment spread over his face when he realized the man he would be negotiating with was the owner of the company he had been shorting.

"Chibueze Ozinwa," said Panzer as the two men shook hands. Panzer's four-inch height advantage and jackhammer handshake did nothing to relax Ozinwa's nerves.

Extricating himself from the third-row seat of the Sienna, Tiberius stepped out of the van. Rising to his full height he was astounded by the young woman who dropped her basket of mangoes and trembled before him. It looked to Diegert like she was going to faint, but instead she took three awkward steps forward and fell into the arms of Tiberius.

"Nikea," he said.

Hands still held firmly, Panzer walked Ozinwa past his two AK armed guards into the recesses of the hangar. "I appreciate that you recognize who I am, and I hope you realize that this process of negotiation, will not be what you might expect."

"Please, I am honored that you are here, Mr. Panzer."

"Not for long you won't be. I can understand that you may want to resell arms that you purchase from me. It's a free market and the merchandise is yours to do with what you want, once you pay me."

"I… ah…um."

Losing patience with the stammering, Panzer blared, "Not paying me and underselling to my other customers, that's very bad for business. And in the business of death, a transgression like that can be fatal."

Ozinwa's apprehension forced a smile on his lips as an awkward laugh relieved a bit of his tension.

Panzer's lips curled slightly, but it wasn't a smile.

Diegert looked at Tiberius, whose eyes were as wide as old DVDs. "She's my sister," he said.

When the other women heard this, great wales of happiness erupted from the previously constrained young women. They jumped up and down, stamping their feet, dancing to a drumbeat of freedom. Their joy burst forth in a cacophony of ululations as they all rejoiced that they might now be freed.

Nikea looked up at her brother through her tears with a hopeful expression she had not felt for some time. "Tiberius, I am so happy to see you. So many terrible things have happened and so much death has surrounded me." Intensifying her gaze and clutching at his thick arms, she implored him, "You are going to get me out, aren't you?"

Tiberius, still reeling from holding someone he had mourned as lost forever, nodded his head. "Yes, I'll get you out of here. Is Althea here?"

At the sound of her sister's name, the tears, which had built up in Nikea's eyes, flooded her face. She shook her head and pressed her head against her brother's chest, taking refuge in his arms. The songs of the other women, elevating their celebration of emancipation, alerted the whole compound that something was going on.

The singing and rejoicing of the women penetrated the hangar, turning the heads of both Panzer and Ozinwa. The self-styled military man stepped away from the tyrant as he headed out the wide doorway, seeing all the activity at the van. Panzer, looking forward, could see Tiberius holding a tearful woman in his arms. Using his satellite phone, he texted Diegert. *"Get the gray duffel out of the back of the van."*

The tallest of the women, the one with the black eye, ran over to Felix. "Come on, brother, we need to make our escape." Indecision and confusion played across the face of the happy van driver. To Diegert it seemed like a facade was falling apart, and Felix was being forced to do something he should've done some time ago.

Diegert's phone buzzed in his pocket. As he pulled it out, he saw a man approaching wearing an overdressed military uniform. Panzer was close behind, followed by four men armed with AK-105s. On his screen he read, *Get the gray duffel out of the back of the van.* Hustling to the rear of the Sienna, Diegert opened the liftgate.

Quickly surmising that the man with the supercilious military costume was Chibueze Ozinwa, Diegert dropped the duffel on the opposite side of the van.

"What the hell's going on?" shouted Ozinwa.

The women stopped singing and stood defiantly, facing their tormentor.

"You don't look me in the eye," bellowed the overbearing military costumed clown.

Diegert stepped behind the van, unzipping the duffel. He was immediately joined by Panzer.

"Who the hell are you," asked Ozinwa as he stepped over to Tiberius, whose sister crept behind him.

Positioning her safely, Tiberius answered, "I am the Evil Prince you were unable to kill."

Panzer said to Diegert, "The drones will be here in five minutes." Unzipping the bag, Panzer extracted an MP 9 Vector submachine gun. Grabbing a belt of extra magazines, Panzer threw the loop over his head, securing the belt to his shoulder. Setting a thirty-round magazine in the pistol grip, Panzer racked the slide, chambering the first round and opened fired on the guys with the AK's. Diegert scrambled to keep up, readying his weapon as he had just watched his father. Rising from behind the van, Diegert saw the women scattering, Tiberius walking backward, pushing his sister behind him. Ozinwa, caught in the midground, held a ready stance with his head on a swivel. Panzer kept firing until all four guards lay on the ground, their lives bleeding out through fatal holes. Diegert realized he was too late to shoot anyone.

Pointing his weapon at Ozinwa, Panzer said with annoyance, "Hands up."

As Ozinwa moved to draw his Magnum, Panzer sprayed the ground with half a clip. The general's hands slowly rose. Panzer removed the big gun from the holster, stepping back with his Vector trained on Ozinwa.

Placing Nikea on the far side of the van, Tiberius ran straight at Ozinwa, striking the man's exposed ribs like a linebacker, knocking the medals off the man who killed his family.

Red dust coated Ozinwa's face as he lifted his ringing head to see Tiberius towering above him. Flecks of spit clinging to his beard, Tiberius snatched the front of the general's coat and hauled him off his back.

Nikea bolted from the van, streaking across the compound in the direction of the large hangar.

As he was pulled up, Ozinwa kicked Tiberius in the hip, forcing the bald man forward at the waist. He then hammer fisted the back of Tiberius's head, sending the big man tumbling to the ground. Kicking dry red dirt into Tiberius's face, Ozinwa shouted, "You fuckers are going to die."

Coughing and spitting dirt, Tiberius tried to stand, but Ozinwa delivered a roundhouse kick to the sternum, driving the bigger man to his back. The general's medals shook as he stomped his boot on Tiberius's abdomen. The compression forced the air from his lungs which Diegert saw as red dust erupting like a volcano from Tiberius's beard. Rolling to his side, struggling to breathe and desperately trying to regain his footing, Tiberius saw his sister approaching Ozinwa from behind.

In her hand, Nikea held a large, dark machete. Without breaking stride, she swung the weapon high above her head and drove it down onto the epaulet of Ozinwa's shoulder. The edge of the blade tore through the fabric into the underlying skin, muscle, and bone. A geyser of blood shot from the wound, showering Nikea with crimson rain as she retracted the weapon.

Arterial blood pulsed from the shoulder as Ozinwa turned to face his attacker. The machete had cleaved the clavicle, severing the skeletal attachment of his right arm, rendering the appendage useless. Dazed into staggering silence, Ozinwa's life was spraying out second by second.

"NO, NO, No," shouted Nikea. "You're not going to die that easily."

Nikea looked into the eyes of evil, framed in a face covered in his own blood. "You are not leaving this world until you have suffered what you did to all of us."

Unbuckling his pants, she pulled them and his underwear down, exposing his genitals. With uncaged fury, Nikea proclaimed, "You destroyed our pleasure, robbing us of a lifetime of joy, leaving us in eternal pain. Now I chop off your dick as I watch you die."

Slashing the blade at the base of his penis, the machete cut through the flesh, severing both the shaft and the balls from his body. Blood gushed from the wound. Ozinwa's cries rose in pitch as he collapsed to the ground where he lay screaming in the dirt. With his face lying in the bloody mud, Ozinwa's cruelty had returned to him.

Tiberius wiped the dust from his face as he got up to embrace his exhausted sister.

The sound of engines could be heard coming up a rutted path west of the big hangar. Panzer got on his satellite phone. "Land the drones to the east of the biggest building on the map." He then ushered Tiberius, who brought Nikea with him, to the clearing on the eastern side of the hangar. Three drones hovered above the clearing. Panzer motioned to the drones, knowing the video feed was going directly to the pilots in his Innsbruck, Austria mansion. The first drone lowered to within twelve inches of the ground. Panzer stepped into the center circle as the drone rose to knee height. In front of him, he extracted a strong strip of nylon webbing from a compartment in the drone's frame. Passing the webbing between his legs, he clicked the buckle into a receptacle on the opposite side of the frame. He repeated this action with a second strip of webbing perpendicular to the first. The crossed webbing created a seat upon which Panzer could sit as the drone rose. He pulled additional web strapping crisscross over his shoulders, securely fastening him for flight.

Diegert ran into the clearing to see Panzer eight feet off the ground. Tiberius had the second drone low and was helping Nikea step in. He set the web seating as Panzer had done, securing Nikea with the shoulder straps. The drone elevated as the young lady's astonished face showed fear and joy.

"You take the next one," said Tiberius.

"No way," said Diegert. "You've gotta help your sister. Hurry up." He waved his hands.

Panzer was now above the forest canopy, once he cleared the trees, Diegert saw his father's drone take off to the east. Nikea hovered at eight feet as Tiberius strapped himself in. Both drones rose rapidly, banking to the east when they reached safe height.

Diegert turned back toward Felix and the other women. Passing the edge of the hangar, he heard the engines of approaching trucks grow louder. Sprinting across the open space where Ozinwa's mutilated body lay in the dirt, he motioned to Felix and the three remaining women to meet him on the opposite side of the van. From the duffel, he handed Felix an MP 9.

"Have you ever fired one of these?"

Felix looked anything but comfortable as he shook his head.

"Well, it's survival time." Diegert racked the first round. "Just point at the enemy and don't shoot us."

The three women huddled by the front end of the van trying to take up as little space as possible.

Into the clearing in front of the hangar pulled two pickup trucks. The green Chevy had a 50-caliber machine gun mounted on the bed. The yellow Ford had a roll bar in the bed that ran across the back of the cab. Each truck had two men in the cab and two more in the bed. The trucks stopped, and the driver from the green one stepped out, moving forward to inspect Ozinwa's body. Realizing who it was, he shouted for one of the men in the back of the green truck to come forward. He shouted again, motioning for the yellow Ford to pull up next to Ozinwa's body. The grisly wounds on the remains of Chibueze Ozinwa held the attention of all the men.

Diegert put his fingers across his lips to silence Felix and the women. Diegert signaled that, at the count of three, Felix should open the door, get all the women aboard and make a run for it. Moving to the rear edge of the van, Diegert peered around to see the men lifting a tarp with Ozinwa's body into the yellow truck. Diegert held up his fist and extended his first, second and third finger. Felix pressed the button on the fob to open the passenger door and the three women climbed in, staying low on the floor. Felix took the driver's seat, started the van and threw it into reverse. Diegert walked next to the van with his MP 9 up and ready. When the van stopped to shift, Diegert opened up, sending bullets into the bodies of the surprised men. Both men in the bed of the yellow truck, as well as the driver, fell dead where they were. One of the passengers in the green truck took a bullet to the shoulder which hit a major artery, sending blood pulsing into the air like a Las Vegas fountain.

Diegert stepped on the bumper of the van as it accelerated. He reached high on to the roof of the van clutching the crossbar of the roof rack. Shots rang out, hitting the back of the van. Diegert took a bullet through the calf of his lower leg. Gutting the pain, he pulled with all he had to lift himself onto the roof of the van. With a vice grip on the roof rack, Diegert slid around facing backwards. Two men jumped into the green truck to chase the van. From a prone position, Diegert aimed his weapon to fire at the Chevy in controlled three round bursts. The truck was gaining on them, but Diegert's fire kept the 50 cal from being brought into the fight.

Felix drove the six-cylinder Toyota as fast as he dared on the uneven dirt road. His navigation of the potholes made a rough ride for Diegert on the roof, who struggled to hold on while also replacing his spent magazine. Diegert's pause to reload allowed the man operating the mounted 50 caliber gun to get into position. He racked the feed, steadying the pivoting gun before firing multiple heavy rounds at the fleeing minivan. Diegert had to keep his face down as the pressure waves of the massive bullets passed over his head. The heavy suspension and V8 engine allowed the Chevy truck to gain on the van. Looking up, as he struggled to reload, Diegert saw the big gun being aimed at him. The 50 cal fired, but the bullet went low. The Sienna's rear window shattered into shiny diamonds as the big bullet burst through the safety glass, continued over the heads of the women, penetrated the center of the dashboard to lodge in the engine destroying several piston rods. Smoke blew back into the cabin and out from under the hood. Diegert coughed as the cloud of acrid smoke enveloped the van. The disabled vehicle slowed, before suddenly lurching to a stop.

With a fresh magazine in place, Diegert pointed his weapon at the truck. Squeezing the trigger he hoped for the best. Watching, as 9 mm bullets left his barrel, Diegert was shocked when the green Chevy pickup exploded into a ball of flame. He looked at his submachine gun, incredulous at the power in his hand.

Klaus Panzer had doubled back to see what was happening. From his position in the air Panzer could see the truck pursuing the van with his son laid out on the roof. The drone was equipped with missiles. Panzer used a reticle equipped pair of glasses to target the truck and lock it into the missile's control panel. Upon release, remote pilots in Austria controlling the flight fins directed the missiles to the designated target, delivering the intended destruction.

The truck's fuel tank exploded sending the rear of the truck skyward, forcing the grill of the vehicle into the dusty red road. The driver and passenger were dismembered as the truck became a twisted piece of flaming scrap.

Panzer climbed to a safe position above the treetops.

Seeing the fireball behind him, Felix exited the van. Sliding off the roof hurt like hell when Diegert's injured leg had to bear weight. Limping, he led Felix, who clung to his MP 9, and the three women into the forest off the side of the road. From his view in the sky, Panzer could see the yellow truck coming up the road. He texted Diegert, *Yellow pick up one KM back, 2 men coming up fast.*

Hobbling as fast he could to the smoking van, Diegert grabbed the gray duffel. Making it back to his group in the woods, he saw the yellow truck approach. With the road blocked by the burning and smoking vehicles. The yellow stopped, the driver remained in the cab as he told his passenger to get out and investigate.

Signaling with this hands, while imploring everyone to remain silent, Diegert instructed Felix to shoot the passenger when he moved forward toward the damaged truck and van. He indicated that with a knife and a pistol from the duffel he would attack the driver to acquire the yellow truck. He handed two of the women the remaining MP 9's, making it clear they should use them only in an emergency.

Diegert took Felix's phone and set the timer for two minutes. He set his own phone for the same period. He informed Felix to shoot when the two minutes were up. He started both timers before sending the tall, thin man forward. Felix's nervous smile and inexperience left Diegert doubting the plan, but his two minutes were counting down. Creeping through the forest to flank the pickup was a painful process. Diegert made a wide circle, crossing the road out of sight of the truck. Once on the other side of the road, he moved quietly, coming up low to the passenger door of the pickup. He drew his knife and checked his phone: 1:50. Drawing slow deep breaths, he readied himself, 2:00.

No shots. *Shit.* Diegert texted Felix: *Shoot damn it!*

Felix was freaking out, *he couldn't kill someone.* When his timer hit 2:00 minutes he started hyperventilating and remained behind the trunk of a very big tree. Receiving Diegert's text he realized he might face an even more dangerous enemy if he didn't shoot the passenger.

Diegert stared at his screen, realizing it would do no good, but frustrated at not being able to influence the situation. A moment later the staccato blasts of the MP 9 ripped through the eerie silence of the forest. Diegert flung open the truck's passenger door with his Gough knife ready. He launched himself across the cab, driving the blade point into the side of the driver's neck. The blade dug deep, passing through muscle and the esophagus. Diegert thrust the sharp edge forward, severing the trachea and carotid arteries.

Felix had never fired a gun before. He had seen it done in movies and figured he'd just go John Wick on this bad guy. Pointing the weapon, with his arm fully extended, he closed his eyes and pulled the trigger. The MP 9, set on full auto, began emptying its magazine as Felix's arm rocked around in an out of control circle. He had all he could do to keep the gun in front of him. The bullets flew, startling, but not hitting the target. The surprised passenger ran back towards the yellow Ford pickup.

Diegert wiped the blade on the man's pant leg as he backed out. He saw the other man returning as he set one foot outside the cab. The passenger, having drawn his gun as he ran back, stopped, raised his barrel and fired at Diegert, who ducked down using the door panel as a shield. Diegert dropped his knife to pull out the Glock 17. He stuck the gun under the truck door and fired. The shots hit the passenger in the boot and the shin. The injured man howled as the bullets tore through his leg and foot, felling him to the ground. Diegert jumped up into the cab, pulled the door shut, leaned out the window, and shot the man as he writhed on the dirt road.

Diegert texted Felix: *All clear, bring the women to the truck.*

Exiting the vehicle, Diegert stepped over to disarm the dead man. Shoving the acquired Berretta in his waistband, Diegert also slipped the guy's phone from a cargo pocket on his pants. The guy had a full beard and wildly unkempt hair, but it was his BH tattoo on the back of his neck that identified him as having completed his training with Boko Haram.

Limping to the opposite side of the truck, Diegert opened the driver's door as Felix and the women arrived. The driver's body fell sideways, Diegert caught the falling body, slowing the descent while the nearly severed head dangled by the vertebrae, and blood spurted from the gaping wound. Dragging the corpse a couple of meters into the forest left Diegert covered in glistening blood.

The yellow Ford's extended cab allowed all three of the women to climb into the back seat. The tallest one, with the black eye, handed Diegert an oily towel from the floor of the cab. Wiping as much blood as he could from the driver's seat and steering wheel, Diegert then rubbed his hands, arms, and clothing. The towel was pretty saturated and did more to smear the blood than remove it. With no other option, Diegert tied the towel as tight as he could around his injured calf muscle. Nodding to Felix, he directed him to drive. Four wheeling around the smoldering Chevy and the smoking Sienna, Felix got the truck back on the dirt road and they all rode in silence even after reaching the LB expressway. Diegert couldn't help but wonder what lay ahead for this strange band of travelers.

CHAPTER 22

The smooth roll over pavement was much more comfortable than the dirt road. Two of the women fell asleep as Felix kept the truck at 60 miles per hour. Lost in thought as the ribbon of asphalt stretched across the Nigerian coast, Diegert had to re-consider his perception of Klaus Panzer. He was so surprised by the decisive action displayed by his newfound father. The old man was extremely aggressive. He instigated and dominated the battle. He was ruthless with his weapons. Why he should find that surprising was perplexing, but having always seen the distinguished German as a power suit executive, left Diegert little room to perceive the guy as an effective combatant. From now on Panzer's skills and abilities to personally deliver violence would never be overlooked. He also had to acknowledge that all five passengers in this truck would have been toast had the 50 cal not been taken out by Panzer's return in the drone.

Snapping his head to the left, Diegert caught the gaze of the tall girl with the black eye. When their eyes locked she did not alter her peering stare. Diegert maintained the contact while asking, "English?"

She nodded.

"How long have you known Tiberius and his sister?"

"All my life."

249

"What's the sister's name again?"

"Nikea." She used her index finger to make a little swoosh in the air.

"What's with the finger?" asked Diegert while mimicking the movement.

The girl reached down, removed her sandal and held it in front of Diegert pointing to the Nike swoosh emblem on the band.

"She's named after a shoe company?"

"They make a lot more than just shoes," she replied, replacing the sandal on her foot.

Smiling, Diegert asked, "What's your name? And don't tell me it's Addidasa."

The girl flinched and then smiled. "I am Kashani," she said with pride. "My name has a long family history and needs no corporate sponsor. Felix is my brother." She let her smile linger before adding, "What is your name Mr. white man and why are you here?"

Diegert looked into the bold eyes of this young woman, struggling to imagine anyone hitting her or keeping her captive. She projected confidence and her spirit seemed strong.

"I'm David and I'm here because my father brought me. I really don't have an explanation or any idea about Boko Haram."

Kashani's smile dissipated. "Boko Haram is a bastardization of Islam. They are criminals masquerading as disciples of Allah. They shit on the Quran with their twisted interpretation of its rules."

The anger simmering in the young woman was now at full boil.

"The man that Nikea killed, kidnapped us, holding us for three years. Chibueze Ozinwa mutilated our genitals and he and his men raped us for pleasure. Nowhere in the Quran are men given permission to treat women with such brutality and degradation. His death was justified and now his mutilated body," Kashani used her thumb to point behind her, "lays in the back of the truck."

Diegert's mouth fell open. "It sounds like you endured real torture."

"The only thing that helped me survive was the strength of my sisters." Kashani put her arms around the two women sitting on either side of her, pulling them close. They both woke up, gradually re-engaging themselves.

Felix announced, "Up ahead there's a police checkpoint."

Conversation halted as all eyes focused on the cones in the road and the gray uniformed officers directing motorists to pull over into the inspection lane or waving them through to continue.

"What's going on?" asked Diegert.

Shrugging Felix replied, "They do this if they're looking for someone, but you can also see it is the nicer cars being delayed." Felix turned his gaze on Diegert, "They're collecting bribes."

"Shit, how much?"

"Two thousand to five thousand nairas."

"I've got a hundred US dollars."

"No, no don't let them know you have dollars. They will arrest you."

"What for?"

"To ransom you."

Diegert's African naïveté was greeted by the ever-present smile of Felix. A thought occurred to Diegert, which if it worked, could solve two problems. Speaking to his fellow occupants he said, "Follow my lead and go along with what I say."

Kashani said, "That's all you're going to tell us?"

With the truck slowing to a crawl in the traffic, Diegert stepped out, "I don't have time to explain." Closing the door, he looked back in. "But I know you're smart."

Vaulting into the bed of the pickup, Diegert unwrapped Ozinwa's bloodstained head. Rearranging the tarp so it looked like a proper set of bed sheets, Diegert made certain only the head was visible.

As Felix approached the first officer, Diegert shouted out, "Injured man, let us through."

The officer kept his hand raised as he stepped to the edge of the truck bed. His suspicious eyes studied Diegert's face.

"He was injured at a construction site near Ado Odo." Diegert stroked the forehead of the corpse, feigning concern and empathy. "We need to get him to a hospital."

"Are you going to Lagos?"

"Yeah."

"That's still a long way. I'm a medic, let me see his wounds."

Diegert said, "He was treated by a specialist before we left, please let us continue."

"I am a police officer and also a medic." Turning to one of his men, he barked, "Go get the medical kit from the truck." He faced Diegert. "Before this truck will pass I am required to inspect the treatment of this man's wounds." Stepping to the back of the truck he dropped the tailgate. Diegert had the Berretta in his waistband, but he knew if he drew the weapon, he and his companions would die.

Lifting the tarp, the officer was aghast to see the man's pants bunched up at his ankles and his genitals, covered in bloody red mud, separated from the body lying between the knees. With the officer's astonished eyes upon him, Diegert raised his hands. "I hijacked this truck and made these people drive me." Surrounding the truck, the other policemen trained their weapons on Diegert. "I have a gun, I will disarm." Diegert used one hand to remove the Berretta, dropping it on the bed of the truck. The officer's Glock was pointed at Diegert. With his hands returned to a raised position, the white American said, "Arrest me, but these people only did what I forced them to."

The officer ordered, "Get out of the truck, lie face down on the ground."

Stepping from the truck's bed he was hit from behind with a rifle. His face hit the dirt hard before he got both feet on the ground. Sucking air, he choked, spitting blood and dust while his arms were cuffed behind him. A boot on his back compressed his chest. Diegert struggled to breathe.

"Good God they cut his balls off," said the officer.

Three men dragged Diegert to a Nigerian Police pickup truck and threw him in. Peering out under the truck's canvas canopy, Diegert saw the police inspecting Ozinwa's body.

Felix leaned out the truck's window with his effervescent smile masking his fear. To the closest policemen, he said, "Do you know who the dead man is?"

The policemen looked at him sternly as he shook his head.

"That is Chibueze Ozinwa."

The surprise on the policeman's face made the smile on Felix's grow even bigger.

"There is a bounty for him dead or alive," he told the policeman.

Returning his attention to the rear of the truck, the policeman stepped over to the officer and spoke in his ear. The officer's startled reaction and raised eyebrows triggered the policeman to locate a photo on his phone and show it to the officer. They stepped closer to the corpse and, upon inspection, the officer ordered the truck that held Diegert to pull up next to the yellow Ford.

"Get the prisoner out and move this body into our truck," barked the officer.

Pulled from the truck and thrown to the ground, Diegert once again tasted the red dirt of Africa. The tarp with Ozinwa's body was moved into the NP truck.

From the ground, Diegert overheard the officer instructing his men, "At the station, keep the body wrapped up. I will file a report and claim the bounty. We'll all share in this prize." The policemen excitedly prepared to depart.

"Don't forget to retrieve your handcuffs."

"Do you want to let him go?"

"He is of no value to us."

Diegert anticipated a bullet in the head, but sighed with relief when he felt the cuffs removed from his wrists.

He remained on the ground until the NP trucks drove away. Sitting up he saw traffic resuming movement on the highway. He wobbled as he stood, the pain in his leg searing through his nerves. Felix, with his beaming smile, helped him to balance while Kashani, looking quite mischievous, held up the officer's medical kit.

Spitting sand as he took painful steps Diegert groaned, "Let's get to the Lagos Airport."

CHAPTER 23

Kashani's medical skills were put right to work as she administered a local anesthetic and began suturing Diegert's leg wound. "I was studying to be a doctor when I was kidnapped," she said. "Now I've gone three years with only experience educating me."

"You have good skills," said Diegert with a hand gesture toward his leg. "Will you go back to school now?"

"We'll see."

"We could've paid for school with the bounty from Ozinwa," said Felix as he glanced into the rearview mirror.

"You knew there was a bounty on that guy?" asked Diegert.

"Yes, of course, everybody knows, but I did not know he was in the back of the truck."

Diegert snorted.

Kashani tugged extra hard on his suture.

"Ouch!"

"It was Felix who told the police that the dead man was Ozinwa. He saved your life," scolded Kashani.

Diegert's expression turned sheepish.

Felix exclaimed, "It would have been nice to get rich off that bad man, but the greed of the police gave us the true prize of freedom."

Diegert reacted under the admonishing glare of Kashani. "Thank you, Felix." His words were not enough for her. She narrowed her eyes and threatened to tug on another suture. Diegert responded, "Your quick thinking was very impressive and saved all of us." Kashani began to smile but did not take her gaze off the less than gracious white man. "I will always be grateful for what you did." Kashani's face blossomed into a beautiful smile that impressed Diegert with its radiance.

Klaus Panzer waited at the Ikeja Air Service Terminal with Tiberius and Nikea. Earlier, when they had returned with the drones, the devices were loaded onto the cargo plane upon which they arrived. The Crepusculous-owned plane immediately took flight, getting the drones out of the country and away from scrutiny. A lack of evidence reduced the effectiveness of any accusations, but of course accusations came. The man was of normal height and stature with a gradually receding hairline and spectacles with circular lens. Dressed in the gray uniform of the Nigerian Police, he conducted himself in a thoughtful, understated manner. "I'm Colonel Nathan Izwali, I am an Investigative Officer with the Nigerian Police," said the man extending his hand as he introduced himself.

Panzer clasped the hand of the shorter man, power pumping it. "I'm Klaus Panzer, pleased to meet you."

"Yes indeed," replied the soft-spoken officer as he reset is shoulders and his glasses. "I am seeking information about sightings of aerial drones with people flying within them. Do you have any information to share?"

A hardy laugh erupted from Panzer before he said, "My good man you seem to be playing a joke on me. Certainly, there is no such thing as drones that can fly with people. Do you have any evidence?"

"We have reports from several reliable sources."

"But no pictures or video?"

"Not that have come forward."

"Well, I'm sorry but I have nothing to add to the speculation that has fostered your imagination... I mean investigation. I would wish you all the best in your search, but I am not a man who wishes fools well on fruitless endeavors."

Letting the sting of the brush off subside, Officer Izwali asked, "May I inquire as to the nature of your visit here to Lagos?"

"You may inquire, but as you know, I am not required to comply, nevertheless I am here to reunite my colleague," Panzer gestured to Tiberius standing beside Nikea, "with his sister."

The officer gazed at the two young people. Tiberius gently put his arm around Nikea's shoulder.

"When are you due to depart?"

The question made Panzer realize he did not want this officer around when Diegert arrived. The presence of another traveler with another group, who would arrive in who knows what kind of condition, all spelled trouble for their departure.

Extracting his phone, feigning a schedule check, Panzer texted Diegert. *"ETA for Airport?"*

"Tomorrow morning," responded Panzer.

Nodding slowly, the officer replied, "If I want to reach you for more questions, how can I contact you?"

From his pocket Panzer produced a business card. "The globe is fully integrated, you contact me wherever I am, from wherever you are." Handing the card over Panzer sought conclusion. "Have a nice day, Officer Izwali." He shook the man's hand as vigorously as before.

Having his upper body again rattled by Panzer's powerful arm, the bookish investigator regretted accepting the man's hand for a second time. Nevertheless, he smiled as he said, "You enjoy your day as well."

The quiet, curious man walked back to the terminal, taking a seat in a waiting room chair.

Diegert's text reply came back, *"ETA 20 minutes."*

"Good" replied Panzer, *"Be prepared for immediate departure."*

"Guess I'm flying out as soon as we get to the airport," said Diegert looking up from his phone.

Felix looked into the rearview mirror. Kashani, having completed his stitches, finished dressing the wound with clean gauze bandages.

"Thank you so much," said Diegert. "Felix saved my life, now you've saved my leg. I'll be grateful to you with every step I take."

Kashani smirked as her skeptical eyes reacted to the cornball nature of Diegert's remark.

"Where will you go next?" she asked.

"I don't know, back to London I guess. What will you do? Is there other family you can stay with?"

"Felix and I will find a home and get our lives back. We will be part of the best generation Africa has ever known."

"Wow, I can't wait to see that."

"You will see it. Africa has a young population. We are educated and eager to make our countries and our continent so much better. We are a huge market and the world wants to sell us their products. We must become wise consumers so our people can grow and our economy is sustainable. Africa is poised for greatness, and I will help make it happen."

"Cue the violins and the cymbals, it's a wrap, and a star is born!"

"Fuck you, Mr. David White Man, you may think it's funny, but you will see the change is coming. Africa will rise and take a prominent place in the world."

"I didn't mean to make fun of you. You're just so pumped after spending three years as a prisoner, yet you see Africa with so much potential. It's amazing that there are so many people, who have so much right in front of them and they see no hope in their future, let alone expect to change a whole continent. You are a very impressive person, Kashani."

Scrunching up her nose as she smiled a beguiling grin, Kashani turned her face away from Diegert, yet he could hear her say, "I just know that without hope there is no future. The last three years taught me that."

Diegert looked out the window as buildings started to get larger and more frequent approaching the metropolis of Lagos.

Panzer spoke to Tiberius, directing him to carry out a plan to facilitate the departure of the plane as well as the truck.

Tiberius found a thick limb and broke it between two closely spaced trees. The pieces broke along a spiral fracture creating two pointed pieces. Moving to the rear exit of the terminal building, he shoved the two pointed ends between the bottom of the door and the threshold. With these in place, the door could not be opened from within.

With a length of strong rope, he tied a loop with a slide knot that would cinch up tightly when pulled. He moved to the set of double doors, which functioned as the front entrance of the terminal. Only the right-hand door was unlocked, accommodating ninety-nine percent of the passages into and out of the building. Tiberius's nonchalance and seemingly innocuous act of placing a loop of rope on a doorknob as if he were tying up a goat, was largely ignored.

As Felix and the yellow truck pulled into the airport's driveway, Panzer signaled Tiberius with three full rotations of his arm at the shoulder. Tiberius circled the rest of the length of rope around both doorknobs, securing the length with a cinch knot that only got tighter as pressure was placed upon it. With the door tied shut, he had denied everyone inside from exiting the building.

Tiberius ran to the truck, parked next to the Gulfstream. David Diegert stepped gingerly out of the truck's cab, limping quickly under Panzer's insistence over to the airplane, and struggled up the stairs. Tiberius joined Nikea and the others in the truck. At the plane's doorway, Diegert and Panzer looked back. Panzer saluted the group and moved inside. Diegert stayed at the door, waving at Felix as he watched the rest of the group arrange themselves in the truck's cab. Kashani's smile appeared out the window and she blew him a kiss, which he caught with a smile as the stairway folded up, turning the entrance into a smooth section of the jet's fuselage.

The truck wasted no time leaving the airport. Panzer's jet taxied to the runway and was airborne within minutes. Both vehicles made their escapes, while the Investigative Officer had to wait for someone to come and cut the ropes before he could exit the building.

CHAPTER 24

The two tired men remained quiet during the rapid take-off and ascent to cruising altitude. When they leveled off and the twin jet engine's locomotive like roar subsided into a gentle hum, Diegert turned to Panzer. "Why isn't Tiberius coming back with us?"

"Now that he's united with his sister, he wanted to stay and see to it that she is safe and well set up. Besides he was never going to go with us to Nairobi."

"Nairobi?! You mean we're not going back to London?"

"Oh my dear son, let me tell you of the real purpose of this trip. You and I are going on a hunting safari."

Although astonished, Diegert appeared impassive. He recalled the time Tom Diegert took him hunting for frogs. As a young boy, it was an emotionally traumatic experience. What would this be like, with this man?

Panzer was excited, "We are going to Kenya to hunt with one of the world's best guides. I've hunted with James Kabeela several times. He is simply the best big game tracker in the world. He will help us locate, so we can kill, the big African animals of our choice."

"You mean this was the real reason we came to Africa?"

"Yes."

"The last thirty-two hours was not our mission?"

"Killing Ozinwa was, of course, a mission but it was primarily for the benefit of Tiberius." A happy smile leaped upon Panzer's face. Diegert shuddered at the unmistakable similarity to Batman's nemesis, the Joker. "We are going to have some good old-fashioned Father-Son fun."

Slowly forcing his cringe into a smile, Diegert braced himself.

"When I was about your age," began Panzer, "my father took me hunting. We got several antelope, a wildebeest and in one of the most thrilling nights of my life," Panzer stretched his words for effect. "A black panther." Catching Diegert's suspicious look, Panzer persisted. "All the trophies are in my office in Innsbruck. You haven't seen my home in Austria yet, but I will have to have you visit soon. Years later, on a trip with Dean Kellerman, I shot a lion. The king of a pride, a fully maned adult male in his prime. He was magnificent and now resides in my office above my desk. Truly an outstanding animal and a tremendous trophy!"

Diegert could feel Panzer's pride in his accomplishments, and he had to admit African animals were the most fascinating. Having been summarily excluded from all Minnesota hunting trips while growing up, he longed for the inclusion and camaraderie which formed when men banded together to hunt and kill animals. It was a fulfillment of the primal testosterone blood lust wired into the human male. Diegert was excited but hesitant.

"Have you been hunting before?" asked Panzer.

"I told you, my father hated me because of you and he never took me on family hunts."

"Right! That ruddy little bastard."

"No, I was the bastard because you were my father. Tom Diegert was an asshole."

Panzer leaned back in his chair and brought his hand to his chin in a thoughtful gesture.

"So your mother loved you, your father and brother hated you, casting your family into constant conflict. Growing up was difficult, but you survived it and now you are stronger for having faced that adversity."

"I'm not an advocate for the experience."

"Nevertheless you are a benefactor because you've grown up in the backwoods of poverty, outside the world of wealth. You've developed tenacity through hardship, and perseverance through adversity. You appreciate the value of things and you recognize that life goes on even if its comforts are lost."

Panzer paused, Diegert nodded slowly. "You're one tough bastard, aren't you?" said Panzer.

Diegert smirked. He snorted, and a chuckle broke from him. Panzer's Joker smile spread but warmed. He too chuckled, then laughed. Diegert laughed, and they looked at each other and both started laughing out loud, hale and hearty. They cracked up at Panzer, the absent father, calling his abandoned son a bastard. As improbable as it seemed, the two men found humor in their deplorable situation. The mutual guffaws bridged a divide and broke down a barrier between them.

"You see," said Panzer, "although your life sucked because I wasn't there, we are now together at this fortuitous time. You have re-entered my life right at the point in which I need to begin preparing an heir."

Diegert held eye contact.

"I'm not going to die any time soon," said Panzer, "but Crepusculous and Omnisphere are complex organizations that rule the world. You have to know what you're doing. You must see the threats and the opportunities and strategically take action to maximize benefits while minimizing loss. Blah, Blah, Blah. But we've got time so I can prepare you. Like we discussed earlier, I need to know you, I need to build a relationship with you and we need to trust one another. We have billions of dollars in cash, even more in assets and we will soon own all the money in the world through Digival. We're in our own jet streaking across Africa to stay at a fabulous lodge and hunt the world's most magnificent animals. I wouldn't want to share all this with anyone other than my own son."

Diegert nearly choked on the lump in his throat.

Panzer said, "Without family, life is rudderless. It's blown by the winds of circumstance into the constant unknown. Actions, endeavors, investments, they serve no purpose and carry no meaning."

Diegert didn't nod, but he did tilt his head.

"I believe a father's love is demonstrated through practical, supportive measures that allow children to grow and flourish," said Panzer matter of factly. "Personal growth is not always, easy, comfortable, or even safe, but a father must prepare his son for the demands of the challenges that await him. Since I wasn't there for your past, I want to be there for your future and share with you everything that is ours. I cannot change the past and although I regret all the lost years, I can provide opportunities for a future that will be the envy of every man on the planet."

Diegert didn't want to choke up, but deep inside a small boy longed for what was being offered. His defenses cracked. The protective internal walls David had constructed were high and formidable, but not impenetrable. They were susceptible to the right application of emotional force. Panzer's words were striking the panels with deft sledgehammers, creating fissures in the emotional fortress behind which Diegert lived. The idea that money would never again be a problem was enticing, but more importantly his life would have purpose and meaning, he would be part of a family. This thought brought shudders to Diegert's emotional walls. He could no longer resist the wobbling and crumbling of his inner citadel.

Panzer sensed the wavering of the young man. He too felt emotions he was not fully able to control since, for him, his words about the value of a son were true.

"When I saw you riding on top of the van, with the gun truck firing upon you, I just went into action. I didn't want to see you die and lose all the hope for the future that you give me. Possessing so much is great, but a legacy that will be carried on by one who shares my blood, my genes, my dreams, matters more to me than anything."

Through a thicker than normal layer of water over his eyes, Diegert dared not blink as he said, "What do you want me to say?"

"There's nothing you need to say. Just let me be part of your life."

CHAPTER 25

The Gulfstream touched down on the Nairobi Wilson Airport where private aircraft are received. An AgustaWestland AW 169 helicopter awaited them and they transferred to the chopper for the one-hour flight to Ololaimutiek Village. The AW aircraft is an Italian design powered by two Canadian Pratt & Whitney turbojet engines with a maximum range of 820 kilometers. With a spacious, comfortable interior, it was ideal for traversing the mid-range distances of Africa. Ololaimutiek Village is located in Kenya not far from the border with Tanzania and the Serengeti National Park. The village is known for its luxurious tourist safari camps. For well-heeled patrons, no expense is spared. All manner of comforts are made available to ensure that guests on safari thoroughly enjoy themselves. The Serengeti is the world's most popular destination for wilderness safaris, on which all the big African animals can be found.

Panzer and Diegert were billeted at the Juma Juomo Resort. The facility's design incorporated the tradition of African hospitality with an architecture that felt rustic while being comfortable and secure. Guests felt like they are "roughing it" in their khaki safari garb, while they ate sumptuous meals in the dining hall and at night, slept in cotton sheets surrounded by sturdy canvas walls providing each guest their requisite privacy. Guide driven vans used radio and drone trackers to locate animals for the tourists to watch in their "natural" habitat. The truth was that, in the Park, every daylight hunt undertaken by the big cats was attended by no less than six to eight vans. For the animals it had been this way for decades. Many of the hunters had never known it any other way. As sure as the vultures showed up once a kill was made, the vans showed up when a hunt has begun.

Panzer was greeted by the staff of Juma Juomo with a warm recognition from his earlier visits. James Kabeela hugged the distinguished man with his great arms nearly lifting Klaus off the floor. When David was introduced as Klaus's son, the surprise was not well hidden. The big African was astonished to have never heard of this young man before. Sensing the awkwardness, he recovered quickly shaking hands and shifting his excitement to tomorrow's outing. He directed the staff to deliver Panzer and Diegert's luggage to their cabanas and led the two men to the dining hall.

Like the sleeping cabanas, the dining hall was a timber structure on a raised floor with a corrugated steel roof and canvas walls. The dining area had a summer camp feel to it, but only if a summer camp served braised water buffalo, wildebeest burgers, mango salad and imported red and white wines, followed by natural cacao mousse torts. Both men relaxed and enjoyed the fully prepared, unlimited meal.

After dinner, Diegert and Panzer walked across the compound with the weight of the African night pressing in. The moonless sky was especially dark while the sounds of the surrounding bush revealed the hunting and fleeing of untamed wildlife. Panzer stopped when the guttural roar of a male lion flooded over the savannah. The call was deep, with repeated bellows that echoed across the plains, proclaiming the big cat's supremacy.

Panzer turned to Diegert, "Tomorrow that magnificent cat will be ours."

Diegert's look remained impassive, shifting his eyes to see the smile on his father's face. The flickering of the torches, lighting the way to their cabanas, cast a devious glow on the cheeks and eyebrows of Panzer's Joker-like face.

"Tomorrow will be a big day for us, but the night has yet to reveal its surprises," said Panzer.

The toothy grin looked even creepier in the flickering lights. Standing in front of David's cabana, Panzer patted Diegert on the shoulder as he gently coaxed him up the steps. At the door, Diegert looked back to see Panzer waiting for him to enter. The staunch German waved as if sending his son off on a school field trip. Diegert nodded, but the vibe from Panzer left him wondering what was on the other side of the door.

The cabana, was on an elevated platform, had a metal roof and dual wall, canvas sides. The walls were supported by wooden timbers, while the door was set on hinges in a sturdy frame. The electric lights gave the canvas a warm glow. Upon entering, Diegert realized he was not alone. Sitting on the bed was a beautiful young African woman.

"Hello," said Diegert.

She was sitting on the bed looking at her phone. She stowed the phone as soon as she heard Diegert's voice.

"Hello," she said. "I am Lindavi, I'm happy to be here with you tonight."

Diegert looked at her bright eyes which flashed with a mischievous shine. She had perfect teeth surrounded by plump lips stretched back into a friendly smile. He cast his eyes over her body. Having risen from the bed and standing at a slight angle, Diegert was enchanted with her hourglass figure. Her hips were wide with full round buttocks. Her ample breasts were covered by a gauzy red button-up blouse, knotted at her trim waist revealing her smooth flat mid-section. She wore a khaki skirt which blended with the safari uniforms others in the compound wore, only hers was short, the hem placed very high on her sensual thighs. Continuing his gaze, he arrived at her bare feet, which had the cutest row of toes he'd ever seen. Pulling his gaze back up, he met her eyes, which sparkled with delight for having pleased him with her appearance. She shook her head and her braided locks cascaded behind her shoulders.

"My name's David."

"I know, I've been waiting for you. Can I get you a drink?"

"Sure."

"Do you like Guinness," asked Lindavi as she crossed the room. "It's a delicious beer that is very... Black," she said as she looked at him with the fridge door open.

"Yes, I like that beer." Diegert held her eye contact with a wry smile.

Lindavi poured the beer into a large glass mug, which she held out to Diegert so he could grasp the handle.

"Cheers," she said. "Please sit."

Diegert sat in a chair upholstered in zebra hide. Lindavi sat back on the bed facing him.

"You traveled a long way today didn't you?" she asked with a sense of concern.

"It is a long way from Nairobi to here."

"I hope you are not disappointed with your welcome."

"So far the trip has been worth it."

She looked at him, wanting to say something but was hesitant. Finally, she spoke. "You are very young. I suspect you are no older than me."

Diegert could see that Lindavi was uncomfortable being so forward, but her words were just as uncomfortable to restrain.

"Well, how old are you?"

She drew in a deep breath while straightening her posture, "I'm twenty-two."

Diegert nodded, "I got you by a few years, but you're right we're about the same."

Her smile revealed her bright white teeth, but she was nervous as she looked to the floor. "Usually the men are older."

When she looked up, Diegert held her gaze as she searched his reaction.

"They are over fifty or even older," she said.

Diegert nodded.

"And they are fat." She giggled. She brought her hand to her mouth until she saw that Diegert was laughing too.

The laughing eased her tension and Diegert asked, "Are the old, fat ones any fun?"

Her smile contracted. "They are not fun, but they are usually fast. I do not like the angry ones who get off by hurting me."

Their eyes locked again.

"You're not going to hurt me are you?" she asked.

Diegert shook his head. "No, I will not hurt you."

Her smile returned as she rose from the bed, undid a button on her blouse and stepped over to him. "It's been a long time since I really made love to a man. This night could be very special."

As she approached, Diegert put his beer on the side table and held out his hand.

She slid her fingers over his palm and up his forearm. She shifted her hips and sat down on his lap. Wrapping his arms around her waist, he pulled her body close to his. Their eyes projected tension and desire. Leaning in, eyes now closed, their lips met. Soft at first, sensitive and eager, but careful and cautious. The kiss was an exploration, an overture to seek the tacit permission to go further. They both pressed forward, eager to wake the passion and arouse the libido. Diegert felt her hesitation giving way as he intensified the kiss. Lips parted and tongues danced in the halls of each other's mouths, sending sensual signals through their bodies and brains. Diegert held Lindavi's face in his hands as the sole focus at that moment was the kiss. Their bodies were heating up as the embrace tightened while the kissing deepened. When they broke the kiss, their panting ensued as they pressed cheeks against necks. Lindavi spoke, "They never kiss me, they never want to."

Diegert brought her face close to his and kissed her again with an open mouth and an eager tongue. With one arm around her back and the other under her knees, he lifted her as he stood and carried her over to the bed. He gently laid her down. Together they entwined, connecting their bodies while the rhythm of pleasure was obeyed in spite of their clothing. Lindavi clasped Diegert's head, holding him tightly while she kissed his mouth with all the passion she possessed. Diegert undid the buttons on his shirt. He pulled his arms through the sleeves, tossing the garment to the floor. Separated, they both stripped the rest of their clothes in a giggling flurry. She laughed at the awkwardness with which Diegert hopped around as he pulled his legs out of his pants. He smiled at her as he stood in his boxers, which protruded in the front. She sat on the bed with her bright red panties encircling her hips. Their laughter subsided as she slid her panties forward over her knees and past her feet. Diegert grabbed the waistband of his boxers and pulled them down.

Her eyes enlarged as her smile broadened. "I usually have to pull that guy out from under the fat."

She looked up to see Diegert returning her smile, as she walked over, reaching out to his throbbing organ. "With most men, I have to bring this soldier to attention, but this brave one is ready for action," she said while gently stroking his erect shaft. Diegert had his arm wrapped around her, with his other hand he caressed her soft, warm and firm breasts. Her stiff nipples elicited a shudder of pleasure when Diegert squeezed them between his fingers. She straddled his leg while standing and forced her pelvis against his hip. Squeezing her sexy butt produced a rhythm with which she pressed her vulva into him. Their erotic sensations crossed into the primal zone where reason and logic give way to lust and desire. Diegert held Lindavi tight, took one long, rotating step and laid her on the bed.

Horizontal now their undulations intensified and they returned to deep passionate kissing. Lindavi opened her legs and centered herself on Diegert's hips. They thrust together for several minutes while their tongues indulged in the pleasurable delight found in the deepest of kisses. When they broke for air Diegert rolled Lindavi to her back. He took her plump, erect nipple into his lips and suckled it. Lindavi arched her back and let out a moan.

Diegert descended down her body bringing his lips to her labia. Lindavi lifted her head. "No one has ever done this to me before." Diegert smiled as he returned his lips to the warm, soft folds of her vagina. He could feel the throb of her clitoris, which was firm and erect. Enveloping her sensitive protrusion in his eager lips sent a shudder of pleasure through Lindavi. She thrust her head back against the mattress closing her eyes while gripping the sheets. Diegert could sense her sexual tension. He could feel the pleasure and excitement building within her. When his tongue caressed her clit, her legs spread wider and her hips thrust forward against his mouth. Lindavi's moaning was deep and primal. She was leaving the physical world and entering a realm of pleasure, distinctly personal and unprecedentedly intense. Diegert sensed her pace and applied just the right pressure to keep her escalating. Lindavi writhed from side to side and arched her back while thrusting her hips. She was moving towards an orgasm, the likes of which she had never experienced before. Diegert knew her moment was approaching as her breathing shortened. He slowed the pace and pressure on her sensitive bud. Lindavi grabbed the back of his head and forced his face against her. Diegert's smile could not be seen, but he sucked on her clit as she exploded with an orgasmic spasm that shook the bed, the cabana, the continent of Africa, and Lindavi's entire world. Her pleasure came in waves which Diegert reacted to with subtle adjustments in pressure allowing her to ride on delightful crests of joyful sensation for several minutes. As Diegert removed his lips, the tension in Lindavi's body dissipated and she entered into a blissful state of deep relaxation.

Diegert crawled back up next to her, wrapping her in his arms. He held her as she snuggled against his chest, resting quietly for several minutes. She ended the quiet by saying, "That was the most amazing thing I've ever felt."

"I'm glad you enjoyed it. It was exciting for me too."

She lifted her head and looked into his eyes. Diegert shifted his head to meet her gaze. He saw the surprise on her face.

"What?" he said.

"You enjoyed doing that for me?"

"Yeah."

The idea had to percolate in Lindavi's mind, and Diegert could see she was struggling with the notion.

He said, "Sex is a two-way street. The pleasure is better when you share what the other person is feeling. I could sense you were enjoying it and that feels good to me."

"Perhaps it's different when it's business," she said.

Diegert had no reply as Lindavi slid her hand down his abdomen encircling his shaft. She stroked it a few times stiffening its already erect state. She positioned herself so she could kiss his erection. She peppered his penis with little kisses and looked up at Diegert with a mischievous smile. Diegert had to smile back as she looked so cute, and he knew what was coming.

She engulfed his shaft in her mouth, sending a wonderful bolt of pleasure throughout his body. Her bobbing motions found a rhythm which intensified the thrilling sensations. As she produced such wonderful pleasure, Diegert thought *was this just business for her?*

Lindavi withdrew him from her mouth and sat on his thighs. She reached to the nightstand and ripped open a condom with her teeth. She unrolled it down his member and pumped the latex covered obelisk, working the lube into a froth. She positioned herself above him and inserted him within her. Diegert looked up at her pretty face and saw the same mischievous smile. Her firm breasts were there for the squeezing and Diegert couldn't resist caressing them. Lindavi began undulating her hips. Her movement was sensual and slow, with an escalating pace. She flexed her spine, thrusting her hips forward and back. She rose and fell while contracting her pelvic muscles. Diegert was entranced with her erotic movements. He was transfixed by the pleasure she was able to pull out of his groin, and he thrust his hips ever so slowly so as not to disturb the rhythm of her sexual dance. He looked up and swore she was enjoying it. He hoped they had crossed a line and were really lovers, not wanting to be just a John. Lindavi picked up the pace and the force with which she moved her hips. As she quickened her thrusts, her smile broadened. Diegert was now completely in her control. She seemed to want him to feel as good as she had felt. Her thrusts became shorter, quicker and more specific. He lost any capacity to resist as his hips began thrusting with intense automaticity. He exploded into her with an orgasm that sent her into the air as if she were riding a zebra stallion. As Diegert pulsed with pleasure, a tremendous lion roar reverberated across the savannah. Diegert's thrusts continued for another minute until he was spent and she was once again stable. She leaned forward, lying on top of him as his breathing slowed into quiet purrs and they both fell asleep.

Together they were blissfully peaceful in the satisfied repose of the sexually spent. As Diegert fell deeper asleep, he began to dream. He saw Lindavi dressed in a beautiful yellow sundress with a tight tank top and a smooth flowing skirt. They were together for the day as they walked through a festival in a park. Lindavi admired the arts and crafts, tastefully displayed in the vendor's tents. Live music pervaded the park, putting people in happy moods. Lindavi found a large hat with a bright band that fell into a draping tail of rainbow colors. Diegert thought she looked fabulous and insisted on buying it for her. She was taken aback and protested the purchase. He persisted and soon they were continuing their walk with her in her lovely new hat. At the food court they got sandwiches and lemonade. Sitting at a table near the entrance to the park, they laughed and smiled, finding it so much fun to be together. From the road a large black van entered the park and drove right up to where they were sitting. The movement diverted Diegert's attention from Lindavi's beauty. The side door of the van slid open and four men exited. Armed with submachine guns and scowling faces, they headed right for Diegert, barrels trained upon him. Diegert froze in the moment. He had no weapon, no escape plan, and no backup. With Lindavi there, he felt a pang of vulnerability, a realization he was not prepared to protect her. The men advanced quickly, Diegert jumped up to block them as they fired at the ground in front of him. Dirt flew up, blasting his face with pinpoints of shrapnel. The gunfire triggered a stampede of people scrambling in the opposite direction. The festival was transformed into a frightened wave of human panic. Diegert turned to see Lindavi, in shock at the horror unfolding in front of her. The buttstock of a gun struck his jaw, knocking Diegert backward, tumbling over their lunch table. Multiple three-round bursts rang out. Diegert looked to see bullets ripping into Lindavi. Her beautiful face and lovely body torn open with hideous wounds from which the flesh gaped and the blood splattered. She fell back out of her chair, the bright fabric of her yellow dress splotched with bloodstains. Her hat on the ground, covered with the contents of her bullet-riddled cranium. Diegert weakened as he witnessed the violence of her death. Struck again in the head, he was dragged off to the van.

The van door slammed shut. Diegert woke on the bed with a full body shudder. Lindavi was shaken by Diegert's body quake. His startled reaction and bewildered look caused her to ask, "Are you OK?" She gently slid to the side, laying down beside him. "I thought the Olduvai had erupted again," she said with a smile.

Diegert was slow to smile but he was relieved that she was OK and his nightmare had passed.

"I have to get going," she said.

"Can't you stay?"

"No, I have to work early, I've stayed longer than usual, and my family will be looking for me."

"Don't they know where you are?"

She reacted with a perturbed startle. "No, and they especially don't know what I am doing. So I must go so there are no suspicions."

Lindavi stood from the bed and dressed quickly. She pulled on her blouse, and Diegert watched as she buttoned up her top, covering her breasts.

"Will I see you again?"

"Oh come now, that's not the way this works. You may see me again, but I will be just another dark girl walking in the red dust of Africa."

Diegert looked at her forlornly, sliding to the edge of the bed, grabbing her hand.

She smiled. "You gave me an experience I had never had before. For that reason, you will stay in my memory, but I am a servant and you are the master, that won't change and I won't deceive myself." She kissed him on the forehead as she slid her feet into her sandals.

Diegert said, "I am a servant too. I have to do what is asked of me even when I don't want to."

Rolling her eyes Lindavi replied, "Come on, you sound like a petulant little boy. You are the son of a very wealthy man. You are an heir to a fortune. You may have to do what you're told, but really your life is nothing like mine," she said with a look of annoyance.

"You have to have sex with men, but I have to kill them."

A quizzical look of concern cast across her face.

"That wealthy man is my father, but I am his assassin. Soon I will be assigned to kill again."

Lindavi looked frightened and stood motionless as the gravity of his admission sunk in. Her phone buzzed in the pocket of her skirt.

"You and I are more alike than you realize," exclaimed Diegert. "What we do is highly valued, but we act in the dark, secret and discreet. In the light of the day, we are shameful."

Looking up from the screen of her phone, Lindavi said, "I may have been your whore, but I am not your therapist." She pointed a finger at him. "I don't want to know anything more about you killing people." She lifted her phone. "I have to go."

At the door to the cabana, she stopped to give him one last suspicious look before escaping into the night.

Diegert pulled the condom off his dick and tossed it in the trash. He pulled the blankets over him. He felt foolish, about wanting to connect with her, to share his struggle. She obviously didn't want anything to do with him once the sex was over. With further contemplation, he realized he was truly alone with his discreet occupation. Tell someone with whom you're trying to form a friendship that you're an assassin, and it's pretty certain they'll want nothing to do with you.

Lying in bed, he heard the long, low guttural bellow of the male lion echo across the dark savannah. A powerful reminder that he was in the territory of a mighty king who ruled with tooth and claw. He was restless for quite a while before falling asleep.

CHAPTER 26

In the morning, Diegert filled his plate from the sumptuous banquet served in the Lodge. He sat down with his breakfast just as Klaus Panzer entered the room. His father came right over to him. "Guten Morgen." He sat next to Diegert. "That looks like a meal fit for a man about to have one of the greatest adventures of his life."

Diegert slid a bite of eggs Benedict into his mouth.

Panzer leaned in to ask, "Did you enjoy your company last night?"

Chewing his mouthful, Diegert nodded.

"I must tell you that I had the company of two last night. There's nothing like the intensity of a threesome."

Swallowing Diegert replied, "Well I'm sure you enjoyed it more than they did."

Panzer's consternation played across his furrowed brow as he stood and went to the banquet table.

Diegert used his fork to break off a piece of French toast and watched as the tall gray haired man greeted everyone he passed with a smile and that German, "Guten Morgen."

Upon return, Panzer said, "Eat well, my son, for today we face the most formidable of opponents. We will hunt a full-grown Black Mane lion."

Diegert thought about the beast he heard in the night. The innate power of that animal to command his kingdom with a lack of fear of any of its inhabitants, except one.

"That sounds interesting." Diegert nodded.

"Interesting?! It will be a lot more than just interesting. When I shot my lion it was the most exciting and exhilarating experience of my life. The trophy is one of my proudest possessions. Taking down the king of the beasts puts you on the top tier of the throne of humanity." Just before inserting a big forkful of pancakes, Panzer said, "I want you up there sharing that place with me."

Again, Diegert nodded, this time with uncertainty As he did on the flight from Lagos, this new father of his was bypassing twenty-six years, Diegert's entire life, to instantly arrive at the much desired, loving Father-Son relationship that so many hope for, but which takes a lifetime to build.

"Let's finish eating and get out to the truck," said Panzer as he sliced his sausage link.

The Land Rover they were taking into the bush was dark green and equipped with an elevating roof so one could stand up and still be covered. The massive tires gave it extra ground clearance and it was tricked out with GPS and satellite navigation systems that allowed communication with trackers in the field. Their guide, James, was a tall man with salt and pepper hair and a trim beard. He was quick to smile and happy to serve.

Upon greeting Diegert, James said, "Ah, you are the prodigal son who has been returned to your father."

Diegert looked to see Panzer, now donning a broad brimmed hunter's hat smiling at them. "Yes, I suppose I am," said Diegert as the shaking of hands concluded.

"This is your first hunt in Africa isn't it?"

"I haven't gone hunting at all in a very long time."

"No problem. You will succeed, I guarantee it," said the tall African seeking to reassure Diegert that he was being guided by the very best. With all their gear loaded into the truck, the three of them took their seats, and James accelerated into the bush.

Even the best Land Rover, once it leaves the dirt roads, delivers a rough ride as it crosses the African landscape. What may look like a smooth expanse of grassland is, in fact, rugged terrain producing a jarring ride that will rattle the bones and shake loose the teeth. Even the heavily cushioned seats in a Land Rover are not enough to make the trip painless.

Diegert and Panzer endured this travel for three hours. Cresting a knoll, James stopped the truck, pointing out a pack of hyenas feasting on a freshly killed zebra. The pack was oblivious as they tore apart the carcass, soaking themselves in the fifteen liters of blood that flows through an adult zebra. Diegert was transfixed by the scene, the primal need to feed and the violence with which these animals transferred the life of their prey into their own bodies was alarming. Panzer too was mesmerized by the vicious competition for the most succulent body parts. Looking to the sky, Diegert noticed the vultures circling. These meat-eating birds did nothing to contribute to the kill, yet they thrived through the killing of others. Gazing upon Panzer, Diegert recognized his father as a vulture. Benefitting from death, while letting others do the killing. The birds look rather stately as they soar high above in the sky. Close up, their pink-skinned heads look hideous. Diegert thought that Panzer also appeared dignified and classy when considered from a distance. Closely observed, the man had his ugly side, there to be seen when you realized what you were really looking at.

"Enough?" asked James. While Diegert and Panzer both nodded their heads, James put the Land Rover into gear, and the truck lurched forward over the uneven surface of the vast savannah. In order to reach the destination James had selected for the hunt, they needed to drive another hour. Along the way, they saw giraffes, wildebeests, impalas and a large herd of elephants. James, though, was seeking the recently claimed home of a pride of lions. The spot was on private land, upon which Panzer had purchased the right to hunt. The land bordered the Maasai Mara National Reserve where hunting was strictly prohibited. The lions had crossed a small spring-fed stream, leaving the reserve to set up their whelping grounds for their young cubs. Outside the Reserve, the lions were game and the license Panzer had bought gave him permission to kill.

James stopped the Land Rover, raised the roof and stood in the middle of the vehicle. Through his binoculars, he observed the pride. All the adults were either lounging or fast asleep. Eight lionesses were arrayed in a haphazard circle in which six little cubs alternated between wrestling with one another and biting the tails, paws, and tits of the adult females. Beyond them, outlined in shade, was the large male of the pride. He was sleeping soundly with his ribs rising and falling in a steady rhythm. Even with just the simple motion of ventilation he was impressive. His muscles rippled as he lifted his head when one of the cubs nipped his tail. His restful calm projected his dominion and his full mane looked as though it had recently been combed. The most striking thing though was its black color. A truly black mane on an African lion was rare. The contrast between the tawny color of the body and the black mane distinguished him from his harem of lionesses.

"We have found him," said James as he ducked back into the Land Rover's cabin. Exiting the vehicle he stepped to the back of the Rover, opened the tail doors and lifted the gun case. Moving forward he passed Diegert and Panzer on his way to the hood of the truck. They stood together as James input the code which opened the case, revealing the length of the rifle they would use today. The firearm was long, sleek and black. The stock was made from a composite plastic while the presence of the bolt handle along with the absence of a magazine receptacle, indicated its firing mechanism was single action. A feature that increased the gun's accuracy but required manual re-loading between shots. Diegert leaned in to look at the stamp plate: *Whitaker LG 650 - .375 H&H mag.* From behind his shoulder, he heard Panzer say, "We manufacture this weapon."

Diegert nodded approvingly.

James lifted the rifle out of its foam cradle and affixed the scope, which was an incredible piece of technology. It used a built-in microprocessor and integrated cameras to capture a digital image of the target. The computer adjusts the reticle based upon automatically calculated distance, angle and wind speed placing the point of impact squarely on the target. It also has a zoom function and the scope recorded video of everything it saw, allowing the kill shot to be reviewed and posted online.

Seeing the device James was affixing to the rifle, Panzer pointed it out to Diegert. "This is one of the most advanced pieces of hunting technology we've ever produced. When you look through the eyepiece you'll be amazed at the HD image."

Diegert looked at the scope, which James was tightening to its mounts. Panzer said, "The use of optics to calculate the range under which the target is being engaged, substantially improves your chances of making a great shot."

Having secured the scope, James handed it to Diegert. Peering through, Diegert aimed at a distant tree. The scope immediately identified the tree's trunk as the target, much like a cell phone camera will focus on a face. Instantly the screen filled the borders with data. Distance, wind speed, altitude the X and Y-axis of the angle of the target, barometric pressure, the position on the compass as well as the relative zoom factor. Diegert knew if he had a bullet in the chamber he could have hit that 317 yard distant tree no problem.

Turning to James and Panzer, he shared a smile with the two hunters.

"Ok." James buckled the belt upon which he had holstered a .44 magnum revolver. "Let's move up to that ridge."

James carried the rifle, Diegert slung the gun case strap over his shoulder and Panzer adjusted his safari hat. They walked about 400 meters through the veldt ascending the final 10 meters to a high spot that flanked the position of the lion pride. At the peak of the ridge, they set themselves in an open area that afforded an excellent view of the pride. From this distance, Diegert could see the family life of the pride displayed before him, with the adults dozing and the children playing.

From the case, James extracted a tripod upon which he set the rifle. Also from the case, he removed a small cube with a perforated metal grid on one side. Upon a second tripod he attached the cube before setting it on a large rock so as to be three feet off the ground.

"This is a speaker which has several prerecorded sounds that are useful for eliciting action from wildlife."

"You mean like a duck call?" said Diegert.

"Yes, only more variety and a bit more specific."

"What works best for lions?" asked Panzer, although Diegert got the sensation his father already knew the answer.

"Hyenas and lions are natural enemies," said James. "They are competitors and although the edge usually goes to the lions, the hyenas will attack if they sense an advantage. The two are constantly on guard against each other."

"So you'll fake an attack."

"Yup, and what will happen is the lionesses will circle the cubs and hold their ground. Those that aren't mothers will come out to defend the territory. The big male though is the true protector. My scouts tell me this one is particularly aggressive towards hyenas. So he will rise to the occasion, seek out the hyenas, kill any he can and chase off the rest."

"And we'll shoot him while he thinks he's defending his family," said Diegert.

"It's the best way to get him on his feet during the day and separate him from the rest of the pride."

Panzer lifted his eyebrow, casting a disapproving glance at his son's last statement. He stepped over to him, placing his hand on the young man's shoulder. "The shot will be yours to take."

James lifted the binoculars he had slung around his neck and looked toward the pride. He said, "Gentleman, do you see that gully that runs towards the east." He pointed in the direction to which he referred and ran his hand as if tracing the gully. "There is a small spring-fed stream that flows to a watering hole about a mile south of us. The stream is the Tanzanian border. On the other side is the Serengeti National Park. If the lions cross that stream, we cannot pursue them." James looked at the two of them, awaiting a response. When none occurred, he asked, "Do you understand?"

Diegert immediately nodded his head. Panzer paused, pursed his lips, gazed upward, then turned to James asking, "What is the likelihood they will retreat to the Park?"

"I think it's quite likely that when the gun is fired they will run in that direction. They used to live in the Park and only recently have they chosen this spot as their new den."

"We're a long way from anyone observing what occurs out here. There's no one to know if we pursue them."

James looked Panzer right in the eyes, "I will know, and I will not allow them to be pursued. Outside the Park, what we are doing is legal, inside we would be poachers. And that is something no one will ever be able to call me."

Panzer never blinked or broke eye contact. "Then we'll just make sure that first shot counts."

The stare down ended, but Diegert could feel the tension between these two as final preparations were made.

"David," said James. "Let's get you sighted in."

Diegert took a knee and comfortably engaged the weapon, positioning himself so he could clearly see through the scope. He was nervous. He recalled the last hunting trip as an eight-year old boy with Tom Diegert, a contemptuous man he mistakenly believed to be his father. The guy hated David, because the bastard child reminded him every day that he was a cuckold with an unfaithful wife who insisted on raising another man's child in his home. That trip ended in failure when Diegert had to choke down his tearful emotions while struggling to kill the frogs they were hunting. Now here he was again, having killed many men, but feeling ambivalent about killing an animal.

James instructed him, "Just pick a spot about thirty yards away from the pride and sight in like you did earlier with the tree. Let me know when you're ready."

Looking through the scope, Diegert saw the pride. He scanned over the group of sleeping mothers. The big male was sleeping in the shade. The cubs, however, were all active. Romping, wrestling, running and chasing each other. It was like a daycare center with the cutest little creatures he'd ever seen. They tussled in the grass, pounced on one another, frolicking in the sunshine, safe and secure amongst the powerful adults who were seeing to it that these playful little bundles survived to be the next generation of Africa's alpha predators. Diegert felt an instant sense of family as he witnessed the scene of daily pride life.

There was a distinct green bush against the dry brown grasses, which Diegert sited in on.

"Have you got it?" asked James in a soft whisper.

"Yeah."

"Ok, open the chamber, and I'll hand you the round."

Lifting and pulling back on the bolt handle, Diegert exposed the interior of the barrel. James handed him the .375 H&H mag. The bullet was hefty and dense with a gleaming brass casing. It slid smoothly into the chamber. Diegert lowered the bolt handle and slid the round forward.

"You ready?" asked James.

Diegert hesitated. He was contemplating the role of a father to these cubs in this threatening world of competitive predators.

Panzer could not stand the silence. "Answer him, David," he spat a little too loudly.

Diegert, startled by the order, lifted his head to look up at the two men. James was patient and impassive. Panzer was gritting his teeth as his jaw muscles bulged.

Slowly Diegert said, "Ok."

James switched on the speaker and an aggressive series of yips and barks were broadcast toward the pride. In the distance the reaction was immediate. All the sleeping adults were instantly on their feet, shaking the sleep from their heads. They were sensing the air and scanning the bush. James pumped a spray bottle emitting a mist that rode the wind down the rise toward the pride. The hyena scent and the continued calls focused the lions on the rise. Diegert returned to the scope. All the eyes of the pride, including the curious cubs, were trained on their position. James's prediction was right. Six of the lionesses surrounded the cubs who were corralled into a protective circle of motherhood. Two lionesses began stalking forward.

Diegert moved the scope to the shady spot where the male had earlier been. From the darkness of the shadow of the tree, stepped the magnificent male with his black mane framing his tawny face. He strode forward with a look of confident determination like no other Diegert had ever seen. His great paws pressed down the grasses as he moved forward without hesitation, nostrils flaring as the air was sensed. His progress was powerful, purposeful and so very impressive that Diegert was spellbound by this magnificent beast. The big male wasn't running, but there was a bounce in his step and an intense gleam in his eyes as he searched to see what he had heard and smelled. Diegert could see how any hyena who was the target of this animal's anger had better have a quick exit plan.

So amazed was Diegert at the true spectacle of the lion that to pull the trigger and kill him seemed totally inappropriate and cowardly. Killing him would remove the pinnacle of a natural chain which had taken years to develop and upon which the next generation depended. Diegert could not justify the loss for the gain. He could not see the big cat's crime that deserved this lethal punishment. The beast was passing through the scope's ideal range. If the shot did not happen now, the rifle would be inaccurate. Diegert's finger would not squeeze, it would not pull, he would not shoot this animal.

Panzer shouted, "Shoot. Fire the weapon." Diegert did not, no report of a bullet was heard. Panzer stepped over to Diegert, yelling, "Shoot him, shoot him now."

Diegert would not look up. He held the gun but moved his eye from the scope, looking at the ground.

Panzer grabbed the rifle.

James shouted, "Hey what are you doing?"

Panzer pointed the gun at the big male charging up the hill. As he pulled the trigger, the barrel jutted skyward as Diegert stood and shoved the rifle up, sending the bullet into the bright blue sky.

The sound was immense as it rolled across the grassland. The big lion stopped in his tracks. He seemed to suddenly be aware that his enemy was not the strange skulking dog-like creatures with whom he shared the savannah, but rather the one enemy he knew his teeth and claws could not defeat.

The entire pride scattered when the bullet's explosive report reverberated across the low valley. The cubs followed the mothers who crossed the stream and dispersed into the park. The big male also headed to the gully, which divided private from public land. Just before crossing, he looked back with his golden eyes to see that his enemies remained on the hill. He splashed through the small stream and disappeared into the bush.

Panzer turned to James. "Give me more bullets."

"No. They've crossed into the park. We're not going after them."

"Maybe you can't, but I will."

"You're not getting any bullets."

Pointing the unloaded rifle at James, Panzer shouted, "Give me the bullets."

In spite of knowing the gun was now harmless, James was very uncomfortable having the barrel pointing in his direction. Putting up his hands, he said, "Look, we've got two hours before we have to start our journey back. If he returns, we may have another shot at him."

Panzer cast a disapproving scowl at Diegert, who turned away, avoiding eye contact. Panzer continued to glare at the young man, his contempt building.

"How is it that you can kill a dozen men, including the President of the United States, yet you can't pull the trigger on this wild animal?"

Diegert looked at the man with rage boiling inside him. "You know I didn't shoot the president. Someone else had control of the trigger, and I'm sure you know who it was."

"My point is you're a natural killer, a trained assassin. Why couldn't you shoot the lion?"

Diegert looked at James, as did Panzer. The guide had an expression of disbelief as if he expected to be let in on the joke any second now. Panzer spoke, "Oh, please excuse me for not making proper introductions earlier." With a wave of his hand, Panzer said, "Please meet David Diegert, killer of men. The world's best assassin."

Diegert's fierce gaze told James he was not happy to be referred to as an assassin. Yet Panzer had more to say. "This failure of the moment," he gestured toward Diegert. "This hesitant, incapable shooter is, in fact, one of the most prolific assassins in the world. He has killed dozens of men, most of whom were taken out upon my orders. He will kill at my direction."

Turning to Diegert, Panzer said, "Please explain what thoughts brought you to ruin this million-dollar opportunity."

Diegert eyebrows shot up, furrowing his forehead.

"That's right," said Panzer. "One million dollars for the license to get us the chance to take down that lion. Why couldn't you kill him?"

"People deserve what they get. They're criminals, they're dishonest or they're violent and they get the retribution they deserve. None of those things are true about animals. And we were not killing that lion for food."

After a long look of consternation, Panzer said, "Why didn't you say this before?"

Diegert shrugged. "I wanted to see wild Africa. I wanted to see the lions. I just didn't want to kill them. Besides you never asked if I wanted to kill a lion."

"You're a natural killer. I never thought I would have to ask."

"You keep calling me that and telling me about NK cells, but I don't feel like that. I know what I've done, but it is not natural."

James stepped back from the pair and drew his .44 Magnum. Pointing it at Panzer, he said, "Sit down."

"What are you doing? We're talking about pursuing the lion. What is this?"

"Shut up and sit down." He turned to Diegert. "Lie down, face in the dirt." Shaking the big gun at him, he said, "Do it now!"

Diegert knelt down and laid face down in the grass. James ordered him, "Put your hands on the back of your head." Diegert slowly complied.

Panzer was still standing with a look of utter disbelief. James stepped over, shoving him to the ground. Panzer fell and rolled into a seated position on the grass.

James picked up the rifle and set it up on the tripod pointing at Panzer.

"This scope with its built-in video camera will record your admission to all the crimes you have committed against Earth and all its inhabitants. Do you think you are the only one who can hire an assassin? I am being well paid to record your final moments, during which you will beg for mercy, only to receive a .375 mag through your chest. The whole world will witness the death of Klaus Panzer, the man who sought to rule Earth." James maniacal diatribe seemed completely unhinged, but his pronouncement was no veiled threat as he chambered a bright brass round into the rifle's breach.

"James, this is crazy. Are you off your medications? We've known each other for years."

"I'm not on any meds. I've known you for years and that is why I know you are guilty of gluttony, greed, lust, envy, and pride. You may not be slothful, but now the wrath of the world's betrodden will bring you to your death. But first you will witness the death of your son."

James swung his arm, pointing the .44 at Diegert. David wasted no time, immediately rolling to his left, scrambling low on the ground, seeking cover behind a large rock. His desperate escape was pursued by booming discharges from the .44. Two misses, but the third struck Diegert's calf muscle, re-opening his recent injury. With blood spurting from his lower leg, he fell behind the rock.

James picked up the loaded rifle as he went after Diegert. Standing at the rock, James commanded, "Come out of there. I want your father to see you die. I want him to see your head explode."

Diegert slowly stood. James pointed the big pistol at his head. The angry man turned to see that Panzer was watching. At that moment, Diegert hurled a stone at James's head, striking him in the temple. James stumbled backward, disoriented, but not down. Diegert limp-hopped around the rock, grabbing the .44, which James held in his right hand while holding the rifle in his left. Diegert had James's right wrist in his left hand and with right jabs, he punched him in the face. The big man took the punishment. He kicked at Diegert's legs, sending pain shooting through his lower body, yet Diegert clung to his balance. Planting his right foot,

Diegert grabbed James's left shoulder as he tripped him over his leg, sending the hunting guide sprawling on to the big rock. The rifle fell upon impact, but James held on to the pistol. Diegert seized James's right forearm, keeping the pistol at arm's length.

Panzer saw that the hunting rifle lay in the firing line of James's pistol, but he took the risk and made a move for the long gun. James caught sight of him and squeezed off two shots. One went wide. The other hit Panzer in the gut, spinning him as he fell. With his left now free, James punched Diegert in the head, neck, and face. Diegert was blocking and punching with his right, while James countered and defended with his left. James fired his pistol one last time, emptying the revolver. He released the weapon and used his hand to free himself from Diegert's grasp. As he stood, he drove his heel into Diegert's calf, nearly blacking out his consciousness. He grabbed Diegert's face, sinking his fingers under Diegert's jaw and just below his eyes. Diegert felt James holding his head like a bowling ball as he tried to drag the big guide to the ground. James released Diegert, making a run for the rifle.

Diegert picked up the stone he had earlier thrown at James. He righted himself and forced a charge at James with the stone in his right hand. As James was turning to point the long gun, Diegert hit him in the face with the stone. The blow stumbled the man, and Diegert hit him again in the side of the head. James lifted the rifle, but Diegert was too close for the barrel to be effective. A missed shot rang out as Diegert hit James with the stone again and again. The big African dropped to his knees, blood pouring out his ear and nose, and a gash opened above his eye.

"Who paid you to kill my father?"

"Thousands," groaned the bleeding man. "You rich bastards can't own the earth."

"We'll see about that."

Diegert hit him one more time with the stone, knocking him unconscious. He pulled James's belt from his loops and tied his arms behind his back. He unclipped the strap from the rifle and secured the big guy's ankles. James lay on the grass, his blood soaking into the ground.

Diegert pulled his own belt from his waist and cinched it just below his right knee to staunch the blood flow from his injured calf.

He hobbled over to Panzer, who lay on his back gasping in short breaths. He was shot in the lower left quadrant of the abdomen. The projectile experienced minimal deformation, creating an exit wound not much bigger than the entrance.

From the Rover, Diegert retrieved the first aid kit. He cleaned Panzer's wound. Panzer asked, "Why such treachery?"

"Apparently he was being paid by some group that wants to stop you from owning the world."

"Ludicrous. They can't stop that."

"If you were dead, I don't think you could own the world."

"Yes, but neither would they. Another powerful person would step in and do the same thing. In fact this whole save the earth bit may be just a ploy to throw us off the true culprit."

Diegert prepared the gauze and ointment for the next step. "This'll hurt."

Wincing, Panzer asked, "What have you got in there for the pain?"

"Ibuprofen."

Panzer rolled his eyes.

Diegert placed gauze pads on both the entrance and exit wounds. He wrapped an ace bandage around Panzer's waist, encircling the wounds, and pulled it tight. That is when Panzer felt the pain. The pressure hurt like hell, but it stopped the bleeding. Panzer's breathing eventually returned to near normal.

"You undoubtedly have organic material inside your body which will set up an internal infection. That could kill you in forty-eight hours," said Diegert with all seriousness. "We need to make the trip back to camp and get you to Nairobi."

"Where did you learn all this?"

"In the Army. Every soldier is certified in combat first aid."

Handing Panzer a water bottle he said, "Now you've got to keep drinking so your blood volume doesn't drop. Here's the Ibu and take this Amoxicillin, it's an antibiotic that'll help."

Panzer gulped down the pills.

Diegert drove the Land Rover over to Panzer and helped him to the truck. "For the roughest part of the ride, you should sit upright."

"Wait, where's James?"

"He's tied up over by that rock."

"Give me the truck's toolbox and bring him over here."

CHAPTER 27

Diegert lifted the bright red toolbox and set it on the hood in front of Panzer who leaned against the truck. He walked over to James, pulled the back of his collar, and dragged him face down across the ragged grass over to Panzer. Diegert flipped the bound man on to his back and stood next to his father. James regained consciousness after his rough handling.

"James, you've injured me quite badly, so I don't have time to waste. I want to know who paid you to kill me, and I believe the quickest way to get the answer is with the password for your phone."

Panzer took a pair of needle-nose pliers and placed one side of the jaws inside James's nostril and let the other jaw sit on the outside of the nostril. He did not press the jaws but just let them sit there, half in and half out of his nasal cavity.

"Son, could you please get his phone from his pocket."

Diegert retrieved the phone.

"Please be prepared to input the password James provides."

"Fuck you," said James defiantly.

"That seems doubtful, but give it a try."

Diegert input the insult. "No good."

Panzer slowly placed his hand on the plier handles and gave them a quick squeeze.

A piercing scream erupted from the big man as the nerves in his nose were compressed between the iron jaws.

"Now that was just a pulse. Imagine how it will feel when I don't let go. Please give me the correct password?"

"You're going to kill me anyway."

Panzer squeezed the handles as hard as he could and held on throughout James's screaming. After a full minute, during which James was reduced to blubbering, Panzer released the pressure. "Now there will be no more attempts at negotiation. Quit all that sniveling. I haven't even drawn blood yet."

James looked up to see Panzer inspecting his nails.

"Give us the password now." Without giving James the chance to answer, Panzer clamped the pliers, twisting them hard, tearing off a bleeding flap of nostril.

The suddenness of Panzer's escalation, and the intensity of the screaming startled Diegert.

"There is no option for you," shouted Panzer as he held the piece of skin in front of James's hysterical face.

Panzer commanded, "Give us the password, or I will dismantle your face with this simple tool."

The blood ran over his mouth, down his chin, and onto his shirt. As James started to speak, bloody spittle shot from his mouth. "Sh-sh-Chicago."

Leaning forward, Panzer clarified, "Chicago?"

James nodded.

"You've never even been there."

James shrugged.

"The man says Chicago," Panzer blared to Diegert.

Keying in the word, Diegert said, "We're in."

Placing the pliers with the piece of nostril on the truck's hood, Panzer approached.

"What should I look for?" asked Diegert.

"Check the texts for Chin Lei Wei."

"What? He's one of the board members."

"He certainly is. One of the main reasons I created Crepusculous was to keep my enemies very close."

Scrolling through the messages, Diegert said, "Hey… Here we go. Yeah, Chin Lei Wei."

Diegert's eyes tracked over the screen, reading the messages in the texts. "Sure enough, the fucker was going to kill us during the hunt. The cheap bastard. Chin Lee got him to do the job for fifty grand."

"We keep the phone as evidence, allowing Mr. Wei's treachery not to be denied."

"What about him?"

"James has killed many animals. I think it only fitting that they get their revenge. Leave him bound, but tie him to a tree."

Diegert recalled Omar Pascal, the NCIS officer he shot in the middle of the Gulf of Aden while escaping Djibouti on the *Sue Ellen*. What if he hadn't shot him and just threw him in the ocean miles from shore? Slowly drowning seemed like an awful death. James would be disemboweled and consumed by hungry carnivores. It seemed worse than drowning, but if he didn't shoot him, he didn't kill him. Tying a rope around James's waist while the man's hands were bound behind his back and his ankles remained secured with the gun strap, Diegert ignored the pleas for mercy as he bound him to the trunk of a nigra bushwillow.

Panzer picked up the pliers, flinging the piece of nostril into the air. Diegert dodged the flap of flesh as he passed Panzer on his way to the Land Rover.

"You're lucky we aren't going to kill you," said the tall gray man looking down on James. Panzer flipped the switch on the small speaker box atop the tripod. The call of hunting hyenas cast across the savannah. "You can use the time to pray to your God before the animals come to prey on you."

"Please, if you take me with you, I'll help you get back at Mr. Wei."

"What a generous offer of cowardice treachery. But through the power of text, I've already deceived Mr. Wei about the successful completion of your mission. I can tell you he replied thanking you."

James's look of hope sagged into crestfallen despair. Panzer squatted down., "He is a man of his word, Mr. Wei. He transferred fifty thousand dollars to your account." He gestured with the phone. "I now have all the evidence I need to force him into a very deep corner. The only assurance I have that you will not betray me is offered by the lion's thirst for blood."

Panzer rose to his full height as he stepped away. "Goodnight, James."

CHAPTER 28

Diegert drove while Panzer rode in the back seat. The GPS guided the route, but the landscape was just as rough as before and the closing in of darkness slowed the pace, making the trip even longer. Diegert twice had to stop the vehicle and tighten the bindings on Panzer's wounds. What took an hour on the way in, took three hours on the way out, but they eventually found the dirt road and finished the trip in two more hours.

Arriving at the resort late at night. Diegert told the manager that a lion attacked them and, in the chaos, both he and his father had been shot. They were able to escape thanks to the quick action of James. On the way home, however, they encountered a tourist van, which had lost radio service and had an engine problem forty-five minutes away. Generous James, the African jack-of-all-trades, stayed to help them. Diegert gave the manager GPS coordinates that were well to the east of where James had actually been left. Panzer was medically unstable, and Diegert insisted the helicopter be prepped for immediate departure to Nairobi.

Once the AW 169 was airborne, Diegert radioed ahead to the Nairobi Wilson Airport, instructing them to have the Gulfstream ready to depart as soon as they arrived. Panzer was able to walk, but he was definitely woozy. As soon as he was in the jet, Diegert used the plane's medical kit to change the dressing on his wounds. He gave Panzer Oxycodone, which took away the pain, allowing the man to sleep. He changed the dressing on his own leg wound, wishing that Kashani was on this flight. He gulped down a couple of Oxies, reclined the big wide leather chair, and slept six hours on the way back to London.

When he woke up, they still had two and a half hours to go. Panzer was awake, sitting across the aisle facing Diegert.

"How you doing?" asked the younger man.

"I'm OK, but they have hospitals in Nairobi."

"They also have Kenyan Police. No way I was risking that. Keep drinking your water, and you'll be fine. I'll make sure there is an ambulance waiting at the airport."

"You're my own little doctor," chuckled Panzer.

Diegert smiled, and the two shared a moment of mutual camaraderie for having survived this ordeal. Diegert found the closeness gratifying and reassuring, but he waited for it to vanish in some derogatory remark. Panzer just kept smiling. He also seemed struck by the moment, caught in the reverie and flummoxed by the feelings he was having. Was it the Oxy or was it the grateful feeling that bonds even the most disparate people when they've faced death and survived?

Panzer spoke. "You saved my life, son."

Diegert shrugged.

"You stopped him from executing me." Panzer almost fought back a tear, but it rolled down his cheek. "He was going to shoot you, then me." Panzer's voice choked up. "He would've killed my son right in front of me."

"Now don't get upset. You have to stay relaxed."

"I know, but when I told you about the NK cells and the threats upon Crepusculous, you now know it's true. You were an excellent guardian, and I'm proud of you, son."

Diegert got out of his chair to take the one next to Panzer. He inspected the wound. Panzer grabbed his forearm. "I want you to know how proud I am of you. You were brave, a man can't ask for any more from a son."

Diegert looked into the cool gray-blue eyes and thought, *was it the drugs?* Or was this man really telling him the kind of thing he had longed to hear his whole life? Was his father praising him, not only for an act but also for his character, his humanity?

"You're the flesh of my flesh, the bone of my bone, and we share the same spirit of survival. I want to face the challenges of life with you," proclaimed Panzer.

Diegert lifted the blanket and tucked it in around his father's shoulders, "You should sleep for another hour or so. It will be very fatiguing once we get to the hospital."

"No hospital. Call Avery and have him set up a surgeon. Get him to send the LPU ambulance."

"OK."

"But, son, I want you to know my words about you are true. You are the son with whom I've always wanted to share my life."

Diegert smiled and nodded. "Thanks, Dad, I'm really glad to hear that. Now get some more sleep."

Returning to his seat, under his warm blanket, Diegert felt like he was cloaking himself with approval, acceptance, and support. Emotional blankets he never had and only now realized how much he wanted. He tried to fall asleep but struggled to rectify his conflicting perceptions of Klaus Panzer.

****

At the airport in London, Panzer was carried off the plane, into the ambulance, and rushed with lights and sirens to LPU Medical. The operating room was standing by, ready to perform emergency surgery.

Avery drove Diegert to LPU in a Range Rover Discovery. He needed medical attention on his leg wound.

"How did this happen?" asked the dark mystic.

"Betrayal. The hunting guide was paid to kill us."

"James?!"

"Yeah."

"He's been guiding Klaus for years."

Surprised to hear his father's first name, Diegert snapped his gaze upon Avery. "We know who's responsible."

Avery glanced from the windshield.

"Chin Lei Wei."

Avery blinked a few times. "Conflict at the height of power is deadly. Cooperation only lasts so long."

"Yeah, right. I imagine my father's response will be even more deadly."

"Perhaps," said the man as he drove through London traffic, "but if Crepusculous is ripped apart, Klaus is going to make sure he retains as much of it as possible."

"This may be the opportunity I need to turn the organization toward something good," said Diegert expectantly.

"If there is going to be war at the top of Crepusculous, we must first survive the oncoming battles. Then we can reposition the organization according to your plans."

"Really, this could be good?"

"When there's blood in the streets, buy real estate."

As Avery's macabre quote resonated in his head, he thought of something Panzer had said a while ago, "Keep your enemies close in order to know their weaknesses." Was his father's *I love you, son* rhetoric real, or beguiling wish fulfillment designed to lower his defenses? Could Avery be trusted? One thing was for sure, gaining control over Crepusculous was going to take persistence and cunning while capitalizing on opportunities.

Avery said, "Every great general starts out as a soldier." Glancing at Diegert, he said, "You're going to have to serve as a soldier in whatever actions are forthcoming, but your success will pave the way to gaining what you want."

Diegert turned from the man's dark eyes to gaze out at the lights of London. Frightening foreboding and thrilling anticipation filled him with an unsettling mix of emotions as he contemplated who his father would next assign him to kill.

Thank you for Reading

Please post a review on Amazon, or the site of your choice. Your review will let the world know how you enjoyed this story.

A review needn't be long.

A sentence of two is sufficient.

I appreciate your time, effort and energy spent sharing your opinion with other readers.

Up Next:

FACE OF THE ASSASSIN

A deceptive appearance is a killer's most lethal weapon.

Book 4 to be released in early 2021

Thank you.

Bill Brewer

ABOUT THE AUHTOR

Bill Brewer writes to engage his readers. Using imagination and research, he creates compelling characters whom he thrusts into dangerous situations. To thrill his readers, Bill sets a blistering pace and keeps the action coming as the plot explodes across the pages. The story reveals its secrets as the characters experience triumph, betrayal, victory, and loss. While you're reading, look for passages filled with anatomical details that this University Professor of Human Anatomy & Physiology uses to bring realism into his story.

When not teaching or writing, Bill can be found seeking adventure, peace and camaraderie, hiking, biking and paddling near his home in Rochester NY.

SOCIAL MEDIA

Please visit my website and subscribe for e-mail updates.

billbrewerbooks.com

Also, please follow me on

- <u>Facebook</u>: Bill Brewer Books
- <u>Twitter</u>: @Brewer Books
- <u>Instagram</u>: billbrewer434

THRILLEX Publishing

Made in the USA
Las Vegas, NV
27 December 2020

14876069R00192